The Last Broken Girl

by

Cynthia Rice

Copyright Notice
This is a work of fiction. Names, characters, places, and incidents are either the product of the author's imagination or are used fictitiously, and any resemblance to actual persons living or dead, business establishments, events, or locales, is entirely coincidental.

The Last Broken Girl

COPYRIGHT © 2023 by Cynthia Rice

All rights reserved. No part of this book may be used or reproduced in any manner whatsoever without written permission of the author or The Wild Rose Press, Inc. except in the case of brief quotations embodied in critical articles or reviews.
Contact Information: info@thewildrosepress.com

Cover Art by *Diana Carlile*

The Wild Rose Press, Inc.
PO Box 708
Adams Basin, NY 14410-0708
Visit us at www.thewildrosepress.com

Publishing History
First Edition, 2024
Trade Paperback ISBN 978-1-5092-5539-9
Digital ISBN 978-1-5092-5540-5

Published in the United States of America

Dedication

To my friends, old and new.

Chapter One

Every parent has a favorite child, whether they'll admit it or not. Erin Moore-Jackson had a framed photo of each of her daughters, Gracie age four and Charlotte aged five, stashed in the top drawer of her desk at work. She pulled them out frequently during the day, and some days she put Gracie's on the top of the pile and some days it was Charlotte. The photo Erin chose depended on what sort of day she wanted to have. With Gracie, she would be critical and exacting. To have a Charlotte day was much more carefree.

Every clinical psychologist has a favorite patient, whether they admit it or not. Erin Moore-Jackson, with her PhD in Psychology in practice in Lake Delton, a small touristy town in south central Wisconsin, knew she was no different, and she would readily admit it after a few drinks, professional ethics be damned.

Erin preferred intelligent, motivated patients who didn't expect her to do all the heavy lifting. They worked on the assignments she gave them between appointments and didn't expect a quick solution to each of their problems. She could have added punctuality, sense of humor, and a healthy respect for the Oxford comma to that, but then she would be as nitpicky as that day's favorite daughter.

It might be logical to assume her least favorite patients were those possessing none of these qualities, but it wasn't the case. Not even close.

Malcolm Ferris, who sat in her patient chair at that moment, fell somewhere in the middle. She'd been seeing him for over a year, usually on a bimonthly basis, and he'd make significant progress with his crippling anxiety. More recently, as Malcolm struggled with critical life decisions, he had upped his visits to once a week, He now sat in his usual spot, staring at the box of tissues on the coffee table in front of him.

Erin knew better than most therapists how disabling anxiety could be. Malcolm had improved to the point that he was in a committed relationship. He'd rented his own apartment, and recently his girlfriend Cheryl had moved in, although he hadn't yet told his mother. He'd even begun to drive over bridges without a full-blown panic attack although he admitted driving forty miles out of his way to find the lowest and least menacing bridge over the Wisconsin River. Now it was all threatening to fall apart over his inability to handle change.

Erin's phone buzzed in her lap. The text could wait. She nodded for Malcolm to continue.

"Cheryl's still talking about graduate school, and now she's been accepted to Loyola," he continued his narration. He sighed dramatically, even for Malcolm. The tall, burly young man leaned forward in his chair, his hands nervously sliding up and down the padded armrests as he spoke. "We both grew up here, you know, a few years apart, but we both went to Baraboo High."

"I mean, we'd end up moving down to Chicago for three years, maybe longer," he said. "She wants to live in a modern high-rise apartment and take the L to school. She could find these same classes online, or even in Madison, and we wouldn't have to move to Chicago."

Her phone buzzed a second time. Erin flipped it over to check how much time was left in the session. She read the text twice. It was a notification from the VINE system, the Wisconsin Victim Notification System, and she could click on the link for more information. "No fucking way. This can't be happening."

Malcolm looked up in surprise. Had she said it aloud?

"Sorry, please continue," she said.

She flipped the screen face down. Erin didn't let personal phone calls interrupt her therapy sessions. Not phone calls from her husband Cody or her sister Lindsey, not even from the school nurse, who had learned to contact her receptionist for immediate attention. Not even Amber alerts, and Amber alerts scared the hell out of Erin. They always would. But this was a warning from the VINE system, and it was a warning she had assumed, or at least hoped, she would never hear. It was too soon. Much too soon.

She was not going to check her phone again. Erin was a professional with self-control. She must be imagining it. She had been trying her best to stay focused as Malcolm droned on and on about moving to Chicago. Had she dozed off and dreamed it? The phone in her lap buzzed a third time a minute later. This time she clicked on the link and froze.

"Parole hearing scheduled for Thursday, June 27th, at 1:40 p.m. in Room 214 at the Columbia Correctional Facility regarding early release for Stanley Duggan III. Please contact the Office of Victim Services and Programs for further information."

Erin checked the time. There were twenty-four minutes left in his forty-five-minute session. She adjusted the coaster underneath her now cold mug of Earl Gray tea and nodded for Malcolm to continue. She could do this. She struggled to maintain a calm expression on her face, even though she was sure her patient could hear her raspy breaths as she attempted to inhale. He didn't seem to notice.

Erin counted her breaths, inhalation followed by a longer exhalation, and it relaxed the tightness in her chest. It usually did. She had expected this eventually, but not this soon. It was five years too early. They had promised…maybe they hadn't in fact promised, but she'd taken their reassurance as the truth.

Twenty-two minutes. She could focus for twenty-two minutes.

"What part of moving to Chicago makes you most anxious, Malcolm?" she asked. "Remember what we discussed in our last two Cognitive Behavioral Therapy sessions. You've been doing very well with it."

But had he really? He'd parroted back the terminology, but had he truly changed his pattern of thought?

He shook his head and stared at his knees. Once again, she noticed his rapid foot tapping which she hadn't seen in months. He moved his hands to his knees and gripped the faded jeans tight as if he could hold them still. She looked down to see her own foot moving in concert with his.

"I can't move to Chicago." He took a deep breath. "I know, I'm supposed to say I prefer we don't move. I don't want to lose Cheryl and she wants my answer by Memorial Day."

"That's ten days away," she reminded him. And how many days away was the hearing? She paused to count. June twenty-seventh was only thirty-nine days away. Or forty. She couldn't remember if May had thirty or thirty-one days. What was that stupid poem? She needed to get a grip.

"It's eleven, if you count today," he said. "It's still early in the day."

Eighteen more minutes.

"Too many people down there and we won't know any of them. It might be too expensive to keep our own cars, and we'd be taking buses everywhere. And I'd have to find a new job. I read about the murder rate online. People get shot waiting to check out at Walgreens, that's what I read. I showed Cheryl, but..." He wiped a tear from his eye. "She claims it's beautiful, and we could go down to the parks on Lake Michigan and walk on the beach. But we've already got Devil's Lake, plus the Wisconsin River, and we can do those things here."

Erin resisted the urge to check the time again. Instead, she jotted a few words down into the notebook. Fifteen excruciating minutes, she estimated, then immediately felt guilty for minimizing Malcolm's distress. She needed to leave the room, to be alone.

Malcolm looked quizzically at her foot, which was now tapping faster than his.

"Are you okay?" he asked.

"I'm sorry, but we're going to have to finish a few minutes early today." She rose from her chair and moved towards the door.

"But what about Cheryl?"

"Next week. We'll get this settled before Memorial Day." Please, Malcolm, just go. It wouldn't end well between Malcolm and Cheryl. She knew it, and so did he. If he moved to Chicago, it would exacerbate his anxiety disorder, likely enough to destroy their already tenuous relationship, and Malcolm would be back, foot tapping and paralyzed. Would it be kinder to tell him some people weren't meant to venture beyond their comfort zone? That the things he worried about were part of Chicago? Cheryl was asking for more than he could give.

"But I've got fifteen minutes left," he said, checking his watch.

"I'm truly sorry, but I'm not feeling well and need to cut it short." She shut her notebook and stood. "We'll go longer next week."

She was pleased he was standing up for himself, even if it was to insist on his full appointment time on the one day she couldn't give in. But the VINE message – she needed to read it again, and hope it said something different the third time. Did Malcolm truly think fifteen minutes would make a difference? This was their second full year of therapy, and he'd already spent twenty-eight years tiptoeing around anything which might provoke unease. She knew all about tiptoeing and comfort zones.

Malcolm murmured something under his breath and arose from the chair. He grabbed the gray cardigan he had draped over the chair back and put it on, impossibly slowly. She clenched her fists, digging her nails into the skin of her palms, to keep from hurling his damn sweater out the door and pushing him after it. Four buttons, each fastened more deliberately than the last. She gritted her teeth and watched as he walked halfway to the door, paused, and adjusted the position of a cheap landscape print which hung from the wall.

"I've been staring at your crooked picture for the last half hour. Hope you don't mind," he said.

Erin shut the door firmly behind him. She could hear his continued lamentations about Cheryl and Chicago as he walked away from her door, heading towards the receptionist to confirm his appointment for next week.

She re-read the notification two more times and saved a screenshot. June 27th. A parole hearing for someone who deserved to die in prison. It was forty-one days away, she decided. Like Malcolm, she would count today.

She'd driven by the maximum-security prison in Portage countless times heading to Beaver Dam to visit her old college roommate. She took little comfort in the stone wall with the deterrent loops of barbed wire topping and guard towers. Prison escapes were not common, but they happened. Why else would they have signs along the highway warning motorists not to pick up hitchhikers? Especially if they were dressed in orange. Were people that careless? But she knew the answer.

Normal people didn't worry about prisoners breaking out. They worried about more mundane things, like their dread of facing their judgmental in-laws over a Thanksgiving turkey, why they couldn't sleep at night, or in Malcolm's case, those perilous Walgreens checkout lanes in Chicago. These weren't inconsequential worries, but they were also not life and death matters. Erin would have traded her concerns for theirs in a heartbeat.

She looked again at the contact number. She had memorized it and could still recite it in her sleep. Her parents had also once known it by heart. They eventually told her it was time to move on, but they had never taken their own advice. She knew how traumatic her disappearance had been for them as well.

But she had been the victim.

Erin heard a loud snap and looked down at her hands, which still clenched a plastic rollerball pen, now in pieces. She grabbed a tissue from the nearby box to catch the red ink as it dripped from her fingers onto the desk.

Chapter Two

Detective Warren Osborne hung up the phone and smiled broadly. He shoved aside the stack of folders on his desk. They could wait. He clasped his hands together like a delighted toddler and stood. Deputy Joshua Lippmann looked up from his computer screen.

"That was Margie Hinshaw from Columbia Correctional," Osborne said. "She was calling about Stanley Duggan. He tried to get a parole hearing five or six years ago but got caught with contraband in prison and they cancelled. No idea where he got the money this time, but it seems he's found an interested legal team out of Madison and is on the docket for late June."

"Who is Stanley Duggan?"

"That's right, you aren't from this area originally. He kidnapped a teen girl twenty years ago and kept her for five months. The victim was Erin Moore. She still lives in town."

"I did hear about that. She has a younger sister, Lindsey. She was in my volleyball league last winter," Joshua said. "She's a few years older than me."

"How old are you?"

"Twenty-eight," he answered.

Osborne nodded. He would have pegged the deputy for a few years younger, with his thick, unruly hair and unlined face. He rubbed his chin, feeling his own five o'clock shadow at ten in the morning. Osborne had turned forty just before the Moore girl disappeared, and he was now past the point he should have retired. The case had aged him, and he saw it every time he looked in the mirror. It was the parting advice his ex-wife Clara had given him when they exited the county courthouse ten years earlier, newly signed divorce papers in hand.

He couldn't give up until he found closure for Erin Moore.

"You were involved in the case?" Joshua asked.

"I was more than involved. I broke it open. I was there the day we found Erin. Duggan was convicted, and they sentenced him to twenty-five years, but he had a female accomplice, a woman who supposedly helped him kidnap and hold the girl for five months. This was according to Erin, at least. We never found any definite evidence this woman existed. And if she did, she was in the wind by the time we found Duggan. He wouldn't give her up."

"I'm surprised they're considering him for parole."

"So am I, but he's seventy-eight now and in failing health. They'd sentenced him to twenty-five years, and he's put in twenty. So, now's our best chance."

"Chance for what?" Joshua asked.

"Let's get something to eat. I'm buying," Osborne said. "I'll tell you on the way."

Joshua followed him out the front door to Osborne's car and they headed towards town, after agreeing on tacos.

"Duggan might be willing to help us find his accomplice now, if he thinks it will help his chances for parole. I'm going to interview him at Columbia and try to make some sort of deal."

"I thought this woman didn't exist."

"The DA didn't think so, but Sheriff Carter's predecessor gave Erin's story the benefit of the doubt, which is why this is considered a cold case and not a closed one. Carter disagrees." Osborne pulled his car behind the taco truck parked around the square and turned off the ignition. "But I was there. The first one on the crime scene when we rescued the girl. Erin was more terrified of the woman than she was of Duggan. The accomplice was real."

"Couldn't the girl give you enough information to find her?"

"She tried, but she was fourteen and was fucked-up, for a long time. She'd been beaten and emotionally abused but claimed Duggan had never sexually assaulted her. Veronica was the woman's name, no last name. Erin thought Veronica was younger than Duggan, and she had long red hair which should have helped. But we still never found any solid leads."

"Which explains why it's still a cold case," Joshua said.

He nodded. "Technically, but we haven't treated it that way. If this Veronica was real, she's still out there. It's hard to understand a woman participating in something like this. She was the crueler of the two, from what the girl said. Erin had a dog with her when she was taken, I think it was something unusual. A King Charles Cavalier. Cute little dog, some type of spaniel. Apparently, Veronica would control the girl by threatening to poison or carve up the dog."

"That's sick."

"If this Veronica exists, I'm going to find her."

They waited in a short line at the food truck and settled with their plates at a nearby picnic bench.

Osborne wolfed down his plate of enchiladas and took a satisfying swig of bottled iced tea. He'd pay the consequences later with heartburn and flatulence, but this was a day to celebrate.

Back at the Sauk County Sheriff's Office, Osborne knocked on Carter's office door. Not only had the sheriff heard about the hearing, but he had known for three months.

"This didn't end well for you last time, did it? Looking for the woman? You still think she exists?" Carter asked.

"There's a possibility she's still out there."

"He hasn't talked to you in the past. I think it would be a complete waste of time," Carter said.

"I'm wasting time right now working on a two-week-old motel vandalism case. Some yokel sliced up the mattresses and left a mess. Let the insurance company pay for the damage and close it out. I'd like permission to formally interview Duggan at the prison. He may be willing to cooperate if he thinks it's going to improve his chances at the parole hearing."

"So, you're asking permission this time? I'm aware you've visited Duggan since he's been in. How many times?"

"I admit I've been there, but that's not against any law. This time it will be an official interview." He nodded toward the deputy. "I'll even take Lippmann."

Carter placed his fingertips together under his chin and stared towards the window. Osborne doubted the sheriff knew how many times he'd visited Duggan, or he'd now be unemployed. As it was, he'd been demoted and reassigned to a subservient role in investigations that should have been his. It could have been even worse if

Carter had known how far he'd gone.

His ex-wife Clara knew how far and was now happily married to an HVAC repairman.

Back at his own desk, Osborne was able to arrange a morning appointment to interview Duggan for May 31st, assuming Duggan's legal team didn't object. He'd hoped for sooner.

"What ever happened to her puppy, the King Charles what-ever-it-was?" Joshua asked.

"It was supposed to be a King Charles Cavalier puppy."

"Supposed to be?"

"Like I said before, the girl was pretty messed up, emotionally, I mean. Moore's mother had a lot of allergies."

Osborne powered down his laptop and looked up.

"There had never been any dog."

Chapter Three

May 17, 6:15 p.m.
BREAKING NEWS – BARABOO NEWS-JOURNAL
by Richard Fitzpatrick/Reporter

In August 1999, Stanley Duggan III, a resident of Baraboo, Wisconsin, was convicted of first-degree kidnapping of fourteen-year-old Erin Moore from nearby Reedsburg, Wisconsin and sentenced to twenty-five years in prison. The victim was held for five months prior to her discovery and Duggan's subsequent arrest. She claimed Duggan had a female accomplice who had assisted in her kidnapping and incarceration. Police investigation at the time failed to uncover any evidence of a second kidnapper.

Now, twenty years later, Duggan is scheduled for a parole hearing on June 27th, to be held at Columbia Correctional Facility where he is currently incarcerated. Had the sentencing occurred after December 31, 1999, at which time the Truth in Sentencing Law went into effect, Duggan would not be eligible for release for five more years.

Reporter Richard Fitzpatrick from the Baraboo News-Journal received a Gold Award from the Wisconsin Press Club for Excellence in Journalism for covering the kidnapping, rescue, and trial.

Dr. Erin Moore-Jackson, the kidnapping victim, returned to Reedsburg after obtaining her PhD in

Psychology at the University of Chicago and practices at the Meadowview Counseling Center in Lake Delton. She is married with two young daughters and currently resides in Reedsburg. Dr. Moore could not be reached for comment.

More details to follow.
Follow on Twitter @FitzpatrickRichard14
# # #

Richard Fitzpatrick proofed and tweaked the news entry three times before hitting send. He hadn't blogged in over a month, despite his editor's admonishments. Was there anyone out there dying to read about the annual crane count at the International Crane Society a few miles outside of Baraboo?

He was the only crime reporter of the only newspaper in the county, but there weren't enough local stories to keep him busy most months. He'd been forced into human interest stories including being forced to participate in the annual crane count, a fun-filled morning of standing out in the rain for two hours early on a Saturday morning. All of this for a 500-word, page 5 piece of shit. He had prayed for an uptick in crime, but he hadn't expected to get this lucky.

He'd been in his late twenties back when Duggan was captured, and it was the only time in his career he had covered a kidnapping story. He'd won one of the most prestigious journalism awards in Wisconsin that year. It hadn't done his career trajectory much good, but he still proudly displayed the plaque on his side of the soundproofing divider.

He didn't need to check his notes. Duggan would be 20 years into a 25-year sentence. Darren Holmgren had provided him with updates on Duggan's incarceration occasionally for the past ten years, when he'd joined the administrative staff at the prison, always at a price, of course. For the first time Fitzpatrick was getting his money's worth.

He had always hoped there would be a follow-up to the story.

Years ago, the public had hungered for details about Erin, the feisty fourteen-year-old girl who had survived five months in the hands of Stanley Duggan III and his female accomplice, who had never been identified or captured. Erin had endured and returned to Wisconsin after college and graduate school, to be close to family. Fitzpatrick would have never come back.

Nineteen years ago, he had outlined a book-length true crime story about the kidnapping and tried repeatedly to sell it, without success. It hadn't helped that the victim had been a minor and her overprotective parents considered her off limits for interviewing, nor that Duggan had stonewalled him completely.

It had been Erin's story nineteen years ago, and it was time for the sequel.

Chapter Four

If Cody noticed Erin's foul mood when she arrived home after work, he gave no sign. She had debated about calling her husband after she had hashed it out with the representative from the Department of Corrections. "Don't kill the messenger," she had been told. She knew her anger was misplaced. One didn't need a PhD in Psychology, even though she had earned that exact degree. In the end, she hadn't phoned Cody. There was nothing he could say or do to lessen her fear. Stanley Duggan III might go free.

Cody had lit the charcoal grill in anticipation of her arrival, and the coals were glowing red and gray. It was a warm night for mid-May and Gracie and Charlotte both wore shorts and T-shirts. Cody was dressed as always in jeans, roomy enough to hide his prosthesis.

"Your sister called a few hours ago," Cody said, when she joined him on the back patio. "Invited herself for dinner."

"Did she give some reason for not calling me?"

He shook his head. "I learned a long time ago not to ask when it comes to Lindsey."

Erin hadn't remembered to pick up the bottle of Washington state cabernet which Cody insisted on for his secret recipe tenderloin marinade, or the second bottle for drinking. Tonight, she might have appreciated a third bottle. They would settle for what was on the wine rack.

She changed out of her blouse and skirt into a loose-fitting t-shirt and yoga pants, and joined Cody on the back patio, a full plastic wine glass in her hand. She had pulled her shoulder-length brown hair up into a loose bun and was barefoot in a nod to the warm night. The girls were playing nearby on the grass with old badminton racquets Cody had picked up at a garage sale, along with a shuttlecock missing most of its plumage. The girls didn't seem to mind there was no net. Both swung and missed often, but they squealed with excitement when they connected, no matter what the direction of flight.

Erin settled on the nearby loveseat, lowered her voice, and spoke. "I got a message from VINE today."

Cody turned and frowned. He set the grill scraper down.

Erin nodded. She cupped the plastic wine glass and took a large swallow.

"Duggan?" he asked.

"Who the fuck else?" she said. Twenty seconds – she silently counted. Four deep breaths. "Sorry, it's just…"

He nodded.

"What'd they say?"

"He's apparently been granted a parole hearing. So much for justice. He is supposed to be locked up another five years, at least. He's convinced them he's dying, apparently." She laughed bitterly. "I should be so lucky."

"But it is just a hearing, right? Not a done deal. It doesn't mean he'll be released. You can fight this."

Cody joined her on the loveseat and wrapped his arm around her. She tried to relax into the embrace, leaning her head against his shoulder. She thought about the last time she had seen Stanley Duggan, pushed his arm away and stood abruptly. She paced back and forth on the stone patio, occasionally glancing over at the girls.

"You can hire an attorney and fight this, Erin," he said. "You must have had an attorney when he went to trial."

"It happened twenty years ago, and I didn't have an attorney. I wasn't on trial. He was."

"Have they set a date for the hearing?"

"June 27th. It's on a Thursday."

"A little over a month."

No shit, Sherlock. She bit her lip and held back this automatic response. She managed a nod.

An errant shuttlecock plopped on the table next to her near-empty wine glass. Five-year-old Charlotte ran towards the table, the racquet held over her head. One of her braids had come completely undone, her red hair flapping with each step. Four-year-old Gracie followed close behind. Cody picked up the shuttlecock and tossed it up in the air over their heads, and they turned and gave chase.

"I'll kill him if he comes by here," she said quietly, instantly regretting she had not been to the shooting range in nearly six months. Sloppy. It was less than a half mile from her office, and she used to go over her lunch break, until her partners complained she smelled of creosote, even after she had washed her hands repeatedly. It didn't seem to matter to them that it was propellant and not creosote. It could upset the patients, they reasoned. And now she had become complacent, and there was a potential price one paid for complacency.

"Maybe he's actually dying," Cody said. "He's almost eighty by now, right?"

Their conversation was interrupted by the sound of a car pulling to the gate, then her less-than-considerate sister blasting the horn. Erin pulled out her cell phone, brought up the security app, and remotely opened the gate.

A few minutes later Lindsey came striding around the side of the house, a bottle of wine in one hand and her phone in the other. The girls briefly abandoned their racquets to hug their aunt, who promised to play with them before she left, if they could find the third racquet which Erin suspected was lost somewhere in the small barn. Cody returned to the grill, and the sisters headed through the French doors into the kitchen.

"There's an administrative assistant job I'm interested in at one of the resorts in the Dells. Would you mind looking at my cover letter?"

"I can't do this tonight. You should have called first."

"I called."

"You called Cody, not me."

"I need to get the letter sent tomorrow. It's written but I need feedback on it. It will only take a few minutes."

Erin said nothing. She pulled containers of deli salads from the refrigerator and put them on a tray.

"You're always the one always reminding me Dad's life insurance money isn't going to last forever and I should get a job."

"Not anymore. I promised you I would stop."

"I could always use what's left to buy a house in the middle of nowhere and erect a prison fence around the perimeter."

"I thought we agreed we weren't going to discuss

this." Erin sighed. "I'm sorry–it's been…" A bad day didn't cover it. "We can go over the cover letter right now."

Lindsey brought it up on her phone. It was better than most of the covers Erin had critiqued, less wordy. She made a few suggestions and handed the phone back to her sister.

After dinner, the girls were in their pajamas watching cartoons in the family room, exhausted after running back and forth with Lindsey chasing after the birdie, while Cody loaded the dishwasher. The women nursed glasses of wine at the kitchen island.

"Glad you could join us for dinner tonight, but what's up?" Cody asked.

"I wanted Erin's opinion on a job application, but mainly I'm here for moral support. I heard about the hearing."

"How did you find out? You hadn't signed up for the VINE notifications, had you?" Erin asked.

"I have no idea what VINE means. But I receive the online alerts for breaking news from the Baraboo paper. It's the same reporter from twenty years ago. I swear it's the same guy. He must be ancient. Richard Fitzpatrick. They included his headshot, but I remember him as short and dumpy, even back then. They ran a half page on Stanley Duggan finally getting a parole hearing." She examined her wine glass and fished out a fruit fly floating on top. "We should all go. It could have a lot of impact on the court."

Erin closed the door to the family room.

"The girls can't know about this, Lindsey," Erin interrupted. "It's not going to be easy facing him at the hearing. You will never understand what it was like, back then."

"Aren't you able to testify before they bring him into the room?" Lindsey asked.

She could do that, she knew. The Corrections Department had informed her she could speak freely, prior to Duggan entering. She would not have to see him. But that was only half of the problem.

Erin lowered her voice to a whisper and Lindsey leaned close to hear. "I'll prepare a statement and testify, but not in front of Duggan. But she'll be there, somehow, watching. She won't miss this opportunity."

"You don't know that."

But Erin did know and had always known, Veronica had made sure of it.

"What if I go in your place?"

"I could go, too." Cody stood in the doorway, drying his hands on a dish towel.

"Thanks for the offer. I mean it, but I'm not sure it would be any easier for you," Erin said. "I also think the judges would be more inclined to listen to the victim.

"We're both coming along. Right, Cody?" Lindsey asked.

Erin nodded glumly and drained her glass of wine. She didn't want to think about Stanley Duggan or Veronica, but she would prepare a victim's statement for the hearing.

Cody closed the front gates after Lindsey drove away, then armed the security system. Erin checked the camera feeds on her laptop, and satisfied everything was in working order, headed off to bed.

She watched as Cody released his stump from the prosthesis and climbed into bed. She grabbed her iPad and leaned back on the pillows.

"It was nice to see your sister. It's been a while."

"It was bad timing."

"Well, the girls were happy to see her. Are you going to read for a while?"

"Another chapter or two. I need to unwind."

"I've got another suggestion on how to clear your mind," he said.

"No, Cody, please."

He turned to face her and stroked her forearm slowly, up and down. She pulled her arm away and tucked it under the blanket.

"I'm just saying, it's been a long time," he said.

"Does today seem like the right time, considering what's happened?"

"Can I at least hold you?"

She exhaled loudly. He nodded and eventually turned towards the wall, like she knew he would.

She powered up her iPad and returned to the exterior security camera monitors, five in all, capturing the front gate, the entrances, and the interior of the barn. Two of the goats abruptly stood in their pen and scurried to the back corner. Erin inhaled sharply. Was there someone out there? She swung her legs from under the covers and sat on the edge of the bed, watching. A few minutes later the same two goats returned to the center of the pen and lay down. The lighting was dim but finally she was convinced there was no intruder in the barn.

She studied the dark shadows cast by the trees, the patio furniture, any cars slowing as they drove by, scanning for any movement. There was none. She would watch, if only for a few minutes. Veronica was out there, and she would be coming again, for Erin or possibly one of the girls. It was simply a matter of time.

Now Veronica might have Stanley Duggan at her side if he succeeded in getting parole.

Erin climbed back under the covers and switched back to the interior cameras. She scanned room by room. Finally, she watched over the girls, asleep in their beds. This had been her routine since they had been born. She leaned back against the headboard and shut her eyes. She breathed in for three seconds, out for four seconds. Over and over. Tonight, the familiar routine didn't help. She finally gave up, sat forward, and snatched her phone off the nightstand.

She turned her attention to the online News-Journal. It was the lead article, as Lindsey had described.

"Convicted Kidnapper Stanley Duggan granted parole hearing with possible release after June hearing."

The article went on to summarize the months of captivity which had destroyed her life twenty years ago and haunted her still. He described the question of a female accomplice, seen only by traumatized young Erin, and authorities were not sure she existed. Duggan had denied having an accomplice. Fuck them. She had no doubt Veronica was alive and watching.

She bristled on reading the bottom of the article.

"Erin Moore-Jackson still lives in the area with her husband and two young daughters, with a Psychology practice with Meadowview Center in Lake Delton, Wisconsin. She could not be reached for comment."

She checked her phone's call log and saw there were no missed calls. The reporter hadn't even tried to reach her, and he had no business mentioning her girls and her place of employment.

After studying each security camera feed again, she

threw off the covers, tiptoed down to the kitchen and topped off another glass of red wine. She settled on the living room couch and wrapped a throw around her legs, clutching her glass so tightly she was afraid it would shatter in her hand as the pen had done earlier in the day. She would not be sleeping that night.

Chapter Five

Erin watched the video Fitzpatrick had posted earlier in the day under Breaking News in the Baraboo News-Journal, mortified as the number of views ticked upward. She resisted the urge to replay it a third time. What were the chances her patients would see this, and would they be looking for a replacement therapist?

Erin had heard the vehicle crunching up the gravel driveway late morning, followed by the opening and slamming of a car door, then a second one. She checked her watch. This wasn't the deep thud of Cody's pickup truck door. She had uninvited guests.

She fumbled for her cell phone. She would have it ready to dial 911. *Damn it, Cody. The security gate works only if you remember to shut it behind you.*

Erin relaxed slightly when she saw the two men approach the house. She didn't recognize the tall black man carrying the video camera, but she remembered Richard Fitzpatrick, the local news reporter, who looked to be in his upper forties, not ancient as Lindsey had implied. He had been balding twenty years ago and now sported a gray goatee to go with it. She remembered how he had hounded her family for two years after she had returned home. Her father saw it differently and credited Fitzpatrick for 'keeping her story alive' until she had been rescued. He felt his daughter had a better chance of being found due to the reporter's persistence. Fitzpatrick had done weekly updates on her disappearance for six months. He had won some reporting awards for it, she knew. Fine, it may have helped. But he had insisted on 'keeping the story alive' after she returned, and she had wanted nothing to do with that.

Erin shouldn't have been surprised he found out about the hearing the same day as her VINE notification– he was a journalist and likely had a contact at the prison.

"Dr. Moore," Fitzpatrick called out, as he walked across the yard towards her.

"It's Moore-Jackson," she corrected.

"Sorry, of course. It's been a few years since we've talked." He smiled and unzipped his light jacket. "If you've got a minute, I'd like to ask a few questions."

"I'm in the middle of a project," she said. "I'd prefer you leave."

He looked up at the house and hobby barn. "You're out in the middle of nowhere here. It was hard to find this place, even with my GPS."

She tried to keep her face neutral and said nothing.

"Do you mind if we tape this conversation?"

Her hand gripped her phone tightly and she still said nothing. Eventually they would go away.

"This is Kenneth, our photographer. He's worked with me at the paper for two years now. Maybe you've seen his work. He covered the disappearance of that lawyer in Tomah last year and won the Abernathy Press Award for photojournalism."

She remembered the case. Another missing person, although it had been a different situation. Following a bitter marital fight, the man had walked into the deep woods, half-buried his body under leaves, and shot himself in the head. He wasn't discovered until hunting season, and she briefly wondered what photographs Kenneth might have taken.

"There was a 'No Trespassing' sign by the front gate. I'm sure you saw it."

"I assumed since the gate was open…" Fitzpatrick smiled. "Just a few minutes and we'll be gone."

Cody would hear about the open gate.

Erin sighed. He hadn't taken no for an answer twenty years ago and he hadn't changed. "A few minutes, but no camera."

The photographer shot a frustrated look at Fitzpatrick but pointed the video camera towards the ground.

"Were you surprised Duggan is receiving a parole hearing?"

She nodded her head. "I thought I had five more years." She and her family would be safe for five more years. The security gate would be enough until then. It had been enough to keep Veronica out.

"It has to do with the Truth in Sentencing Law which went into effect year end 1999. His crime just snuck in under the wire. If he had taken you nine months later, he wouldn't have been eligible for release until he'd served the full twenty-five years."

"How fortunate for him," she said, no expression in her voice. Erin hadn't remembered hearing that, but she'd been very young. Maybe her parents had known. It didn't make it fair.

"I understand what a shock this must be, and I'm not here to harass you or make your life more difficult," he said.

"Then don't," she said. "Leave now." She stared at the reporter, waiting for more.

"The crime Duggan committed against you, against your family was unspeakable, but it was a long time ago. People need to be reminded. There needs to be an outcry, a raising of voices in the community, to prevent this man from being released. With your help, I can raise the public awareness."

She considered this, wondering who would rally behind her. Her coworkers? They would be supportive, but rally was a strong word. She had a few close friends, sure, or at least she had at one time. The parents of her middle school friends would remember. It could have been their daughter. Could there still be enough public uproar that she could avoid going to the parole hearing herself? She doubted it.

"You do know you are entitled to address the parole board, and you can do it without Duggan being present."

Erin nodded as she mopped sweat from her forehead with her sleeve, hoping the reporter wouldn't see her hands shaking. She forced herself to slow her breathing, in and out but the tightness worsened. She needed to get rid of Fitzpatrick and his photographer before they noticed.

"That's all the time I have." Her voice was hoarser than it had been a minute ago.

"Just a few more questions. Have you had any contact with Duggan's female accomplice?

Erin stiffened and shook her head. Veronica. She had never been captured, even with Erin's detailed descriptions of the woman. She hadn't seen her in the twenty-one years since her rescue, and she often tried to picture how Veronica would look, two decades older. Erin wished she were dead, of course, but the woman was not much older than her dad. She was almost certainly still alive. There had been all those reminders. Yearly postcards on her birthday, on the girls' birthdays. There hadn't been a signature, but Erin knew they were from Veronica. She hadn't shared these with Cody since the first few years of their marriage. She had stopped taking them to Detective Osborne for the same reason. It hadn't made any difference, and she wasn't sure either man believed her.

"One more question. Then I promise we'll leave."

Erin shook her head. She noticed Kenneth's camera was now pointed in her direction and wondered when he'd started recording. "Get off my property now."

"Just a few more minutes."

She couldn't answer any more questions. She wanted these men to go away and never return. There was not some community outrage coming to save her from Duggan's release. And Cody would adjust the gate and make it automatically shut every time a car pulled out of the driveway. Surely that was possible.

Erin walked a few feet to the side of the house and cranked the water spigot wide open. She unfurled the coiled garden hose, aimed the sprayer in Fitzpatrick's direction, and released a blast of cold water.

Fitzpatrick swore and jumped out of range.

"Dammit, Erin, we're both on the same side here." He dried his notebook on the sleeve of his jacket.

"Get out!"

Fitzpatrick cursed loudly, turned, and walked back to his car.

Award-winning Kenneth caught it all on video.

Chapter Six

"Never give up, do you, Osborne?" Stanley Duggan said. He sat in an interview room at Columbia Correctional Facility, his hands cuffed to the table in front of him. "Looks like you've put on some weight since your last visit. Twenty pounds? Thirty?"

Osborne ignored the dig. Why should he care what this asshole thought? It had been thirty-five pounds, but his girth wasn't any of Duggan's business. He sucked in his stomach and sat taller, reminding himself to drop his shoulder blades back like the massage therapist he had dated a few years ago had instructed. It was the only positive thing to come out of that relationship. He and his deputy took seats on the opposite side of the table.

"And you brought a Mini-me with you this time."

"This is Deputy Joshua Lippmann, also with the Sauk County Sheriff's Office."

"I don't really care what his name is." Duggan stared up at the ceiling. "You're wasting your time. Again."

Osborne studied the man. Unlike himself, Duggan had lost considerable weight in the past two years and his prison-issued orange shirt hung loosely on his frame. His once full face was lean and haggard, and his skin tone tinged with gray. His unjustly thick head of hair hadn't changed, while Osborne now had to arrange his own every morning in the mirror for maximum scalp coverage, but he noted with satisfaction the prisoner now had pronounced creases around his eyes and mouth which were new. Maybe the failing health described in the petition for parole was real. Twenty years of prison food had to take a toll.

On his past visits Duggan had stonewalled him completely, had sat with his arms across his chest and never said a single word. He was talking today, even if it was to insult him, which could only work to Osborne's advantage.

"June twenty-seventh. It's coming up fast, isn't it?" Osborne asked.

Duggan shifted his gaze from the ceiling to the two men. "What about it?"

"It took you twenty years to get this parole hearing. I heard you've got a top-notch attorney involved. I wonder who's paying for that."

Duggan shrugged. "Does it matter?"

"I'm sure your legal team has advised you to show penitence at the parole hearing and apologize for the harm to that poor girl."

"It seems like a sensible strategy."

"It wouldn't help your chances for release if Erin and her family show up to testify at the hearing, would it? I'm sure she'll write a victim's statement. I mean, why wouldn't she? But it would be exponentially worse if she shows up in person to testify, even brings her family along so the parole board can remember the frightened looks on the faces of her two little girls while they're deliberating."

Duggan was paying attention this time.

"It also might not help if there's a letter from the Sauk County Sheriff's Department outlining your continued refusal to provide information on your accomplice. The woman. The girl said her name was Veronica."

"Tit for a tat, is that what you're offering?" Duggan asked.

"I'm offering nothing. Nothing at all. Merely stating a fact. A letter from the sheriff's department advising the parole board you've finally cooperated after twenty years and aided in the capture of a wanted felon might carry some weight. That's all I'm saying," said Osborne. He knew Sheriff Carter wouldn't write such a letter in a million years.

Duggan turned toward the deputy and studied him intently until Joshua's face reddened. Duggan smiled, clearly enjoying the young man's discomfort.

"Is this guy teaching you everything you need to know about detecting?" Duggan tilted his head to indicate Osborne.

Joshua said nothing but peeked sideways at the detective.

Duggan hunched forward towards the deputy and said in a loud stage whisper, tapping his index finger on the table. "Follow the evidence, that's critical. Write it down."

Joshua still said nothing.

"Enough," said Osborne. "Good luck with your hearing." He stood and picked up the folder in front of him.

"Wait. Detective. You know I've read the court transcript of the girl's testimony. Read it a dozen times, because what can I say, I have had a lot of time on my hands for the past twenty years. And I've seen the results from your crime lab after their unjustified violation of my home. A man's castle, am I right? Again, I've had lots of time. Too much fucking time."

Duggan began to cough until his face was deeply flushed. They waited for him to stop.

"Your point?" Osborne remained standing.

"This phantom, this red-haired lady, this Veronica, who lived with me for the few months I had shared with Erin…"

"Five months." Joshua finally spoke. "It was five months, not a few."

"Whatever, five months. The crime lab found no evidence of a red-haired woman, not a hairbrush with tangles of red hair, no red hair in the shower trap, nothing at all. No DNA other than mine. And Erin's, of course. I'm not denying I had the girl. The neighbors never reported seeing a woman at all come or go, least of all one with long red hair."

Joshua looked inquiringly at Osborne.

"That's true, but we're talking twenty years ago. The techniques for crime scene processing and evidence handling have evolved in the past twenty years."

"Not a single red hair. Not a pube in the sheets. Not an eyelash."

"You're still implying Erin made her up?" Osborne asked.

"Well, if you ever find the spaniel puppy, the one we supposedly threatened to keep the girl under control, let me know." Duggan turned to the open door and yelled for the guard.

Osborne and Joshua turned and left. They retrieved their service weapons and headed for the parking lot.

"Is it true what he said about the lack of evidence? No proof there had been a woman there?" Joshua asked, as he turned the key in the ignition.

"Unfortunately. But we didn't use the state crime lab back then. We had our own guys. Let's say there were some…irregularities. The house wasn't processed properly."

"Is that why you're still convinced she's real?"

"Partially, but you weren't there." Osborne shook his head. "You didn't hear the girl's testimony. You couldn't have listened to her tell her story and not believe every word."

Chapter Seven

Erin leaned up against her white Volvo SUV, scrolling through her e-mail messages and ignoring Lindsey's running commentary on the other parents waiting in the school drop-off circle.

They had come directly from the shooting range, Erin's third time in two weeks, and her two handguns were locked in a gun box in the back of the vehicle. She was getting better, but she never should have stopped target practice. It had been three years, and she'd lost accuracy. Cody hadn't handled a gun since he'd left the military, and now he couldn't legally own one. She didn't want him shooting on their property, not with the girls around, and he wouldn't be welcome at the range. Lindsey had missed the target completely with most of her shots. It was up to her.

It was the last day of the spring term and summer break loomed ahead, at least two and a half weeks of it, until the summer camp at Heritage Learning Academy began. Charlotte and Gracie had begged to stay home with Cody for the summer. After all, what good was it to have a father who didn't work if you couldn't sleep in and watch cartoons all summer? Just a week ago Cody had left the gate open on a run to the hardware store. So much could go wrong if you weren't always watching. Erin was home alone the morning the reporter and his cameraman had gotten in, but what about next time? The girls would be safer at school.

"There isn't a car in sight worth less than fifty grand," Lindsey said.

"Not true." Erin pointed to a weathered green pickup truck across the circle. She didn't tell Lindsey it belonged to one of the teacher's husbands, who ran a small organic farm a few miles outside of Baraboo. It was a private school, tuition sixteen thousand a year. What did her sister expect?

She checked the time. It was 3:15 and the girls should be out any minute, laden down with grocery bags of art projects and a year's accumulated detritus from their desks and cubbies.

"Erin, how are you?" A short dark-haired woman dressed in too-tight yoga pants and a Namaste t-shirt smiled and held out a handout.

Erin recognized the woman as the mother of one of Charlotte's classmates but couldn't remember her name.

"Fine, just picking up the girls." She took the light-blue paper from the woman. "Have you met my sister Lindsey?"

The nameless woman smiled and extended her hand, "Pleased to meet you. I'm Glenda Albright. I've got a son in Charlotte's class and a daughter Gracie's age."

Glenda. She would remember it next time.

"It's Leo's birthday in two weeks, and we're throwing a party. You only turn six once. It will be Wednesday afternoon, since the kids are off school. June nineteenth. I am hoping both girls can come. We're going to have a bouncing castle, or it might be a pirate ship, but I don't think the kids care which."

June nineteenth, one week before the parole hearing. She had not yet decided if she was going in person or writing a letter. This woman was planning a child's birthday party, blissfully unaware of the potential dangers ahead.

Erin knew without checking her calendar she had a full patient schedule that day, like she did every Wednesday. The party was the week before the summer session started, and she knew the girls would love a bouncing whatever. Cody would have to drive. She would insist he stay for the entire party.

Erin smiled at Glenda. "The girls would love to come, but I do have to check our family schedule."

They turned to the school, hearing shrieks of laughter and happy chattering, as a horde of small children spewed from the front door, dressed in their matching uniforms.

Charlotte came running for the car, wearing a backpack and toting a grocery bag in each hand. Gracie followed ten feet behind, a backpack and a small plastic bag at her side. The girls hopped in the backseat and buckled up, while Erin loaded the bags into the back of the car. Gracie's small bag contained a few carefully folded art projects and a few half-empty bottles of hand sanitizer. She pawed through Charlotte's bags. She could see at least three shoes, none of which she recognized and one significantly larger than her daughter wore, and a half dozen items of clothing.

"I'm starving," Charlotte said, before Erin had even shut her car door. "They had sloppy joes for lunch and there wasn't enough for seconds. Can we stop for ice cream?"

"Ice cream," echoed Gracie. "Lindsey loves ice cream, don't you? Let's vote."

They all raised their hands, and Erin headed towards

Robby's Custard Stand.

"Did Leo's mom tell you about the party? We can go, can't we?" Charlotte asked.

"I have to check my work schedule and talk to your dad."

"Dad will say yes."

Erin said nothing. Cody always did say yes.

After the ice cream, they returned home, where the girls jumped out of their safety seats and barreled for the family room for cartoons. Lindsey helped Erin carry in the backpacks and remnants of the school year.

"Glenda seemed nice enough." Lindsey extracted a half-empty bottle of Chardonnay from the refrigerator and grabbed two glasses from the cupboard. "You're not planning on letting them go to Leo's party, are you?

"I said I'd have to check with Cody. And I'm worried about his driving with the girls."

Lindsey stared at her sister and leaned forward. She dropped her voice to a near whisper, "Are you afraid he's using again?"

Erin shrugged her shoulders. She didn't have hard proof.

"If you smother them like this now, what are you planning to do if he gets out?"

Erin whirled around and faced her sister. "Smother them? I'm only trying to keep them safe."

"At what cost?"

"I know what it's like to have a childhood destroyed." Erin reminded herself to breathe. Slow in, slow out. How many times had they fought over this? "And now he might be getting out of prison. It's not going to happen to my daughters."

"You were fourteen, and your life had been a piece

of cake up until then. Mine, too. You do know both of our childhoods changed that day, don't you?" Lindsey said quietly. "Mom and Dad couldn't focus on anything but your disappearance for five months. I understand. I don't blame them for it. But you need to remember I was ten and needed them, too."

Erin had heard variations of this for the past twenty years. She poured herself a half glass of wine and sat across the kitchen island from her sister. She said nothing.

"Even after they found you, things were never the same."

Not for any of them, least of all Erin.

"What I'm saying is you can't let this ruin their childhoods, like it did yours. Like it did mine."

Erin studied her glass, took a sip, and said nothing.

Chapter Eight

"I told you it was a mistake to include Lindsey." Erin reached for the radio dial and turned it off, seconds after Cody had switched stations. "She doesn't go anywhere unless she's guaranteed to be the center of attention."

"You know she gets migraines. Cut her some slack."

Erin pulled out of the parking lot and set her GPS for Columbia Correctional Institute. He was right and if she were in a better mood, she would admit it. "I'm sorry. I'm on edge."

"Me, too."

"She could have called before we pulled up outside her apartment."

"Agreed."

Erin took a quick glance at Cody, who was staring out the front passenger window, watching the billboards and businesses as they passed. She'd seen him searching the pockets of his sweatshirts and jackets in the foyer closet before they'd left home that morning. Looking for something, and she doubted it was spare change. She didn't ask anymore. If he was back on the pain meds, he'd only deny it and it would end in an argument. She couldn't take him storming out of the house in anger the day of the hearing, nor could she handle a long drive-in complete silence while he fumed about her suspicions.

"We've got two hours till the hearing, an hour and a

half before they'll let us in," Cody said. They drove past the prison entrance, did a U-turn, and headed back into Portage, a few miles down the road.

"We passed a few small cafes in town," she said. Her stomach churned at the thought of a greasy spoon hamburger. What she wanted was a drink, a large one. Not her usual wine, but whiskey. Deaden the anxiety a notch or two. She was surprised at the strength of the craving. She rarely drank anything other than wine. There were more than the usual number of empty wine bottles in the recycling bin the past few weeks and she'd flattened a small Amazon shipping box over the top to conceal them. She'd get it under control. She had no choice.

They settled on a small diner with cheery red painted chairs and checkered red and white plastic tablecloths and ordered. The food came quickly, and they ate in silence.

She studied the other patrons and wondered if anyone else was here for a visit to the prison, either for parole hearings or to visit family or friends. An older couple in Packer's sweatshirts too warm for late June slumped over cups of coffee at the counter. A young woman with a toddler and a small infant took up considerable real estate in the corner, with a stroller and a highchair pulled up to the table. The kids were quiet, subdued. Were they going to see their father? No wonder the waitress kept her mouth shut.

Erin pulled out her wallet and left cash for the server, including a hefty tip for not asking any personal questions.

"Do you think you'll recognize Duggan?" Cody asked on the short drive back to the prison. "It's been more than twenty years."

She would remember his eyes most of all, the palest, iciest blue she'd ever seen, would ever see, and unblinking. She shuddered. How was she going to look into those eyes?

"I'll recognize him." There was no doubt.

"Are you sure you want to be in the hearing room? It's probably not too late to ask for the remote testimony."

"I want to face the bastard." She pulled into the visitors parking area and turned off the car. Did she really want to see Duggan, who had usurped a good deal from whom she had been and was now? She needed to face him, boldly stare him down and speak. The parole board would hear her, and they would deny him early release.

But could she confront him? She remembered the smirk on his face the last time she had seen him in the courtroom after her testimony. He had held her gaze, and then licked his lips slowly and shook his head imperceptibly. That same leering stare had recurred in her nightmares for years. Would they start again after this encounter, whether or not he went free?

Was she making a huge mistake coming? Her fists clenched the steering wheel, and she felt a numbness slowly ascending her arms to her shoulders. She could control this.

"Are you all right?" Cody asked.

Was she? It had been more than ten years since her last full blown panic attack, but was it coming back? She struggled to inhale and felt her heart racing, pounding in her chest. She glimpsed into the rearview mirror and saw her entire face was red and perspiring. She opened the car door and vomited her Cobb salad onto the pavement. Cody handed her a lukewarm water bottle and she rinsed her mouth and spit it onto the ground.

"You can still do the remote testimony. You don't have to see him."

"But he'll see it, won't he?" Her voice was hoarse and quiet.

"I don't know if he sees it, or if the parole board reviews it before he comes in. What difference does it make?"

"Osborne's going to be there. I wonder if he's going to testify," she said.

"I would assume so."

"When he stopped by the house last week to talk about the hearing, I got the distinct impression he was trying to discourage us from attending."

"He said he didn't think it would be necessary, that's all. I assume he doesn't think Duggan's got any chance of getting parole," he said. "I think you're reading too much into it."

Erin knew it was more than that. Osborne had gone as far as to tell her not to bother sending a letter to the parole board. She didn't trust him, and apparently his own deputy didn't either. He had texted Erin a few hours after she'd met with them, and Joshua strongly advised her to send a letter to the parole board if she wasn't going to attend in person. She'd saved his information to her contact list, just in case.

Erin sat and watched the clock advance. It was now twenty minutes after one, and they would need to get signed in, go through metal detectors, show ID, whatever else they would be required to do. She reached for her purse, removed the handgun, and slipped it into the glove compartment.

"You took your gun into a restaurant?" Cody asked.

"I take it everywhere these days," she said.

After a few minutes she said, "I can't do it." It was barely a whisper. Her arms tightly encircled her chest and she tried to stop the shaking.

Cody opened his car door and climbed out. He stuck his head into the car and said, "I'll testify. They need to know, Erin."

She nodded and he walked towards the visitor's entrance. She opened the glove compartment. She retrieved the gun, verified it was loaded and clasped it close to her chest. And tried to breathe.

Chapter Nine

Fitzpatrick stashed his notebook in his messenger bag and hurried after Cody immediately after the hearing ended.

He'd watched Cody throughout after purposefully taking a seat in the same row, a few chairs away. The man was jittery, tapping his good foot continually, rubbing his thigh muscles, and squirming like a bored child. He repeatedly wiped the sheen of sweat from his forehead with the sleeve of his shirt. Cody wasn't getting enough of whatever he had been taking, and he was restless as hell. Oxycontin. Fitzpatrick would bet on it. He knew Cody had run into legal problems in the not-too-distant past after forging prescriptions for narcotics after losing his lower leg in the service. He knew he should be sympathetic, but what an opportunity.

Lucky for both of them, he had come prepared. He felt in his jacket's inner pocket for the small envelope. Still there. He smiled, headed down the hallway and took a right at the corner like Cody had done.

"Cody! Hold up," he called.

Instead, the man bowed his head farther and picked up speed. Fitzpatrick caught up with him a few yards short of the exit to the parking lot, grabbed his arm and pulled him into a small alcove.

"What the fuck?" Cody asked.

"Easy, easy. I have a few questions."

"You were there. You saw everything," Cody said. "Osborne—I can't believe he did this. Erin's going to freak out."

"Where's Erin? I was sure she'd come, or at least testify over the closed-circuit system. She didn't even write a letter to the board," Fitzpatrick said. "How hard would it have been to write a letter?"

"She planned to be here in person," he said.

Fitzpatrick released the grip on his arm and Cody massaged the area.

"She didn't write a letter because she was going to be here and testify," Cody said. His voice lowered to a whisper. "But in the end, she couldn't do it. She's out in the car. Please don't try to talk to her. She's... not well."

"I'm not trying to hurt her. In fact, I think it will help her if her story gets out there. That's all I'm trying to do."

"She was livid you stopped by our house," Cody said. "And blamed me for leaving the gate open."

"Detective Osborne's testimony was unexpected, wasn't it?"

"What an asshole. He came by the house last week and told Erin it was unlikely Duggan would get parole, and if he did, not to worry because the guy was on his deathbed. He told her there was no real reason to come and testify. Of course, now I know he didn't want her in the courtroom when he supported the parole."

"Interesting he would do that. Did he at least talk to her about sending a letter?" Fitzpatrick asked.

"No, but his deputy suggested it, texted Erin, because apparently, he didn't want to say it in front of Osborne. We should never have trusted him."

Cody fidgeted and scratched his neck.

"Duggan looked older than last time I saw him, of

course, but he didn't look chronically ill. Certainly not on his deathbed."

"I've got to go. Erin's been waiting this whole time."

He turned down the hallway and Fitzpatrick followed.

"Buddy, wait up," he said.

He stopped, turned, and stared at the floor.

"I would never tell Erin you didn't speak up at the hearing."

Cody teared up, leaned against the wall, and slid down to a sitting position on the institutional tile floor. He gripped his head tightly in his hands and sobbed softly. Fitzpatrick checked the time. He needed to speak to Osborne before he drove away, but there was more to gain from Cody.

Finally, he spoke. "I just…froze. I hadn't prepared anything because Erin was going to do the talking. My role was the supportive spouse at her side. Shit, I can't even do that anymore."

"Erin doesn't need to know any of that. I think she'll be adequately enraged by Osborne's testimony, and you'll get a pass on this."

Cody smiled weakly. "Right. I'm just the second shittiest person in the room."

"Third, if you count Duggan."

Fitzpatrick extended a hand and pulled him to his feet. Cody smoothed his pant leg over the prosthesis. The reporter pulled a small brown envelope from his pocket and handed it to Cody.

"What's this?"

"To tide you over. No one should detox in the middle of a shitshow like today, or like the next few months might be for your wife, for your family."

"What is it?"

"Oxycontin."

Cody hesitated, but finally reached for the packet. He nodded his thanks and headed for the exit. Fitzpatrick turned back towards the hearing room, hoping he could still catch Osborne. He didn't know what game the Detective was playing, not yet.

# # #

Detective Osborne gathered his messenger bag and bottle of water as the hearing room emptied out, watching as Duggan huddled with his attorneys, whispering back and forth. Duggan made eye contact with Osborne and smirked.

"This could end badly for Erin and her family," said Joshua. "I hope you don't come to regret this."

Me too, he thought. He had taken a huge risk, but it was a calculated one, he told himself. The sheriff wasn't going to be pleased but there wasn't much he could do about that, other than fire him.

"They had their chance to be heard. She didn't even submit a letter. Her choice."

"Her husband showed up. He was in the back row."

"I saw him, sitting close to the reporter," Osborne said. "He could have spoken up."

Osborne watched as the attorneys filed past him and out the door looking pleased with themselves. Two guards approached Duggan, who held out his hands for the handcuffs. He stood and slowly backed away from the table, ankle shackles limiting his movements. The guards flanked the prisoner as they led him out. Duggan paused in front of Osborne and Joshua. He looked taller, bulkier than he had during their visit to the prison a few weeks earlier. The sickly pallor to his skin had improved. His blue eyes, watery and bloodshot when they'd seen him in May, were now clear, piercing and cold. Had he been played?

"Gentlemen, good to see you again."

"Duggan," Osborne replied.

"Detective, a very wise woman once told me to be careful what I wished for," he said. He nodded at Osborne and Joshua over his shoulder as the guards led him out the door.

They made their way through the parking lot back towards the cruiser. Up ahead, they saw the reporter leaning against their front fender, shielding his eyes from the sun as he scrolled through his phone.

"Shit, I hoped he had left," Osborne said. "Don't say a word. That's the reporter I told you about."

"I saw him hightail out of the room after Cody. Do you think that's who is feeding him information for those news releases?"

"I haven't read them."

"Maybe you should have. You might not have been as willing to support Duggan's release."

The reporter put away his phone as they approached and pulled a small recording device out of pocket.

"Detective, do you mind if I . . .?"

"Shut it off, Fitzpatrick."

"Off the record then," he said and slipped the recorder into his pocket.

Osborne couldn't tell if he'd powered down the device, but off the record meant off the record. Nothing he said should end up on the blog. Who was he kidding? He reminded himself to read the damn things when he reached the office.

"Detective, how confident are you that Mr. Duggan presents no danger to the community, and specifically, no threat to Erin Moore-Jackson and her family?"

"I'm not worried about Duggan committing any crimes."

"What about the accomplice who was never captured? What are the chances she'll join forces with Duggan after his release?"

Osborne hesitated. That's exactly what he was hoping, not that the pair would join forces exactly. Duggan's release could draw the woman out from wherever she'd been hiding for the past twenty years. If she existed at all. There was still significant doubt. Osborne reasoned he had rescued Erin twenty years ago, and he could keep her safe now.

"There's no reason to think the woman is still in the area, if she existed at all. It's been twenty years."

"Duggan's attorneys were from a large Madison law firm, Beres, Scott and Mulcahy. They wouldn't take a case like this pro bono. Where is the money coming from? Could his accomplice be bankrolling this effort?"

"That's doubtful, but I don't know who paid for the lawyers," he said and looked over at Joshua. Erin's descriptions of an unkempt, overall-wearing Veronica two decades ago made it unlikely she was wealthy, but a lot could change in twenty years. He'd need to follow the money. If Veronica could afford to hire pricy attorneys, she also had the resources to help Duggan disappear.

"One last question, officers. Do you plan to meet with Dr. Moore-Jackson to discuss your testimony? Or are you leaving it up to her husband?"

Osborne and Joshua ignored the question, climbed into the car and pulled away, leaving the reporter standing alone. Osborne flipped through the preset radio stations, then turned it off. Why hadn't he given more thought as to who was paying for Duggan's defense. Could it be Veronica and if so, what did it mean? Was Sheriff Carter right? His ex-wife? Was he so preoccupied with finding the missing woman that he'd lost sight of the bigger picture?

"I don't understand. Do you believe there was a female accomplice or not?" Joshua asked. "Because if you don't, there was no reason to let this guy out five years early."

Osborne ignored the question and drove towards Baraboo.

"He's going to put two and two together, you know. The reporter." Osborne said. "He's going to realize I'm using Duggan to draw Veronica out."

"If I were you, I'd worry about what Erin is going to say when she realizes you're using her and her family for bait."

They rode back to the sheriff's department in silence.

Chapter Ten

June 28
BREAKING NEWS – BARABOO NEWS-JOURNAL
by Richard Fitzpatrick, Reporter
On June 27th, the State of Wisconsin Parole Board Commission met at Columbia Correctional Facility in Portage to consider the parole and early release of Stanley Duggan III, who was convicted of first-degree kidnapping of fourteen-year-old Erin Moore, a resident of nearby Reedsburg. Duggan served twenty years of the twenty-five-year sentence and presented for his second parole attempt, represented by the Madison law firm of Beres, Scott and Mulcahy. The law firm was contacted regarding who is providing the financial backing for their services and declined comment.

Erin Moore-Jackson, who still resides in Reedsburg did not appear at the parole hearing and submitted no written or oral testimony for consideration. The original arresting officer Detective Warren Osborne, currently a detective with the Sauk County Sheriff's Department, addressed the Commission, citing the advanced age of the prisoner and considerable time served. He voiced no objections to Duggan's release. He also discussed the availability of halfway houses and ankle monitoring to ensure public safety. A brief interview with Detective Osborne following the hearing confirmed his support for release.

The Parole Board Commission will notify all parties of their decision in writing.

I interviewed Dr. Erin Moore-Jackson and her husband Cody Jackson in their home the day following the parole hearing and they have no further comments.

Follow Breaking News for further updates.

Follow me on Twitter @FitzpatrickRichard 14.

Chapter Eleven

When Osborne had refused to discuss the parole board's decision over the phone, Erin knew it was bad news. She'd barely pulled into the driveway after dropping the girls off at their summer program when he arrived. She reflexively shut the security gate behind him and climbed out of the car.

Cody joined them on the back patio. The morning dew still clung to the blades of grass but would burn off as soon as the sun rose above the tree line to the east of the house. Osborne accepted the cup of coffee and sent Cody back into the kitchen for sugar before she could climb out of her chair.

"The parole board's decision was announced Monday afternoon," Osborne said, once Cody had returned with his sugar, and he'd spent a ridiculous amount of time stirring it into his coffee. "I've never heard of their decisions coming down this fast. I supposed they wanted to get things wrapped up for the July fourth holiday."

"You found out this morning?" she asked.

"Not exactly, but there wasn't time…" He stopped himself. "I'm here now. Unfortunately, they have granted Duggan parole, but the good news is they are keeping him on a truly short leash."

"Such as?" she asked.

"Ankle monitor, first of all, for six months. And he's

been assigned to live in a halfway house in Baraboo, at least for now. That's sixteen miles from here, give or take. He's only allowed a five-mile radius, which allows him to check in with his parole officer once a week. That's for at least five years."

"Five miles is a pretty long leash," Cody said.

"It doesn't reach Reedsburg or your clinic. Or your daughters' school."

"Ankle monitors won't keep him at the halfway house if he chooses to leave. It only makes him easier to find after the fact," Erin said. "It also allows him to see Veronica if he chooses."

"That's assuming she's still in the area, or even still alive," Osborne said.

He didn't mention the third option. She had never existed in the first place, but Erin knew what he was implying. He was still questioning her credibility, after all these years and all she'd been through. She abruptly rose from the table and stomped into the house. She returned two minutes later with a manilla envelope and emptied the contents on the table. Three postcards, one each showing the Wisconsin Dells, the Madison Capitol building and the Mississippi River.

"These were all postmarked in Wisconsin. They started coming the week after Duggan was granted the hearing. They're from her, I'm sure of it."

Osborne reached into his pocket and pulled out a pair of latex gloves. He flipped the cards over and examined the postmarks. Handwritten address and a simple short message.

"See you soon."

Same message on all three. No signature.

"Why didn't you report these?" Osborne asked.

"How many postcards and birthday cards have I turned in over the years, fifteen? It never went anywhere. Never any usable fingerprints. Nothing you could trace. I stopped bringing them years ago."

"I assumed they'd stopped coming. Anyway, you can't be certain they're from her."

"I didn't bother bringing them in because that was your response. Anybody could have sent them, you said. But I know they're from her." And they made Erin's skin crawl every time one showed up in the mailbox.

Osborne gathered the postcards into a pile and slipped them back into the envelope, which he slid into his canvas bag.

"Another factor to consider is Duggan's age. He's 79 years old and in failing health. He's a shadow of the man he was twenty years ago. You should have seen him at the hearing."

Erin *should* have seen him at the hearing, remembering how incapacitated she'd been sitting in the car for an hour, rocking herself and tightly clutching her gun. She should have testified as she had planned and had rehearsed. She felt her face redden and she crossed her arms across her chest. Cody squirmed in the chair next to her and rubbed his knee. If she had been stronger… Her eyes filled with tears, and she hastily brushed them away with her sleeve.

"I had a visit from the reporter, the one doing those news releases about Duggan and about my family. He was at the parole hearing."

Osborne glanced at Cody who stared down and said nothing.

"Fitzpatrick said you testified in support of his release. It was even in his blog."

"I simply made the point he'd served twenty years, which is a longer sentence than most kidnappers receive, and the victim and her family hadn't taken interest in coming forward."

You bastard. He'd discouraged her from attending and was now using it to blame her for the outcome of the parole hearing.

"You've delivered your message. I want you to leave," Erin said. Her voice was low and quiet. She dug her fingernails into the palms of her hands to conceal her trembling.

The detective drained his coffee cup, stood, and left without another word. She closed the security gate behind him, and when she returned to the back patio, Cody still sat staring at the ground, his coffee untouched.

"At least tell me why." She sat and stared. "You were at the hearing and didn't tell me anything about his testimony. Why did the reporter have to tell me Osborne stabbed us in the back?"

"I've been having more problems with my leg," he said. He pushed away his cup of coffee and stared off towards the barn. "I know you don't believe that's all that's going on with me."

She sighed and turned her gaze away and watched a crow perched on the top of the fence.

"Fuck this, I need a meeting."

He stood and hobbled back into the house. A few minutes later, she heard the front gate slide open and his truck pulled out of the driveway.

Erin checked the schedule of local meetings he kept taped to the inside of his bedroom closet door. There wasn't a meeting for eight hours.

Chapter Twelve

Cody took his usual seat near the side door of the small meeting room, avoiding the busy corner with the coffee urn and plate of chocolate chip cookies where most of the men and all the women congregated before and after the meeting. He nodded to some of the regulars. He knew their first names from the times they'd shared their stories. Very few knew his name, other than two or three friends of his original sponsor who had introduced him around his first meeting but had since died with a needle in his arm.

He knew he should find another sponsor. It had been a few years, but he couldn't bring himself to approach anyone new, not after Terrence's overdose. Cody had been partially to blame and was still on probation. He had initially resisted coming back to the meetings, not sure anyone in the room who knew his history would have anything to do with him. He'd been wrong. On his return, he'd been met with a mix of indifference and a few understanding nods.

He hadn't shared since, but once he'd heard enough of the other men's narratives, he knew he was in the right room. They'd all been in similar dark places, like the night Terrence died in his arms.

"I'm Mike, and I'm an addict."

"Hello, Mike." Twenty-some voices in unison, including Cody's.

It was a typical meeting, the sharers with their accounts of painful backsliding and their small victories, and the listeners. There were lots of vets in the room, many Cody's age, some with visible battle scars like his. It brought him no solace. Tonight, the experiences they shared were out of sync with his own, and he walked out halfway through the meeting.

###

Fitzpatrick picked up Cody's truck a few blocks from his house and followed him all the way to the church basement in Tomah. The reporter had taken a chair at the back of the room near the entrance and watched, hopeful Cody would speak at the meeting. Fitzpatrick had attended several meetings for sex addicts ten years earlier, when he still thought his marriage was worth saving, if only to avoid a financial bloodletting.

It hadn't worked out for his marriage, although he found the stories he'd heard fascinating. He'd kept on going more out of curiosity than looking for a solution to his problem. He'd never acknowledged it as an illness, not to himself, well, because it wasn't. He had a healthy sex drive, and his wife didn't. She was the one with the problem.

He'd debated using kernels of the other men's anecdotes in a novel, changed up enough to stand up to scrutiny, and he still kept his notes. Maybe after the true crime novel about Erin was published and he had an agent, he'd dig out the files. Sexual deviancy in a small-town setting—it was bound to sell.

The reporter listened to the men as they stood at the front of the room and bared their anguish and pain. He didn't understand why they would splay themselves open for others to see. He'd never spoken at any of the meetings he'd attended.

He stood and squeezed past the back row of chairs to the side exit, following Cody out into the hallway in time to see the door to the outside swing shut. He caught up a half block later.

"Cody! Slow down a minute," he said.

Cody stopped and turned to face him, frowning as he recognized the reporter. "What are you doing here? Did you follow me?"

"No, I saw you leave the church. I was visiting a family friend down the street. There's a coffee shop a half block up. Can I buy you a cup?"

Cody looked at him warily. He clearly didn't buy the coincidence angle. He'd have to be a complete idiot to believe it. Still, he slowly nodded in agreement. They walked in silence down the sidewalk to an old-fashioned diner and took a booth in the back.

A few minutes later, the waitress dropped off two cups of black coffee. They waited until she moved out of ear range.

"I'm assuming you were attending a Narcotics Anonymous meeting at the church."

"It's a mix. AA and NA at this meeting."

"I thought it was more likely you'd be going to meetings at the VA instead. It's only a few miles from here."

"I do occasionally. Depends on the night. This was the only meeting scheduled tonight." Cody paused and sipped his coffee, watching the waitress move around the room. He turned back towards Fitzpatrick and leaned forward. "Why are you really here?"

"Coffee with a pal, that's all. Thought we could get to know each other a little better." Fitzpatrick smiled in what he hoped was a disarming way. "I get the feeling neither of us have a lot of friends in the area."

"How about the one you were supposedly visiting down the street from the church?"

The reporter chuckled. He'd forgotten his own cover story in five minutes. "I'll introduce you some time. You might get along great."

"Can you cut the bullshit?" Cody asked.

Fitzpatrick reached out his hands, palms upward as he leaned back against the red vinyl of the booth. "I was hoping to talk to you about Erin, that's all. I know how stressful these past few weeks have been for her, especially now Duggan's going to be released."

Cody nodded.

"I want to know more about Erin from her teen years and her twenties. I want to understand how she dealt with the trauma of the kidnapping, and how she's recovered to this day. She must be an incredibly strong woman to return to Reedsburg, after all the bad memories."

"Why? So, you can put it in your blog, or whatever you call it? She hates that you're writing about her. Why do you think I would help you?"

"I promise nothing you tell me will end up in the News-Journal. This is all off the record." He meant it, at least until he started to work on his true crime novel.

Fitzpatrick reached into his shirt pocket and adjusted a small manilla envelope until the top half inch was visible. He tapped on the packet and smiled. Cody sighed and leaned back in the booth with his eyes shut. He inhaled deeply and exhaled for nearly a minute, in and out. The reporter watched in silence.

Finally, Cody said, "What do you want to know?"

Fitzpatrick smiled and took out a small leather

notebook and pen.

"I mentioned her returning to Reedsburg earlier. I know her sister lives here, but both of her parents have since passed. Why would she stay in this area to set up her practice?"

Cody took a slow sip of his coffee before responding. "Erin said it was easier here because everybody already knew her story, what happened to her back then. She never had to worry about being found out."

"What do you mean, found out? She hadn't done anything wrong. She was the victim."

"When she went off to college, Luther College in Iowa for her Psychology undergrad degree, nobody knew her story, and she loved that. No one treated her with kid gloves. They didn't regard her as damaged."

"Damaged. That's pretty harsh."

"Her words, not mine. During her junior year, one of her sorority sisters found clippings online somehow and everything changed for Erin. All her friends found out. Even the professors knew, and they called her in for counseling. She hated it. The same thing happened when she was at the University of Chicago for her PhD and again during her clinical internship year."

"I don't understand why that made her come back to the area."

"Everyone here already knew. She said elsewhere she'd be waiting for that last shoe to fall, and eventually it would. She didn't have that here."

"When did you two start to date?"

"About the time she started grad school. We knew each other from high school, but we started to hang out together when she came home to see her family. Then I deployed, met an IED six months later in Afghanistan, and I moved back for my rehab at the VA. We got married after she'd been back in practice for a little over a year."

The waitress topped off their cups and dropped a bill on the table, with an obvious glance at her watch to remind them of closing time.

"How do you deal with what happened to Erin back then?" Fitzpatrick asked.

"I'm not sure what you mean. I love Erin, try to support her and I'm doing a pretty shitty job talking with you right now."

"Tell me this. This Veronica, Duggan's alleged accomplice back then. Was she real? Does Erin ever talk about her?"

"She's real. I don't doubt it at all. And from what Erin's told me, she was by far the worse of the two."

"There. Was that so difficult?"

Fitzpatrick slid the small envelope out of his pocket and across the table. He pulled eight dollars out of his wallet and left it on top of the tab. Cody wasted no time retrieving the packet from the table, glancing around the restaurant as he did.

"If you want to know the truth, Erin and I probably wouldn't be together if she hadn't gone through what she did. I mean, look at her. She's smart, beautiful, and educated. Look at me. See what I see in the mirror every morning. I'm missing part of my leg, got no job and I'm selling my wife out for dope. She calls herself damaged and maybe she's right, but without that, she would be way out of my league."

Cody stood without another word. The little bell above the diner door jingled as he left the café.

Chapter Thirteen

Erin escorted her last patient of the morning to the waiting room and grabbed her lunch from the breakroom. She took a diet Coke from the fridge, hoping the caffeine would counter the lack of sleep. Back at her desk, she shifted lettuce leaves and chunks of artichoke around the container aimlessly for ten minutes, until she finally pushed the salad off to the side. Erin knew she should eat, but she needed carbs more than she needed lettuce.

Three more hours of appointments were on the afternoon schedule, and she had once again skipped breakfast. A few days earlier Lindsey had pointed out that she looked thinner since learning about Duggan's hearing, and even then, she was surprised when the bathroom scale showed she was down fifteen pounds.

Erin leaned back in her desk chair and shut her eyes. She should finish the charting on her last two patients, increasing the chances of getting out on time. She checked her wrist fitness tracker. Her resting heart rate was in the high eighties, and she could feel every beat in her chest as well as a throbbing in the back of her head. She'd once been a runner back in grad school, before the girls, before Cody, and she wondered if she would ever get in shape again.

She checked her phone for messages for the fifth time that day but still nothing from Cody. They had argued that morning when he caught her looking through his wallet while he showered. Once more he had stomped out of the house, fuming at her lack of trust, this time in front of the girls. He was right on both accounts. She had no right to search his belongings and she didn't trust him. This had made her fifteen minutes late for her first patient, since he had promised to drop the girls off at summer school that morning. It wasn't the first time she'd wondered if the girls should be riding with him at all. If she got busy with her charting, she could still get out on time and pick up the girls.

In approximately seventy-two hours, the series of locked doors at the prison would slide open and Duggan would be escorted back into her world and there wasn't a damn thing she could do to stop it. No more overlapping loops of barbed wire across the top of the fence. No guard tower or orange jumpsuit. Just an ankle monitor replacing the shackles.

Erin grabbed her water bottle and gulped down half the contents. Her stomach had been churning most of the morning and she regretted that second cup of coffee. She jumped when her phone buzzed, announcing her next patient. She gathered up her napkin and remaining salad and tossed them into the garbage.

The next client was a scheduled child custody evaluation. The divorce had been three years earlier, but now the father was challenging the fitness of the mother for continuing joint custody. Erin hadn't done many of these evaluations in her practice. They usually went to one of her partners, Beverly Simrock, but since she was on medical leave following back surgery, Erin and one other psychologist were filling in. Fortunately, Beverly had provided a template for evaluation and reporting, and Erin had access to the formal complaint the father had filed with the Sauk County Court. She'd likely have to testify in Family Court, since one of the parents was almost certain to contest her recommendations.

It would mean another visit to the courthouse in Baraboo. The building was considerably larger than it had been twenty years ago, occupying much more of the old-fashioned town square, but the older part of the edifice was much the same, at least from the outside. She remembered the old cannon with a plaque honoring WWI veterans at the north end of the square, remembered sitting on a nearby bench with her parents while Lindsey climbed on the cannon on the first day she appeared in the courtroom. She hadn't been back since her testimony twenty years ago. She and Cody had intentionally driven to the next county for their marriage license.

She remembered the hard, oversized oak chairs in the conference room where she'd been allowed to hide with her parents before going into the courtroom. They'd even brought Lindsey along, afraid of leaving her with anyone else. She remembered how quiet her sister had been for weeks after the trial, even though they'd never spoken about it.

Erin could still picture the jury, thirteen strangers averting their eyes as she testified. Stanley Duggan, cleaned up and dressed in a suit and tie at the defendants table next to his lawyer, staring, unblinking. Smirking at her. She knew his attorney was still in practice in Baraboo. Was he doing family law? Is it possible that he'd be cross-examining her on the witness stand for a second time? She tried to swallow but couldn't.

Erin flipped open the file and scanned the

paperwork. She didn't recognize the name of the attorney who was representing the father, but she would never forget the mother's attorney. It was Victor Fenske, the man who had represented Stanley Duggan. He had asked her questions she couldn't bear to remember twenty years later and was now representing the allegedly unfit mother, who waited steps outside her office door.

Erin broke into a sweat and squeezed her eyes tight. She closed the file and placed it on the desk. A wave of nausea swept over her, and she vomited into the garbage can. Fenske. He would remember her. She couldn't face him a second time. She felt a tightness in her chest. Surely this was what a heart attack felt like.

She was a psychologist and had studied human behavior as well as basic physiology. Intellectually, she knew there was nothing to fear from Victor Fenske. As she'd taught her patients through therapy, she needed simply to recognize an unfounded fear and use coping mechanisms. She took a deep breath in, closed her eyes, and concentrated on her breathing. This would ease up. It didn't and the odor of vomit wafted up into the room. She reached down and tied the garbage bag shut but it didn't help.

She'd ask another one of her partners to take the evaluation. She reached for her desk phone and called the receptionist. When Avery answered, Erin stared at the phone in her hand, and no words came out.

She slammed down the receiver, grabbed her purse, and ran for the back door.

Chapter Fourteen

Stanley Duggan III walked through the open gate, his posture erect and his head held high. He was neatly dressed in a gray guayabera shirt which hung over neatly pressed dress slacks, looking like he was ready for a Tinder date. Osborne had picked up ex-cons after discharge from the prison over the years, and this wasn't standard issue clothing. The outfit likely cost more than his own uniform and again he wondered who was footing the bill. Duggan was clean-shaven and his hair looked freshly cut. He held the bright orange plastic bag with his prison belongings.

Osborne suspected the fifty dollars of gate pay was tucked deep into his pocket. It would have to hold him over until his social security payments started up again, although he might have money stashed away in bank accounts law enforcement hadn't uncovered twenty years ago. Clearly, there was some source of money.

Duggan still owned the small hobby farm outside of Baraboo where they'd found Erin, and the property taxes were up to date. Osborne had checked over the years, and they'd always been paid with an untraceable cashier's check. There was money somewhere, and someone on the outside with access.

Osborne had driven by the farm occasionally, most recently a week ago, and a chain still hung low across the driveway, the no trespassing sign nearly rusted into obscurity. He'd parked on the road and stepped over the chain. He was entitled as an officer of the law, and he argued it was his job to make sure there hadn't been a break-in on a long empty property. The paint had weathered to a soft gray on the wood siding of the small two-story house, but the doors and windows were intact. A thick coating of dust covered the furniture and floor visible through a window from the porch. No footprints in the dust.

He'd walked the periphery of the property including the small pole barn behind the house. No windows in the barn and both doors were locked. The padlocks looked new, and he'd wondered who had replaced them. Veronica? Who was keeping up with the property taxes? And what was locked up in the barn?

At his parole hearing, Duggan had declared his intent to move back to the hobby farm, plant a vegetable garden and raise chickens, and catch up on twenty years of cable television shows. He hoped to lead a simple life, he told the panel. He didn't have to provide proof of work opportunities, not at his age. His attorneys smiled and nodded. He'd stayed on script. He would have adequate funds once his social security payments started up again.

Fortunately, the parole board decided he belonged in a halfway house at least initially, with an ankle monitor and weekly visits to his parole officer in Baraboo, with the first visit the day after his release, then every Tuesday for five years. It was a long monitoring duration, especially for someone as old as Duggan, and a first-time offender, but his single crime had been heinous.

Osborne climbed out of the police cruiser and stood

on the sidewalk, blocking the path for Duggan to exit to the street.

Duggan turned his face back towards the prison gate and squinted up at the bright sunshine, then turned back to the detective.

"Are you here to harass me, Osborne?"

"No, it's a courtesy call. I wanted to offer you a ride into Baraboo."

"Where's your sidekick?"

"He's off today. Can I give you a lift?"

Duggan shook his head no, made a circle around the detective and ambled down the sidewalk away from the prison. There was a bus stop about a quarter mile down the road, and he knew the new releases always received a free bus pass if there weren't going to be family members at the gate. He didn't blame Duggan. The man hadn't had the opportunity to walk a quarter mile in one direction, uninterrupted, for the past twenty years.

Osborne recognized the same reporter who'd attended the hearing, as he pulled up alongside Duggan halfway to the bus stop and hopped out of the car with a camera man. Duggan paused for Fitzpatrick. They spoke for a minute, then he motioned for the reporter to leave him alone.

The detective continued to follow him in his cruiser, and every few minutes Duggan looked back, expressionless. He walked about one hundred yards past the bus stop and sat on a bench. A half hour later, a late model gray sedan with government plates stopped, picked him up, and drove away. Parole officer, he thought.

\#\#\#

"I should have known Osborne would be here,"

Fitzpatrick said. "Let's see how Duggan reacts to him."

They watched as Duggan ignored and walked around the detective, who then climbed back into his car. He couldn't make out their voices, but he imagined Osborne was there to badger or threaten him. Duggan might be more responsive to a friendly reporter.

"Jesus Christ, Kenneth. Is this thing even on?" Fitzpatrick tapped on the microphone, finally convinced it was recording. He cleared his throat and turned to half-face Duggan as he approached.

"Mr. Duggan, after twenty years behind bars, do you have anything to say to our listeners?"

He eyed them warily, shook his head and kept walking. Fitzpatrick and the camera man followed him down the sidewalk.

Duggan saw Kenneth was filming the exchange and he held up his middle finger to the camera.

"Fuck off and leave me alone." He glowered at the reporter, spit on the ground and continued his walk to the bus stop.

# # #

July 16

BREAKING NEWS – BARABOO NEWS-JOURNAL by Richard Fitzpatrick, Reporter

Stanley Duggan III was released from Columbia Correctional Facility yesterday following a successful bid for parole on June 27. Duggan had served twenty years of a twenty-five-year sentence for first degree kidnapping of fourteen-year-old Erin Moore, whom he held captive for five months prior to her rescue.

Video footage attached shows Detective Warren Osborne with the Sauk County Sheriff's Department talking to Duggan after he exits the prison. Osborne had been involved in the arrest of Duggan two decades earlier. No audio is available, and the detective subsequently refused to discuss the nature of the conversation. As seen on the video, the encounter ends with Duggan turning away from Osborne with an accompanying hand gesture.

This reporter attempted to interview Duggan, who acknowledged he remembered him from the original trial twenty years prior. He declined a ride to his halfway house and subsequently was picked up in a vehicle licensed to Sauk County, presumably his parole officer.

Duggan will initially live in a half-way house in Baraboo, Wisconsin and ankle monitoring and extended parole period were conditions for his release.

Attempts to contact Dr. Erin Moore-Jackson, who practices Psychology with an office in Lake Delton were unsuccessful.
CUE VIDEO

Chapter Fifteen

"Erin will hate me if she finds out I've been talking to you." Lindsey lifted the glass of Sauvignon Blanc and sipped.

She was dressed in a low-cut black silk blouse and a tight pair of jeans. Interesting choice. Did she think this was a date or was she planning to meet friends after their drinks?

"We're a forty-five-minute drive from her house. She'll never know," Fitzpatrick said.

She'd already smelled of wine when she arrived, after he'd asked the waitress to remove the snacks from their high-top table. The higher her blood alcohol level, the better.

"She's barely leaving the house these days, except for work. And the gun range. It's been this way since she knew he was getting out."

"She shoots?" he asked. "Does she have a concealed carry permit?"

She nodded. "She's had it for a long time, but ever since they announced his hearing, she's gotten serious about it. Of course, she's careful to lock it up at home, around the girls. She's even made me take a lesson, but there's no way I'm carrying a gun around."

Evidently Erin wasn't as helpless as she seemed. He'd file that nugget of information away for now. His thoughts went back to the day he had surprised her at her house with his camera man, and he now wondered if there had been a holster tucked underneath her gardening shirt. He'd have to go back and check the video footage.

Fitzpatrick held up his glass to Lindsey and they clinked. "To freedom of the press," he said. To secrets, he thought. And betrayal.

She gave him a lopsided smile.

"You look great tonight, by the way."

Her smile widened.

"Thanks," she said. "I wasn't sure how dressy this place would be. I couldn't tell from their website."

"You look perfect." He paused for effect and put on his best Walter Cronkite face. Lindsey was so young–would she even know who that was? "I'm sure you understand that the public is interested in what your sister, your entire family went through twenty years ago, how it changed all of you."

"Sure did," she said. "Erin never saw it that way, but of course that's true."

"What was it like for you back then? You're three years younger, right?"

"Four years and a few months. Almost no one asked me that, you know, what it was like for me? Sure, my parents had me see a therapist for a while afterwards. My dad cared, of course. But my mom passed away during my senior year of high school."

"You were eleven when Erin was kidnapped?"

"I was ten." She took a gulp of her wine. "At first, I was part of it, the investigation I mean. That detective talked to me a couple of times since I was right there when it happened. He's the same one who testified that it would be fine to let Duggan out of prison at the parole hearing. My parents didn't let me out of their sight, even after we got Erin back. And the kids at school, once I went back, peppered me with questions, but they were only about Erin. After a couple of weeks, it was like I faded into the background."

"Did you blame Erin for that?"

"Of course not. She never asked for what happened. I mean, I was the lucky one, wasn't I? We were both on our bikes that day, and she pedaled much faster than me. I'd also got a cast removed from my arm two weeks earlier and was still cautious about reinjuring it. I was an easy target. But she turned around and sped back when she saw I was in trouble." Lindsey's eyes filled with tears and a quiet sob escaped her throat. "It might have been me."

Fitzpatrick signaled the waitress for another round and handed Lindsey a cocktail napkin. It had been a miscalculation to ask her about childhood shit. This was old news and he needed to redirect before she wallowed any deeper. He'd always wondered why they hadn't snatched both girls. It never hurts to have a spare.

"I don't mean to get sloppy on you," she said and sniffed.

"I'm sorry to dredge up such painful old memories." He was sorry, but not for the reasons she would imagine.

The waitress brought their drinks and Lindsey obligingly gulped the last inch of her first glass of wine and handed her the empty.

"Tell me how Erin and Cody are coping now. They must be concerned after his release."

"Erin's been freaking out ever since they announced the parole hearing. I think you can imagine how she's doing now that he's finally back in Baraboo. They are considering sending the girls to stay with Cody's mom for a while."

"And what's her name?" he asked, hoping for another source of information.

Lindsey hesitated and chewed on her lower lip. "I can't give you that."

He'd try again after she finished that second drink, or maybe a third glass.

"Has it been hard on their relationship?"

Lindsey snorted. "They don't openly fight about Duggan, at least not in front of me, but they fight about everything else. Erin doesn't exactly depend on Cody for anything, you know. She hasn't in a long time."

"I know Cody has had some problems in the past." He'd done a deep dive through the Wisconsin Circuit Court records. Narcotics possession for which he'd done time served, followed by court-mandated rehab and of probation. The Moore-Jacksons were all too familiar with the court system.

"He's a good guy, sincerely trying, you know? Erin doesn't appreciate that sometimes."

"He was injured in the service?"

"Afghanistan. Before they were married, even before they were dating. He doesn't like to talk about it, but he lost part of his leg," Lindsey said. "He got into trouble with pain meds a few years ago, when the girls were toddlers."

"I'm aware of his criminal record."

"Erin hasn't said anything, but she may be worried he's using again." She lowered her voice and leaned forward. "Erin has a close friend she sees from time to time, and she may have confided in him."

"I'm glad she has someone she can trust. Have you met him?"

Lindsey finished the second glass of wine in a few swallows and put the glass down on the table.

"He's a friend of hers, that's all. I don't know his name. Look, I need to go. I want to be off the road before that second glass of wine kicks in."

"I can drive you home or call you an Uber. Stay for a few more minutes, please?"

"No, I'm fine. Please forget what I've said. It was the wine talking."

Lindsey grabbed her purse and hurried to the door.

Forget it? Not likely. Erin had a close friend, and it was a man. He wondered if Cody knew.

Chapter Sixteen

"Your neck muscles are tighter than usual," Alex said, as he continued to massage her shoulders and neck. He drizzled warmed oil over her upper back and kneaded. "You need to try to relax."

Erin had secretly never liked massages. Not from Cody. Not from the massage therapist at the overpriced spa outside of Wisconsin Dells that she occasionally visited. Not even from Alex. They hurt, and pain was never relaxing. That's what it came down to.

"Does this feel good?" he asked. "Should I go firmer?"

"No, it's perfect," she lied. His fingertips were already indenting her flesh by inches. "I think it's feeling better."

Erin flipped over and sat up in bed. She reached for her silk robe at the foot of the bed and stood. The light fabric clung to the still oily patches of skin. Alex climbed off the bed still naked and headed towards the shower, without his usual invitation for her to join him.

His condo had the biggest shower she had ever seen, plenty of room for two with four shower heads, penetrating water pressure, gorgeous marble tile from floor to ceiling, and a window overlooking the lake below.

She debated about following him, but he'd been less talkative than usual the whole afternoon and she didn't want to push him. She finally tucked her bare legs back under the covers and waited for him to finish. Ten minutes later he emerged from the bathroom, a towel wrapped around his waist and headed into his walk-in closet, shutting the door behind him.

"Everything all right, Alex?" she called out.

A muffled 'fine' came through the door. She gathered her underwear and dress and took them into the bathroom. After a quick shower and change, she met Alex in the great room. He stood behind the kitchen island and opened a bottle of cabernet with practiced efficiency.

"Can I get your advice?" she asked.

He grimaced and poured wine into each glass.

"What?" she asked. "Sorry if I'm imposing on you by asking your opinion."

"I didn't mean it that way," Alex said. "I'm understandably tired of hearing about Duggan, that's all. I understand you're on edge. I get it. But that's not what these afternoons are supposed to be about."

"You know, Cody thinks I'm seeing a therapist," she said. "He thinks I've got standing appointments every other Thursday."

"Sometimes you treat me like one."

"You'd prefer this should strictly be about sex? Slam bam, thank you ma'am?"

"Don't be crude. You know that's not what I meant."

"Why don't you explain it to me then?"

Alex said nothing but picked up his glass and walked to the glass doors leading to his balcony. He'd chosen madras shorts and a pale green shirt, and she wondered if he was planning a round of golf as soon as she left.

She sipped her wine in silence and checked the time on her phone. It was nearly four o'clock. Cody wouldn't be expecting her home until five. She'd been allowing Lindsey to pick up the girls from their summer program with the understanding that she took them directly home and stayed with them until Erin returned, even if Cody was home. Sometimes it was convenient that Lindsey was still unemployed, and she briefly wondered about her sister's job interview the week before.

"It's about Cody," she said, wondering if Alex would answer. "Not Duggan for once."

He turned towards Erin, silhouetted against the sunshine streaming in the window from behind.

"I'm hardly the best person to advise you on your relationship with your husband."

He settled into one of the gray leather chairs flanking the natural stone fireplace, and she joined him. She carefully positioned her wine glass on the coaster and sat back. The chair was too low and deep to be comfortable, but little in the condo had been designed for comfort, including Alex.

"I suspect he's using again," she said. "There have been a couple of times in the past few weeks where he's irritable and shaky, breaking out in a cold sweat."

"Like he's going through withdrawal."

She nodded.

Where do you think he's getting it from?"

"I have no idea, but if you've got money, there's usually a source. He had no problems finding it in the past."

"True."

"I worry about his ability to take care of the girls."

"That's why you've been trusting Lindsey to pick them up? She's the lesser of two evils?"

"She isn't that bad. I don't think I give her enough credit for how much she's changed over the past couple of years."

"Maybe you should tell her that."

She nodded. "I haven't confronted Cody. I've looked through his drawers for his stash, but I'm not sure what I'm going to do if I find it. I did buy a naloxone nasal spray in case."

"He's still going to his support group at the VA, isn't he? Maybe there's someone there you could talk to."

She shook her head. "Patient confidentiality, and Cody wouldn't sign off on my having access to his treatment records. I tried a couple of years ago."

"Sounds like he trusts you as much as you trust him."

Erin flinched. She hadn't attributed Cody's refusal to a lack of trust, but Alex was likely right.

"You really don't need my advice on this. You know your choices. This is what you do for a living, isn't it?" He yawned and his arms stretched over head. "You either confront him, or you don't. And he agrees to go back into rehab, or he doesn't."

"And I either leave him or I stay," she said softly.

Alex nodded, stood, and picked up both glasses of wine, an inch remaining in hers which she had planned to drink. He poured it down the drain, rinsed the glasses and placed them into the dishwasher. He corked the bottle of wine and slipped it into a bottom cabinet, maintaining the clutter-free appearance to his kitchen.

"That's for you to decide, but I do want to be clear. This has nothing to do with us, with our arrangement. I don't want anything more than we've got right now."

"I didn't imply that."

"We will never be a couple, not in any sense of the word. You understood that from the start. I love these…" He paused to consider the wording. "I'm going to call them trysts."

A tryst, she thought. What was that old expression about putting lipstick on a pig? She knew these afternoons were nothing more than a rendezvous for sex, and Alex was hardly her first. Like the others, he had been quick to accuse her of wanting more.

Erin slipped on her sandals and retrieved her purse from the nearby table. She had known from the beginning Alex had no interest in her outside of their arrangement, no interest in seeing photos of her kids, going out to dinner or anything else. She had never stayed overnight. She knew nothing about his own family other than he was currently on his third wife, although there was never any sign of another woman in his pristine condominium. He always made sure she left nothing behind and perhaps he did the same with his wife.

"See you in two weeks?" she asked.

He said nothing. She left and closed the door behind her.

Chapter Seventeen

"It's me," Erin phoned Lindsey as she pulled out of the condominium parking lot. "Anything I should pick up on the way home? I'm about thirty minutes away."

"Cody just left. Hold on a second."

Erin could hear the cartoon voices and music become softer as her sister was taking the conversation out of the girls' hearing range.

"He wasn't happy I picked up the girls from school today when he was available. I thought you two had worked this out. He was home when I arrived, and the gate was wide open. He complained about you not trusting him right in front of Charlotte."

"I'm sorry. I'll talk to him." Again.

"Cody also insinuated you weren't in fact at a therapy appointment. In front of your daughters."

And she'd need to talk to her girls.

"He stormed off into the barn and stayed there for an hour or so. Then he came in to change his shirt and left without saying a word to me or the girls."

"How did he look?"

"Angry. I didn't get close enough to say more than that."

"I'll see you in thirty minutes."

"There was nothing in the fridge for dessert. I can't believe you expect the girls to eat those carob cookies. Any chance you'll be passing Robby's?"

"Four chocolate sundaes coming up."

It was a warm July evening and Erin should have expected a long line at the drive through. She pulled in behind a minivan packed with kids and waited. She'd seen the help-wanted sign in the window as well as splashed across the marquee, right underneath the flavor of the day and wasn't surprised the line moved at a painfully slow pace. She pulled out her cell phone and checked for new messages. Nothing, not even an angry text from Cody. Nothing from Alex, which was no surprise.

Erin watched as an older woman climbed out of a weathered green Subaru and strolled towards the entrance. She'd probably get faster service inside, but it was too late for Erin to change. The drive through lane had a short cement fence separating it from the rest of the parking lot. She was stuck, unless the six cars behind her all backed up.

The woman had a pixie cut with straight gray hair and looked to be in her sixties. She was short and heavy-set, dressed in an oversize t-shirt with a cartoon cat on the front and wearing cut off denim shorts.

As she passed Erin's car, the woman stared through the windshield and a broad smile spread over her face. Erin froze. She'd seen the facial expression before, or one like it. She turned in her car seat and craned her neck to follow the woman's route to the door.

"Get a grip," she said aloud. There was nothing but the faint resemblance in the smile. This wasn't Veronica. It was some older lady coming for ice cream on a hot summer night. Her hair was gray, and Veronica's had been long and red. Twenty years ago. The woman was considerably heavier than her nemesis had been, but again, it had been two decades.

Erin looked at the dusty Subaru the woman had climbed out of. It was parked at an angle, and she couldn't get a clear view of the license plate. Her hands trembled as she grabbed her phone and brought up the camera. She climbed out of her car, and after another peek at the restaurant door, darted across the parking lot. She snapped a photo of the Wisconsin license plate, then examined the inside of the car. It was strewn with junk, fast food wrappers, soda cans and free advertisers. Nothing to give away the identity of the woman.

Horns blared from the drive-through line and Erin turned to find the cars ahead of hers had moved up considerably. She ran back to her car and moved it up thirty feet. She had a better view of the Subaru from her new position, and she watched for the woman to return. Erin inched forward and ordered the ice cream sundaes, hoping the woman would exit before she had to turn the corner for the pickup window. Maybe she was eating dinner inside and would be in there for an hour.

Erin was turning the corner when she saw the woman return, carrying a white bag of food in one hand and a beverage cup in the other. There was still a foot-tall barrier, and she was trapped, or at least her car was. She shifted into park and opened the door. The lane was narrow, and she had to exhale to squeeze out. The green Subaru was backing out of the parking spot and Erin ran towards the car. She pounded on the driver's window.

Again, the older woman smiled, locked the car door, and stared back at Erin. Erin motioned for her to roll down the window and she shook her head.

"Lady, move your car."

Erin turned to see a man her age dressed in a dirt-covered baseball uniform.

"Hold on a minute…"

Horns blared from the cars in line behind hers. She turned back to the woman in the Subaru, who now looked nothing like Veronica. The eyes were larger, closer together. Her lips were fuller. Veronica had never worn glasses, and this woman had thick black frames. But that smile.

The woman in the Subaru flipped up her middle finger and pulled away. Erin bolted back to her car, pulled forward to the pickup window, paid and snatched the tray of sundaes from the teenager. She sped up once she was free of the barrier and pulled out onto the street in the direction taken by the Subaru. Her Volvo zipped down the road, but there was no sign of the other car. She sped ahead for five miles, realizing the Subaru might have turned off at any number of sideroads.

Finally, she slowed, pulled into the parking lot of a closed insurance agency, and put the car in park. Her heart was still pounding in her chest. She clenched her fists and smacked the steering wheel. It wasn't Veronica, she told herself over and over. Then why hadn't the woman rolled down the window and talked to her? She hadn't seemed afraid and had beamed that repulsive and miserable smile at her. Veronica was twenty years older now, and she would likely have gray hair at this point. She'd likely gotten tired of the long length and cut it.

She vacillated back and forth. It couldn't be Veronica, but why such a blood-curdling smile? And why flip the bird to a stranger?

Erin had the license plate number. She wasn't sure Osborne would run the plate for her, but his deputy might.

She put the car back into drive. The tray of sundaes hadn't tipped in the car chase, but they were melting and running down the side of the tray. She headed for home.

A text message pinged on her phone. Cody.

"*Sleeping at a friend's after a meeting. Don't wait up.*"

One less thing to deal with that night.

Chapter Eighteen

Osborne's patience wore thin. He'd been sitting in his car for two hours down the street from the halfway house, binoculars and a camera with a telephoto lens in hand. He reluctantly phoned the parole officer for an update and learned Duggan had been given permission to move back to his small farm a few miles outside of town. Overcrowding, he'd explained apologetically.

There had been no notification of the sheriff's department or the victim, he'd fumed. Osborne knew he should call Erin with this update.

The parole officer also informed him Duggan had recently purchased a white minivan, and he forwarded Osborne the license plate number. There was no change to the five-mile driving restriction, now measured from his farm. This allowed him to reach the parole office, a grocery store in town and the Walmart out by the highway, but not much farther. It also allowed him to reach the middle school, one of the elementary schools, and God knows how many daycares and playgrounds, but since he wasn't a registered sex offender, these locations hadn't been restricted.

Osborne drove to the property and noticed the chain barricading the driveway had been removed, with fresh tire tracks in the wet sand driveway. A new mailbox stood askew at the end of the entrance, its pole wedged into a cinderblock and with stick-on numbers displaying the address, but no name. He parked the cruiser at the end of the driveway and headed toward the farmhouse on foot with his camera. Duggan's white nondescript minivan was parked close to the house, and he verified he had the correct license plate number. The door to the pole barn was open a foot, with a light shining from the interior.

Osborne crept towards the structure, hugging the side of the yard. His path would still be visible from the kitchen window, but he was certain Duggan was out in the barn. He heard a slow, rhythmic clanging of metal hitting the concrete floor, over and over. What the hell was he doing in there? He reached the door and took a quick peek through the opening.

Duggan was completely naked with his back to the door, performing deadlifts with a bar and weights, grunting loudly with each motion. A large wall rack of additional hand weights was attached to the wall, and there was a punching bag hung from a rafter nearby. He'd only been released from prison ten days earlier, and Osborne assumed he'd had the home gym set up recently. He tried to remember what had been in the barn twenty years ago. He might have missed the weights, but there definitely hadn't been a punching bag. At least part of the setup was new.

Duggan was training hard, and Osborne could see his well-developed back, leg and arm muscles, something he'd missed entirely on his earlier assessment when the man wore the baggy prison garb. Osborne doubted if he could have lifted the bar and weights, and he was nineteen years younger.

At the back of the barn, in a dimly lit corner, he could still make out remnants of the cell, constructed with wood, metal poles and cinder block, where Erin had spent part of her captivity. Once the weather changed, they moved her into the basement of the farmhouse. He thought the pen had been completely dismantled during the investigation. It should have been destroyed.

He had underestimated Duggan. The man was not only healthier than he'd believed but had significantly less supervision. There was no way to change his release now, but he wasn't going to let Erin or her family pay the price.

# # #

The next day Osborne was back in the office cleaning up paperwork. He received a call from one of the deputies that Duggan's white van had been spotted on the north end of the Baraboo central town square. Osborne and Joshua reached the location in less than ten minutes and spotted Duggan sitting with a woman at a picnic table on the lawn. They parked a half block away, behind a large utilities truck.

Joshua retrieved the camera, headed across the park, and positioned himself behind a delivery van thirty feet from the picnic table. Osborne headed closer, ducking behind the row of parked cars as he approached. He pulled out his binoculars and watched. Joshua gave him a thumbs up signal once he started snapping photos.

They looked like a couple on a date. Duggan was wearing a long sleeve blue shirt, with the cuffs rolled up to the elbows, and khakis. From a distance he looked clean-shaven. The woman had shoulder length brown hair and wore a sleeveless green dress. He could only see a third of her face, but he knew Joshua's photographs would have a good frontal view. From his vantage point, she looked to be in her late fifties, considerably younger than Duggan. She smiled near continuously, leaned forward and placed her hand on his forearm multiple times and nodded every time he spoke. Duggan looked bored and checked his watch every few minutes. It reminded Osborne of the last few dates he'd been on, although he hadn't been the uninterested one checking the time. Near-empty deli containers and half empty soda cups had been pushed aside to clear the table.

After fifteen minutes, Duggan stood, grabbed the empty plates, and said goodbye. He headed straight for his van. This woman wouldn't be Veronica. Their interaction was all wrong. This looked like a first date, not a reunion, and the woman had likely insisted on a public location for safety.

They knew where to find Duggan, but they needed to get an identification on his date, to be sure. She pulled a book and reading glasses out of her purse and settled in to read. Osborne moved to a nearby picnic table and sat, studying the digital photographs Joshua had forwarded to his phone.

Erin had never been able to give a helpful description of Veronica back then. She had long red hair, was average height, not fat or skinny, and wasn't as old as Duggan, but they had very little else to go on, and nothing was easier to change than hair color.

Osborne followed when she finally put away her book and left the park. She jaywalked mid-block, flicked a finger in the direction of a honking car, and slipped into a small bookstore. A half hour later she emerged with a heavy bag and went straight to a late model Lexus sedan a few doors down. He snapped a photo of the license plate as she drove away and then met Joshua back at the cruiser.

#

By Friday afternoon, Duggan had met with three different women, all in the same park. Joshua printed up photographs of the three, although they had only been successful in identifying two of the women. Friday's lunch encounter crossed over to the supermarket a half block off the square, went in the front door and apparently exited unseen out the back.

The first two women had willingly talked to Osborne and confirmed he was correct; these were first dates. Madeline Pfeiffer, the book reader/jaywalker/bird-flipper had driven up from Madison for the encounter. She'd met him through a dating website a couple of days after he was released on parole, and they'd talked a few times on the telephone before meeting. She readily provided Duggan's cell number. The parole officer hadn't known he had a phone. Duggan had given her his correct name, and his username on the site was EveryStepYouTake! Madeline didn't follow the news and was unaware Duggan was a parolee. Osborne doubted if dating was forbidden while on parole, even for a dirtball like Duggan.

Woman number two, Caroline Fait, knew about his recent release from prison and had even written love letters to him for the past five years. No, he hadn't called her back since their date, but it had only been forty-eight hours, she said. She did confirm the same contact number for Duggan.

"She had fallen in love with him from his letters. I'd be curious to see what he wrote. She was hurt when I told her he'd been using a dating website. She figured she would get first crack at him when he was released," Joshua said.

"What did Madeline say when she found out he was recently been paroled?" Osborne asked.

"She was shocked. I had her open her laptop and showed her how to check the Wisconsin Circuit Court records. I pulled up Duggan's name and showed her what she was looking for."

"I'm surprised she wasn't aware. Every woman I've met uses it, as soon as they know the guy's full name.

"She brought up Duggan's profile on the dating app and printed it out for me." Joshua slid two sheets of paper across the conference table. "I'm hoping I'm never desperate enough to use one of those sites."

Osborne looked at the profile pictures, which consisted of three poorly lit selfies with different backgrounds, inside and out. He shook his head with disgust after studying the last picture. It was shot in Duggan's pole barn and showed a corner of Erin's lockup structure in the background. He listed his hobbies as fitness, reading and cooking. What had Osborne expected? Making license plates?

"I think we should try to get access to his account. We can see if there are other women he's been corresponding with," Joshua said.

"We'd need a subpoena, and at this moment we don't have any grounds."

Osborne had a profile on a competing internet dating site for the past two years, although he would never admit it to anyone at work. He hadn't posted any photographs because of his occupation, and he knew profiles without pictures got fewer hits. He hoped this explained how few messages he received. Stanley Duggan, fresh out of prison for a capital offense, had more dates in one week than he'd had in the past six months. One more reason to hate the man.

"Caroline lived in Alabama twenty years ago, but Madeline is a lifelong resident of Madison. There's no way to reliably exclude either of their presence in Baraboo that many years ago," Joshua said.

"I don't think either of these women is Veronica," Osborne said.

Joshua slid the unidentified photo across the table.

"What about her? She snuck out the back door of the grocery store. She may have seen us."

"It's a good photo. I think we need to show it to Erin. We'll show her all three."

"She's going to love this, not to mention when she finds out Duggan has already been released back to his farm."

"He still has the ankle monitor."

"You don't plan to tell her, do you?"

"She'll be more cooperative the less she knows." Osborne said.

Chapter Nineteen

Erin cursed aloud after shutting her office door. The day had barely started but couldn't get much worse. Gracie and Charlotte argued all the way to summer school drop off about what they would name a puppy if they ever got one (they wouldn't), and she was now thirty minutes late for her first appointment. Again. The patient had hung around for a while, but finally left a few minutes before Erin arrived, promising to reschedule. She'd stood him up two weeks before, and she knew he wouldn't be back.

She returned to her small office after escorting out her second patient, finally having time to unpack her messenger bag and enjoy a cup of coffee. She'd have ten minutes before the next appointment, enough time to finish her charting if she didn't waste time.

She froze when she saw the colorful postcard on her desk, sitting atop a few other pieces of mail. It was the first time a card or letter had come to the office. She lifted it carefully by the edge. She hadn't completely given up on fingerprints, even though two people in the clinic had likely already handled it, plus the mail carrier, and who knows how many others.

It was a picture of a mother racoon and two babies. Cubs or pups, maybe kits? She didn't remember what they were called. Gracie or Charlotte would know. They'd recently finished a week studying animal babies in summer school. The symbolism wasn't lost on her. She flipped over the card and saw it was addressed to Dr. Erin Moore-Jackson. The other cards were addressed to simply Erin Moore, who she had been twenty years ago when she'd been taken.

There was a short message. 'The tribulations of motherhood. It wasn't directly threatening but still took her breath away.

A card arrived almost every week since the parole hearing was announced. She hoped they would stop once Duggan was released, but they'd continued.

Cody told her he had ferreted out the location of the halfway house where Duggan was staying in Baraboo. He'd driven by and said there was a row of rocking chairs on a large front porch, filled with old men sitting in white T-shirts. The building was set back from the road, and he couldn't tell if Duggan was one of them. He planned to go back with binoculars. To what end, she wondered? These cards weren't coming from Duggan. They were coming from Veronica.

She studied the racoon family, minus a father, one more time. When she flipped it over the second time, she noticed there was no stamp. She gasped and dropped the card onto the desk. It wasn't mailed. Veronica had been close enough to drop it off in person. There was no security camera at the front door, where a large mail slot was positioned. Veronica had been at her clinic. She had been that close. Erin's legs felt weak, and she reached for the desktop to steady herself as she slid into her chair.

She reached for her phone. Who would she call? She and Cody hadn't spoken a word to each other over breakfast, and again she suspected the girls noticed. Once more he'd been angry when she insisted on driving the girls to school since it was going to make her late. Lindsey was off to Las Vegas for a short vacation with friends, and Erin would have to get out in time for school pickup.

Erin used to have friends before Charlotte was born, and she still met for coffee occasionally with the mothers of her daughters' schoolmates. How long had it been? Months? These women knew about her past trauma. Everyone in town knew, but they had no idea what Erin was going through right now.

She debated calling Alex. That was a hard no.

She wouldn't call Osborne. He had taken the last pack of postcards, but she doubted he had ever done anything with them. She thought about Deputy Joshua Lippmann. She trusted him more than Osborne. She remembered the text he sent her before the parole hearing, warning her to send a letter to the parole board if she wasn't attending. It might have made a difference. She could call Joshua.

It was the deputy and not Osborne whom Erin had called to trace the license plate number of the green Subaru from Robby's drive in. He had informed her the next day the plate was reported as stolen from a BMW belonging to an anesthesiologist in Green Bay earlier in the summer and was a dead end in terms of tracking down the driver. That made her even more suspicious. Had it been Veronica? He wasn't able to narrow it down with her description of the car. She'd been watching for green Subarus ever since.

Her intercom buzzed and short-circuited her thoughts. Next patient, she assumed, and she hadn't even signed into the charting application. She was wrong.

"Doctor, I'm sorry to interrupt, but your husband is

here to see you."

Cody, bad timing.

"Your eleven o'clock appointment called and she's running five minutes late. She should be here any minute."

Her office door burst open, and an agitated Cody limped in, followed closely by an indignant receptionist.

"I asked him to wait," Marla said.

"It's all right. It shouldn't be more than a few minutes. Buzz me when the next patient arrives."

She nodded and pulled the door shut.

"A few minutes? That's very generous of you," he said.

"You can't show up here without calling." Erin went to the door and locked it, then returned to her desk. She shoved the mail including the raccoon postcard to the side. She jumped in her chair when he slammed his fist down on the desk.

"We should have finished it this morning, at home, but you needed to get to work."

"I didn't want to fight in front of the girls, and for your information, I was already running a half hour late. The first patient had already bailed on me."

"Sorry, Erin," he said. "We all know how very important your job is, more important than anything else in the world."

"One of us has to pay the bills." She regretted it as soon as she'd said it, but it was true. He looked stunned.

"Cody, please, can this wait until tonight? I promise, right after the girls go to bed."

"No damn it, it can't wait. Why don't you trust me with my own daughters, Erin? What have I done?"

"We can't talk about this here."

"I'm not leaving until we do." He sat down in the consultation chair and crossed his arms over his chest.

She noticed the beads of sweat on his brow.

"Are you back on the Oxy?" she asked, her voice low. "Or are you using something else this time?"

Cody averted his gaze and slumped forward in his chair.

"How can you ask that?"

She studied her husband in silence for a minute. The buzzer on her desk sounded.

"You haven't answered my question? We can get you help if that's what's going on."

"I've got to get to a meeting," Cody said. He stood and stepped toward the door. "It was a mistake, thinking we could talk."

"Can we get you a new therapist? You keep going to the same meetings and it doesn't seem to be helping. Would you consider seeing a private addiction specialist? I can get you an appointment."

"I'm clean, Erin. Your suspicion and ugly insinuations that I'm using again might be a major part of my problem."

"I want to trust you."

"And I'm happy with the VA. There are guys I can identify with in the group." He stepped through the door into the hallway, then turned back angrily. "Your private therapist every other Thursday doesn't seem to be doing you any good, does he? Maybe if would help if he was talking to you instead of fucking your brains out."

He turned and headed to the lobby. Erin hurried to the door to assess the damage. The receptionist, her next patient and one of the other psychologists were standing nearby, their mouths agape. She didn't have to wonder how much they'd heard.

###

The triage desk rang Osborne's landline as he finished lunch. There was a visitor, an angry, inebriated male visitor, demanding to see him.

"Did you get an ID?" he asked.

"Sure did. Cody Jackson. Do you know him?"

Osborne crumbled the wrapper from his sub sandwich and threw it away.

He sent Joshua to the front entrance, who escorted Cody back to an interview room as far from the main work area as possible, out of earshot of the other officers. Sheriff Carter had been angry Duggan was given parole. He didn't want this to get back to Carter. He'd have to handle it quietly, discreetly, and get Cody the hell out of the department as fast as possible.

Osborne met the two men in the small interview room with a cup of hot black coffee for Cody.

"Sit down," he said, pointing to a chair furthest from the door.

"He should never have been released, never in a hundred years." Cody slurred his words when he spoke. "And he wouldn't have been if you'd done your job."

Joshua pulled out a chair and gently helped Cody sit.

"I did my own research on these hearings. The District Attorney should have been there."

"Amundsen retired ten years ago, and the new D.A. didn't take the time. Nothing I can do about that, is there?" Osborne said.

"But you didn't have to say those things. It was a pack of lies. That he'd served his time and Erin would be safe. Because she's not safe. She's not. She's got a gun in her purse, two more in the house," Cody said. "Does that sound safe to you?"

"How much have you had to drink, buddy?" Joshua asked.

Cody ignored the question.

"If Duggan comes near Erin, or my kids, anywhere near us, I swear I'm going to kill him. Tell him that. I'll shoot him if I see him."

"Easy, Cody," Joshua reached out and rested his hand on the man's shoulder.

Cody jerked away, nearly falling from the chair, and sloshing most of the hot coffee onto the conference table. Joshua left and a half minute later returned with a stack of paper towels.

"Sorry, didn't mean to do that," Cody said. "But I swear I'll kill him."

Cody reached for the paper towels and spread them out over the spilled coffee. Then he folded his hands in his lap and stared at the wet mess. His agitated expression faded into defeat.

"I promise Duggan isn't going to come anywhere near your family. He's monitored continuously. You're being paranoid. He's an old man," Osborne said. An old man who deadlifts two hundred pounds and had already returned to his farm. At some point the Moore-Jacksons would find out Duggan had been released from the halfway house, but he wasn't going to be the one who told them.

"You lied to us. When you told Erin you'd be at the parole hearing, you should have told her you were taking his side."

He hadn't lied. Erin failed to ask him what position he was taking on the release.

"I don't know if you were in the hearing room from

the start, but I looked back and saw you sitting next to the reporter when the Commissioner asked if Erin or any family members wished to speak," Osborne said.

"Yes," he answered. "I tried…"

"You didn't try, not as far as I could tell. Or as far as the parole board members could tell. How fair is it to blame me for their decision when all you needed to do was speak up?" he said.

Cody opened his mouth to speak but nothing came out. He shook his head, tears brimming in his eyes. He grabbed a half-dry paper towel and swiped them away.

"Erin could have sent an e-mail or a letter if she didn't plan to attend. Why didn't she do that?" Joshua asked gently.

"She planned to be there. That's why there hadn't been a letter. And she was there. We drove there together, but then she freaked out in the car, thinking about seeing him again," Cody said. "And I didn't do much better, did I?"

Joshua patted him on the shoulder again.

"He'd be out in five years anyway, which isn't far off. They were never going to keep him locked up forever," Osborne said.

Cody stood and turned towards the door. He nodded at Joshua and left.

"That was unnecessarily harsh," Joshua said, rising and heading after Cody. "I'm going to catch him and give him a ride home. The last thing he needs right now is a DWI."

"Take him out the back."

"I should parade him right by Carter's office."

Osborne glared at the deputy as he led Cody Jackson towards the back door. Was Lippmann going to become as big of a problem as Duggan?

Chapter Twenty

When Erin returned home Sunday morning, she saw the sheriff's department vehicle waiting in front of the gate. Osborne was the last person she wanted to see. At least his deputy had come along. She'd had her worst performance at the shooting range since the middle of May, when she heard about the hearing. She blamed a lack of sleep.

Cody had left for a meeting in the midafternoon the day before and texted her about seven to let her know he was staying with a friend for the night. It was the second time he didn't come home in an already horrific week, which included Cody airing their marital problems in front of her clinic staff and a patient, and his being chauffeured home by the deputy in an intoxicated state. The girls witnessed their very drunk father vomit on the foyer rug. She needed to make a long overdue decision about her marriage.

Fortunately, Lindsey agreed to spend the night, after calling from the airport in Madison. She'd arrived at the house two hours later, suitcase in hand, looking sleep-deprived and hungover after three days in Las Vegas. She'd sacked out in the guest room as soon as the girls went to bed.

Erin had made coffee and roused Lindsey before she headed to the range. She wanted to be back before Cody returned, assuming he would come home later in the day.

Now, instead of enjoying the rest of the morning with Lindsey and her girls, she would once again meet with Detective Osborne, who didn't even have the courtesy to call ahead. She used her phone to open the security gate and then followed the police cruiser into the circular drive.

"I tried calling first but there wasn't an answer," Osborne said, climbing out of his car. "I thought you might be at church."

"Shooting range," she said. Prayers weren't going to keep her tormentors away, but bullets might. She pulled out her phone and saw two missed calls. She always wore protective shooting earmuffs and hadn't checked the phone when she returned to the car. It wasn't like Erin to be careless. What if Lindsey had called with an emergency? At the very least, she could have told Osborne to stay away or meet him somewhere else, away from the girls. Deep breath.

Osborne and Joshua followed Erin into the foyer. She could see through to the family room, where the girls were watching cartoons. She pointed to her office for Osborne and Joshua's benefit, then headed back to the family room. The girls were holding plates with toast on their laps and still in their pajamas.

"Mommy!" Gracie waved and turned her attention back to the cartoons.

"What are you drinking?" She eyed a plastic cup of beige liquid on the table in front of her daughters.

"It's coffee. We're old enough," Charlotte answered.

Lindsey came in from the kitchen carrying her own plate of toast. "Don't worry, it's two tablespoons of coffee and the rest is milk."

Erin smiled. Exactly what they needed, caffeine. "Can you stay a little longer? Detective Osborne showed up at the door without calling and I have to talk to him for a few minutes."

Lindsey, who was still in her pajamas with a full plate of toast and a cup of much darker coffee, nodded, yawned widely, and settled down on the couch next to Gracie. She looked significantly less hungover than when she arrived at the house the night before.

Erin sat down at her desk and retrieved a plastic bag from the top drawer. She pushed it across the desk to Osborne.

"This came to my office Wednesday morning. It must have been shoved into the mail slot. See, there's no postage. Same handwriting." She watched as he picked up the postcard and examined both sides. "She's here in town."

"I'll send it for fingerprints," Osborne said, "But I'm not optimistic we'll find anything of use. The only fingerprints we've ever found on any of the other cards were yours. Time after time, Erin."

"I picked them all up to read them. Later, I was more careful and tried to handle them from the edge, like I did with this one."

"Not even a fingerprint from your mail carrier on any of them."

"Are you implying I sent these disturbing cards to myself? Why would I do that?"

"You're the psychologist. Why don't you tell me?"

"Jesus Christ, Osborne," Joshua said.

Erin clenched her fists and resisted the urge to punch the detective. She folded her hands on the desk blotter. "Why are you here today? I'm assuming you didn't make the drive over to insult my mental health."

The detective slid the bag containing the card into his messenger bag and pulled out three photographs. He spread the pictures out on the desk. In each shot there was a clear view of a woman's face, sitting with Duggan, once in a coffee shop and twice at a picnic bench in the town square.

Erin shuddered when she recognized him. She hadn't seen him in person since his discharge, not since the day he was sentenced to twenty-five years in prison. She hadn't attended most of the trial, but her parents brought her to his sentencing, hoping it would give her closure. The closure remained elusive, even twenty years later.

"What's this?" she asked, examining each photo carefully. Who were these women?

"We've been keeping Duggan under tight surveillance, like we promised."

"But you should know he's no longer at the halfway house," Joshua said.

Osborne shot him a dirty look. "That's true, unfortunately. He moved back to his farm, which is not any closer to Reedsburg than the halfway house. He can't come anywhere near here with a five-mile restriction."

"And these women?"

"We haven't identified the third one, with the short black hair, but we were able to track the plates on the other two. They were very cooperative," Joshua said.

"Do you recognize any of these women?" Osborne asked.

Erin examined each photograph, trying to block out the image of Duggan and concentrate on his companion. Nothing. They were complete strangers.

"Do any of these women resemble Duggan's accomplice?" Osborne asked.

She shook her head. She was relieved they were tracking Duggan, but had this been the plan all along? Did Osborne facilitate the release to use him as bait to find Veronica?

"Tell me about the two you've identified?"

"The woman in the green sundress is Madeline Pfeiffer, who currently lives in Madison. We talked to her the day after this was taken. She met Duggan through an online dating website. Said he was charming, and she hoped to see him again. Her opinion changed when we revealed his record."

Erin held out the second photograph.

Joshua took the shot from her. "This is Caroline Fait. She knew about Duggan's history and started writing him letters while he was in prison. She said she was thrilled to finally meet him in person."

"That's sick," Erin said.

"Happens more often than you'd like to think," Osborne said.

"I know. I've seen it in my line of work," she said.

"We followed the last woman into a supermarket, but she left through a back door. We never got an ID."

"It's not her. Doesn't look anything like her," Erin said. "You planned to use Duggan for bait all along, didn't you? That's why he's out."

"Erin, I gave a short summation stating the Sauk County Sheriff's Department had no objections to the release. That's it. All you needed to do was to write a letter to the parole board or come in for a testimony."

"I planned to be there, but it didn't work out." Instead, she'd been shaking and sniveling in the car, trying to catch her breath for the better part of an hour. No, it hadn't worked out.

"Your husband was there in the hearing room for the entirety. They asked for victims or family members to come forward, and he didn't say a word," Osborne said. "If he'd spoken up, Duggan would likely still be locked away."

She had wondered but wouldn't ask Cody, too ashamed of her own decompensation. She could hardly blame him for his.

"What happens if Duggan doesn't draw her out? Then I'm left with both of them back in town. You've essentially made me the bait, haven't you?" she asked. "You deliberately set this in motion, and for what? Your own reputation with the sheriff's department? Your clearance rate?"

"It wasn't like that," he said. "As far as the department was concerned, it's just a cold case. I'm very close to retirement, and I don't care about statistics."

"Then why in the hell are you following Duggan to find her? And what other reason do you have for supporting his early release?"

"We're following him to err on the side of caution, that's all."

He ignored her question about supporting the early release.

"Don't show up at my home again without talking to me first. Now, please get out," she said.

God damn him. She didn't understand Osborne. He seemed to believe her, to believe in Veronica's existence, or he would have had no reason to get Duggan released. Yet he still had the audacity to question if she sent the postcards. It was insulting and contradictory.

Osborne gathered the photos and tucked them back into his bag. Erin slammed the front door behind them and shut the gate inches behind their car.

She returned to her office and shut the door. What did those photos mean? Duggan was clearly dating, but did it mean Veronica and he weren't together at all? If that was true, why was she still hanging around the area? Did it have less to do with Duggan and more to do with Erin? With her daughters? Then his early release did nothing but increase the jeopardy her family faced.

She realized since he was back living at the farm, where she'd been held for months, it would be easy for Veronica to come and go as she pleased. She couldn't imagine the woman tolerating an open relationship, not after she had waited for him for twenty years, but maybe she didn't realize what he was doing. Erin decided her headache was at least partially due to caffeine deficiency and hunger and headed for the kitchen.

Lindsey and the girls were dressed, and the dishes were been piled in the sink by the time Erin finished with the detectives. The girls begged to watch a few more cartoons and Erin agreed. She and Lindsey poured another cup of coffee and sat outside on the stone patio.

"Do you think Cody will be back tonight?" Lindsey asked.

"I'm assuming he will. He made a scene at the clinic on Wednesday. It was beyond humiliating. I couldn't even go into the breakroom the rest of the week. Every time I did the conversations stopped immediately."

Lindsey pushed for more details, but Erin shook her head. She still hadn't talked with her daughters about Cody's drunken episode.

"We've barely spoken to each other since then. It

would be easier if he didn't come home."

"The girls don't feel that way."

"Of course not. He holds it together in front of them most of the time, but I have no doubt he's using again."

"Have you talked to him about going back into rehab?"

"Of course, but he denies everything. Turns it back on me, claiming I'm paranoid and should trust him more." First Cody questioned her mental health, and now Osborne was doing the same thing. Damn them both.

"I'm sorry."

Lindsey reached out and clasped Erin's hand. She squeezed her eyes tight and blinked back tears.

"It's worse than I thought," Erin whispered. "He knows about Alex."

Lindsey eyed her sister with a puzzled expression.

"Sweetie, everyone knows about Alex. I thought you realized that."

Chapter Twenty-One

Joshua stuck his head through the doorway into Osborne's office Monday afternoon.

"I'm heading over to the Dells. They've asked for more help interviewing guests at the waterpark. Anything you need me to do before I leave?" he asked.

"What the hell happened over there? Between the Dells police force and our guys, they called in eight units."

"Apparently there was a fight at one of those indoor water parks out near the highway. It was supposed to rain all day, so the pool area was packed. A bunch of the mothers began drinking early in the day and started to brawl, or at least that's what I heard over the radio. I'm hoping there's more to it than that," Joshua said.

"Not necessarily. Mix stupidity, being stuck inside with your kids and alcohol," Osborne said.

"Did you send Erin's last post card off for fingerprint analysis?"

"I'm doing the paperwork right now. I checked back in the file. Over the years we've sent six of these cards to the State Crime Lab."

"Maybe we'll get lucky this time."

"Come in and take a seat for a minute. Shut the door."

Joshua stepped into the office and sat.

"How did Erin seem to you yesterday?"

"Yesterday?" He feigned deep concentration. "Do you mean when we show up at her home unannounced on a Sunday morning, when she's with her kids? Or when she realizes you let her kidnapper out of prison five years earlier than necessary to help you clear this case before you retire?"

"That's not what I did, and you know it."

"Or wait, do you mean when you shamed her and her husband for still having anxiety issues about the worst time of her life and not speaking up at the parole hearing?"

"Fuck you."

"Or possibly when you implied she was a nutcase and a fraud and had been sending these creepy postcards to herself for the past twenty years." Joshua was practically shouting by this time. "Personally, I think she showed admirable restraint, especially for a woman who was fresh off a shooting range."

"If you'd like I can have you reassigned, and this won't be your problem anymore."

Joshua stood and headed for the door.

"Maybe you should. I expect I'll be tied up at the waterpark for the rest of the day. See you tomorrow."

After he left, Osborne rose from the chair and slammed the office door. What an arrogant asshole. The deputy was barely out of the academy, and he had the gall to question his ethics. He'd talk to Carter about getting Lippmann assigned to another detective. He booted his wastepaper basket across the room and left it upturned.

Back at his desk, he reviewed the form he'd filled out for the postcard. He'd never seriously considered whether Erin could be sending the cards to herself, but this led to the next question. Only Erin had ever seen Veronica. There was no female DNA other than Erin's at the farmhouse, or out in the cage constructed in the barn, although there were problems with evidence collection. Duggan claimed repeatedly he'd acted alone, twenty years ago, during interviews throughout his imprisonment and again a few months ago, when coming clean about an accomplice could have helped him get parole.

Had there ever been a Veronica? He had always believed she existed, but what if he was wrong? Had he been fooled by a fourteen-year-old traumatized and unhinged girl? If so, he knew it wasn't an intentional deception, at least not initially. But what about the postcards? Was Erin so ashamed of concocting a story about Veronica that she couldn't let it go, twenty years later? It didn't seem likely.

He would never admit it to Lippmann or anyone else, but Erin's accusation was correct. It has always been about clearing the case. He'd never given up on finding Duggan's female accomplice, and it had cost him. He had been demoted and his wife (unfairly in his mind) blamed his obsessions with Erin and Duggan for their divorce.

What if it had all been for nothing, if there had never been a Veronica any more than there had been a King Charles Cavalier pup? His ex-wife called it his personal fool's errand. What if she'd been right?

He swore loudly and tore up the fingerprint analysis request.

Chapter Twenty-Two

July 31st
BREAKING NEWS – BARABOO NEWS-JOURNAL
by Richard Fitzpatrick, Reporter
For any readers unfamiliar with past events, local teenager Erin Moore was kidnapped at the age of fourteen approximately twenty-one years ago. Stanley Duggan III was arrested and found guilty at trial, and he served twenty years of a twenty-five-year sentence, freed recently (July 15th) after a successful parole appeal. Mr. Duggan has since been released from his half-way house in Baraboo to his family farm outside of town, still with ankle monitoring.

At the time of the original trial, the victim recounted that there had been an accomplice, a middle-aged female she referred to as Veronica, involved in the crime. No evidence of a female accomplice was found on further investigation. Sources close to Erin remain adamant Veronica was in fact a real person and not a figment of a traumatized fourteen-year-old's imagination. In fact, the female accomplice was the more abusive of the two captors. She allegedly forced the captive teen to mix and consume animal feces with her morning oatmeal and other atrocities.

Sources close to Dr. Erin Moore-Jackson report she has been receiving threatening postcards she attributes to this alleged accomplice on a yearly basis since her release. These postcards were sent while Duggan was incarcerated, although the frequency has increased since his release. Efforts to track the origin of these postcards over the past twenty years have been unsuccessful.

Dr. Moore-Jackson requests privacy for her family.

Chapter Twenty-Three

Erin pushed her way past the protesting receptionist and scanned the small newsroom for Fitzpatrick. She spotted him hunching over a laptop at the back of the room at the only occupied desk. He was dressed the same as every time she'd seen him, wearing a poorly fitting wrinkled button-down striped shirt. Erin had taken a chance coming over the lunch hour, but she couldn't afford to cancel any more patients. It worked out to her favor. Fewer witnesses, and no one pointing a video camera in her direction.

A coworker, Lindsey, and Alex all texted her during breakfast about the latest blog and she hadn't been able to concentrate on her patients all morning.

She marched to the back of the room and stood in front of his desk, her shadow falling over his keyboard. It was still a minute before he looked up.

"Busy ruining someone else's life?" she asked.

"Erin," he said, clearly surprised to see her. "How did you get in here?"

He looked over at the entrance, where the receptionist stood, wringing her hands. He gave her a little wave.

"I usually don't conduct interviews here in the newsroom," he said, "but it looks like we've got the place to ourselves."

"News? Is that what you call the bullshit you've

been putting in your blog?"

"You've been reading my news updates? The subscriber list climbed over two thousand since I started covering Duggan, increasing every day. That's enormous in a small market like this." He was clearly pleased she was one of the readers.

"Who told you about the fucking postcards?" she asked.

"I'm sorry, but again, I can't reveal my sources."

"Who told you they're from Veronica?"

"Again…"

Erin swept her arm across his desk, knocking his pencil holder, can of Mountain Dew and a small, framed picture onto the floor. He snatched his laptop off the desk and held it to his chest. She remained standing over him.

"Was it Osborne? He wasn't too impressed with the postcards. He even suggested I might be sending them myself."

"You can ask him if you'd like, but I'm hard-pressed to come up with a single reason Osborne would share information with me," Fitzpatrick said. "If you sit down and cut the theatrics, we can discuss this further. Interesting he thinks you're sending them to yourself. That's rather insulting."

"That had better not appear in your next article," she said.

She wanted to vanquish his smug smile with a slap but knew she'd read about it in his next news release, or worse yet, he would press charges. Erin remained standing for another minute. This wasn't accomplishing anything, she thought, glancing at the spreading puddle of lime soda on the floor. She sat in the chair opposite him and exhaled noisily. He kept his laptop out of her reach.

"Why are you doing this to me?" She clenched her fists to control the trembling.

"I'm a reporter and I'm merely doing my job here," he said. "The public has a right to know if the female accomplice may still be in the area. Now if you'll excuse me, I'm trying to make my deadline on an unrelated topic."

"No one but my husband and Osborne knows how long the cards have been coming. I'm sure Cody wouldn't have told you."

"Do you mind if I ask you a few questions about the postcards? Some of my blog subscribers have submitted them in their remarks under the comment section."

"I'm not telling you a thing." She hadn't noticed there were comments following his blogs and wondered how much worse they were than the reporter's words.

"Erin, have you thought about getting out in front of the story instead of running from it? Tell me what's happened since they announced the parole hearing. The readers want to know how you're doing, how you're coping. This is your chance to tell your version."

"How the hell do you know about Veronica forcing me to eat contaminated food?"

"I can't imagine how difficult that must have been."

"It never came out at trial. I never told Osborne back then. I was too…mortified. I never told my parents, not even Cody."

"You're not denying it," he said.

No, it was true, along with scores of other horrible things, especially from Veronica. How had Fitzpatrick known and what else did Duggan share with him? She sat and stared until he could no longer make eye contact.

"I communicated with Duggan by letter while he was incarcerated. He finally agreed to put me on his approved visitor's list, and I interviewed him a few times. You're right, I know things about your months with Duggan I haven't shared with my subscribers. I'm saving them for the true crime book I'm hoping to get published. Duggan was interested that I'm writing a book about the events, although I haven't been successful in getting an interview since he's been released."

"I don't want you to publish a book about the worst year of my life. I'm never going to give you an interview. I'll sue or get a restraining order. I'll stop you one way or another.

"It's a small town though, isn't it? Secrets rarely stay that way in a place like this."

"Please, stop." She shut her eyes and willed him to shut up.

"Everyone knows if someone loses their job, is getting a divorce or might be having an affair with a married man. Maybe all three. In a town like Baraboo, everyone eventually knows."

"Are you trying to destroy me?" she asked quietly, wondering how much he suspected. She hadn't lost her job, but things weren't going well at the clinic. And did he know about Alex?

"I'm looking for the truth. It's that simple. Certainly nothing personal." he said. "Like you said, it was the worst year of your life. You survived that and you were just a kid. This will be a piece of cake."

Erin stood and turned towards the door. Tears streamed down her cheeks, but she wasn't going to let this jerk see her cry. She brushed them away brusquely and checked her watch. She would be fifteen minutes late for her next appointment.

# # #

Erin bolted towards the parking lot after the door shut behind her last patient. She had struggled through her afternoon appointments, her brain still stuck in the conversation with Fitzpatrick. Nothing personal, he'd said. Her life was falling apart around her, and his blogs were a big part of it, but it shouldn't bother her because it was nothing personal. Fuck him.

She cranked up the air conditioning as she drove the two miles across town to the school. She'd still have to do her office notes that night, once the girls were in bed, but she was picking the girls up on time for a change. There had already been several warnings from the summer school program about fines for late pickup.

She counted a dozen or so cars ahead of her in the circular pick-up line and a few pulled in behind her. She was not dead last for a change. Erin leaned back against the headrest and let out a deep breath. She rolled down the car windows and could hear the excited chatter of the kids waiting up ahead. Hopefully, her daughters would be in a better mood.

Erin turned on her satellite radio to a pop station the girls liked, and her car inched forward as the summer camp teachers loaded the students, car by car. Erin was a quarter of the way to the front when she saw it, second car from the front of the line. It was the green Subaru. She couldn't make out the driver or license plate from the distance, but she was sure it was the same car. She froze. Was it Veronica and was she coming for Gracie and Charlotte? Surely the camp teachers wouldn't allow it, and her daughters knew better than to climb into the car with a stranger, didn't they?

Erin pulled out her phone. She had to decide immediately, before the Subaru reached the front of the line, where her daughters were waiting.

Erin dialed 911 and reported a wanted fugitive in a green Subaru wagon at Heritage Learning Academy in Lake Delton. She gave her name, hung up and pulled out into the left lane of the pickup circle, ignoring the speed bumps and indignant honks, and she drove to the front of the line. The Subaru was now at the designated pick-up spot, and Erin could see a child being escorted to the back door. She pulled in front of the Subaru, blocking both lanes and hopped out of the car.

Erin apologized profusely to the elderly, Hispanic man driving the Subaru, who was picking up his granddaughter after camp. She tried to explain the extenuating circumstances to the school pickup attendants and to the police officers who descended on Heritage in a manner of minutes. It wasn't the same driver, the same car, or the stolen license plate. In the end, Erin's daughters were the last summer campers to be loaded into a car, and Erin received a written warning from the Lake Delton police.

Her daughters slumped down in their car seats and didn't say a word on the drive home.

Chapter Twenty-Four

"We don't need to do this," Cody said for the third time that morning. "And we certainly can't afford it right now, can we?"

He was right on the second account. Money was getting tight. It was day two of childcare interviews, and there was one more candidate on the schedule. The other four women Erin had interviewed had all fallen short, either only able to work an occasional day or wanting full time work even though Erin's ad was very specific.

Her hours had been trimmed back further at work, temporarily she was assured, and she was now down to the bare minimum to qualify for health insurance. Some of her patients were reassigned to other clinicians, and she was not to accept any new patients until things stabilized, whatever that meant. When Duggan died and Veronica was captured? When the girls were off to college far from Reedsburg and were finally safe?

Betsy Simmons arrived a half hour late. She was tall and athletic looking with her long blonde hair pulled back into a ponytail. She was dressed in very short cutoffs and a t-shirt with a UW-Madison logo. Betsy followed Erin and Cody to the back patio and described her experience with childcare. She had grown up as the eldest of seven children in Milwaukee and recently moved to the area to be with her boyfriend, who was working at one of the resorts in nearby Wisconsin Dells.

She warned them upfront she was looking for a full-time job with benefits, and if one came along, she'd give them two weeks' notice. Erin had checked. No criminal record or significant history of driving infractions, and most importantly, she could start Monday.

Erin hired her on the spot, despite her late show, once Betsy assured them she could cover the afternoon summer school pickups Monday through Wednesday. Erin's clinic schedule was now reduced to one full day and two afternoons per week, and if she canceled any more appointments even that was in jeopardy. Cody sat quietly through the brief interview.

Erin called the girls out onto the patio and introduced Betsy, who would be picking them up after camp three days a week and getting them snacks until Erin came home.

"Why can't Aunt Lindsey pick us up?" Charlotte asked.

They had stopped asking about their father.

"She's working now and doesn't get off in time." It wasn't exactly true, but she needed to save Lindsey for emergencies, not three times a week school pickup.

"Cool." Gracie shrugged and headed back to the cartoons.

"What do you expect me to tell the girls when there's a babysitter here and I'm home? And what is Betsy going to think?" Cody asked, after Erin closed the gates behind the sitter's car.

Erin studied him closely. He was clean-shaven, and his clothes neatly pressed. His eyes were clear. She was relieved Betsy saw this version of her husband but wondered how long it would last.

"It's your choice. You could always run errands,

maybe visit Jeff or Reilly. You haven't seen them in a while, have you? Or go to a meeting." It would be better if he wasn't home when Betsy arrived with the girls, especially if he'd been using. She didn't need the girls or their sitter to see him like that.

"Come on, Erin. They've cut your appointments in half. We can manage on less money, but it's going to be tight. I can be there for the girls.

"You're to blame for my losing hours, Cody. You realize that don't you? You show up at my clinic clearly high as a kite and make a scene in front of my coworkers, not to mention a regular patient who switched over to a different therapist, you should know. Don't put this all on me."

Cody sat back into a kitchen chair, deflated.

"It wasn't drugs—I was drunk. And I apologized for that."

"Yes, but you didn't do anything to fix it, to keep it from happening again. You've got to go back to rehab."

"It cost fifteen grand last time."

"If it helps, it's money well-spent. You know it's getting worse. We can dip into savings for a while."

Cody said nothing. They both knew they'd been cutting it close financially for years, especially with the cost of the private school tuition for the girls. They had spent most of Erin's father's life insurance on security for the home without much left in savings.

Cody changed the subject.

"I got a phone message from the school yesterday afternoon, from the headmaster's secretary. They were looking for you, but you weren't answering."

"It's been taken care of." Erin felt the temperature rise in her cheeks and she turned towards the window overlooking the backyard. They had no business calling Cody, about the incident on Friday or anything else. She had removed his name from the family contact list. She hoped they hadn't called Lindsey as well, whose name remained on the official approved directory.

"What was it about? I have a right to know. They're my daughters, too. Was there a problem with one of the girls?"

"The girls were fine. Are fine. It was a misunderstanding about pickup, and it's been handled."

"The message from the secretary didn't make it sound handled and it was already pretty late in the afternoon."

Erin welcomed the interruption when Lindsey drove up to the gate, and she buzzed her sister in, even though she shared the code months earlier. She even gave the code to Betsy, although she'd leave a reminder note to shut the security gate behind her on Monday and change the gate code if Betsy didn't work out. If the gates were open when Erin came home, it would be Betsy's last day of employment. She sighed. She needed Betsy and there might be undeserved second and possibly third chances.

The girls greeted their aunt more warmly than they'd responded to Betsy, and Lindsey dragged them into the kitchen, each clinging to a leg and giggling.

"Thanks for coming. I wanted to get to the shooting range at least once this week," Erin said, reaching for her purse and phone.

"Not a problem, but what's going on at the school? I got a call from someone in the office there yesterday demanding I find you immediately and have you call them."

"I talked to them. It was a misunderstanding about

pickup time."

It had been mortifying. Alex would have correctly called it a clusterfuck. Neither of her daughters asked any questions about the police presence at school pickup or Erin's role yet, but a few of their friends and quite a few parents witnessed the debacle and would likely bring it up. She was hopeful the school wouldn't ban her daughters from the summer school program after the misunderstanding, but unless that happened, there was no reason to discuss it further with Lindsey or Cody.

Her sister seemed to accept her explanation, but Cody looked at her and shook his head. He wasn't buying it.

Lindsey pulled out her phone and brought up Fitzpatrick's latest update from three days earlier.

"I won't hold you up, but I felt awful when I read his last blog, about that horrible woman feeding you dirty food. Why didn't you ever tell me?" Lindsey asked.

"I don't know where he got his information," Erin said. "I don't think I even told the police, although it's possible I did. I know I was a mess after the rescue, and I don't remember everything I said."

"You never told me either," Cody said.

"Who told him about the postcards?" Erin asked. "He said sources close to me. Did one of you talk to him?"

"I haven't spoken to him," Lindsey said.

"Someone did and I think it was one of you."

"Maybe it was Osborne or someone from his department," said Cody. "They knew about the cards. Why do you assume it had to be one of us? Because Fitzpatrick said so?"

"If you don't trust me, you should find someone else

to watch the girls today. In fact, I remembered an appointment and I can't be late." Lindsey gathered her purse and water bottle and stormed out the door, slamming it behind her.

"Wait, I didn't mean it like that," Erin called after her.

"Sure, you did." Cody gave her a half-smile. "You've always distrusted the ones who love you the most."

He grabbed his truck keys from the hook near the door.

"You never told Lindsey or me about the tainted food they made you eat. The reporter knew about it, which means he obviously used somebody other than us as his source. Why is it hard to believe the same source didn't tell him about the postcards?"

Erin considered the remark and finally nodded.

"I'm sorry, Cody. I'll call Lindsey. I was out of line."

"You were," he said. "Maybe it was your therapist."

"What do you mean?" she asked.

"Your Thursday afternoon therapist appointment, the one whose bill never shows up on any of our insurance statements. It seems like he knows you better than I do. Has he been talking to the reporter?"

Cody closed the door softly behind him and he headed for his truck.

Shit. She *had* told Alex.

Chapter Twenty-Five

"Turn right at the next corner," Osborne said.

"The GPS tells me to go straight for another mile," Joshua countered.

"I know, but I've been out here more times than I can count. This way is shorter," he said.

Joshua muttered under his breath, but he turned. Osborne ignored it. A few minutes later they approached the driveway entrance to Duggan's farmhouse. The chain was in place across the entrance with a 'No Trespassing' sign back in place. Joshua hopped out to unhook the chain. He checked the mailbox and found it empty.

As they approached the house, they spotted Duggan's white minivan parked next to the house. Osborne climbed out and walked around the vehicle, looking in the windows. He felt the hood and it was cool to the touch. Duggan hadn't driven in the past hour. It was empty other than fast food wrappers on the floor of the front seat. He tried the doors and found them locked.

"The parole officer said his ankle monitor shows he's home," Osborne said.

"Maybe he just forgot the appointment. He's elderly. Did they try calling?"

"They believe he doesn't have a phone."

"Bullshit. The two women from the park give us a phone number," Joshua said.

It was a good point. He'd tracked Duggan on two

more encounters, always at the same park in Baraboo, although he hadn't shown the additional pictures to Erin. He'd have to make sure the parole officer had the number.

They climbed the three steps to the sagging front porch, which groaned under their weight, and they flanked the front door. There was no doorbell. A worn welcome mat was coated with dried mud and hadn't welcomed anyone in a long time. Duggan likely used the back door which was close to where his van was parked.

Osborne rapped loudly on the front door and called out, "Duggan, it's the sheriff's department. Come to the door."

They waited a minute with no response, then he yelled out and pounded on the door with his fist. He tried the doorknob, and it turned in his hand. He remembered the shiny padlock on the barn and doubted Duggan would keep the front door unlocked, especially after twenty years in prison.

Osborne pushed the door open slowly and called out again. They both drew their weapons and walked into the living room. It was empty. The television set was turned on to a home improvement station, the sound muted. Flies partially covered a half-eaten piece of pizza sitting on the coffee table, their buzzing the only sound in the room.

"Duggan?" Joshua called out.

No response.

Osborne pointed to the doorway leading to the kitchen and nodded. He led the way with his gun drawn. More flies buzzed around the rest of the half-empty pizza box.

"That looks like blood," Joshua said, pointing to a

faint smear on the small kitchen table. He leaned close and inhaled. He regarded the nearby food container. "I'm pretty sure it isn't pizza sauce."

Osborne walked out onto the back porch and scanned the overgrown backyard. The pole barn's door was shut, and the padlock was in place. He joined Joshua in the kitchen. They went upstairs and entered the first bedroom.

"This must be where he's sleeping," Osborne said. A worn blue blanket was bunched at the end of the double bed, with rumpled sheets which may have been white at one time. An ashtray filled with cigarette butts sat on the nightstand, next to a small battery powered alarm clock. Old copies of Hustler were piled on the floor next to the nightstand, the pages yellowed with age. He checked the date of the top magazine, September 1993, purchased before his prison sentence.

"Can you still buy Hustler?" Joshua asked.

"I have no idea," Osborne said. Yes, it was still in publication, and he knew it, but he resented that his deputy thought he would know.

He followed Joshua down the hall as they cleared the next two smaller bedrooms. At the end of the hallway, they inspected the tiny bathroom which looked as if it hadn't been cleaned since Duggan went to prison. A comb, shaving razor and toothbrush were scattered on the filthy vanity top. It was unlikely he'd left town without his toiletries, meager as they were. But where was he?

"Maybe we should call in backup," Joshua said. "We may need to search the woods behind the house."

Osborne nodded. "First let's take a peek out in the barn. We'll have to break the lock."

Joshua retrieved bolt cutters from the car trunk and cut off the padlock. He flipped the light switch inside the door, and they went in. Nothing appeared to have changed since the day Osborne spied on Duggan working out. The equipment hadn't been disturbed. They searched behind piles of lumber and tools and found nothing. No Duggan. No additional smears of blood.

Joshua stared at the fragmented cage at the back of the barn. As they approached, they saw a small army cot still set up inside.

Why hadn't this been removed and destroyed twenty years ago? Osborne entertained a second and much more disturbing thought: What if this was a replacement?

"This is where…?" Joshua couldn't finish the sentence.

"For the first few months. He moved her into the house once the temperatures dropped."

"Where in the house? I didn't see any padlocks on those two spare bedroom doors?"

Osborne stood puzzled. His mind raced back to the spring day twenty-one years ago. Erin had been handcuffed to the kitchen table. Duggan made a run for it, sprinting into the trees at the back of the property. They'd left a young female deputy with the girl and Osborne and the other two officers chased him down, catching him a half mile from the farmhouse. The detective hadn't sprinted a half mile since.

"She would be locked in the basement at night," Osborne said. "We missed the basement. Let's go back in."

They opened a few doors revealing near empty closets, and finally found a door leading down a dark stairwell. Osborne flipped the switch but the bare bulb at the top of the stairs was burned out. He pulled out his tactical flashlight and studied the stairs. They were wooden, as old as the rest of the house, but looked sturdy enough. After a few steps, his light reached the bottom of the stairs, where Duggan's ankle bracelet lay surrounded by a pool of dark red.

"It's his ankle monitor. Somehow, he got it off."

"Without cutting the signal? That's supposed to be impossible."

"There's a lot of blood."

Osborne grabbed the handrail and eased the rest of the way down, stepping over the congealed blood. He shone the flashlight around and found a ceiling fixture a few feet away, with a string attached. The bare bulb was low wattage and coated with a thick coat of dust, and while it helped, they kept their flashlights on.

"Is that a wallet?" Joshua directed his flashlight beam into a corner near the bottom of the stairs.

"Don't pick it up until the crime scene team comes through," Osborne said. "Let's see if his phone is down here."

Duggan had contacted those women and there had to be a phone somewhere.

They searched the rest of the basement and found nothing but empty canning jars and a few dead mice.

Joshua went out onto the front porch to call the sheriff. Osborne came back up to the kitchen and put on a fresh pair of gloves. He looked inside Duggan's refrigerator, and unfortunately, it reminded him of his own at home. A few takeout containers, eggs and bread, a six pack of beer and a few condiments, little else. He knew he should leave the crime scene undisturbed, but he would be very careful. Nothing of interest in the kitchen cupboards. The garbage can was empty other than a few beer cans and crumpled up paper towels.

He spied a small dark hole in the door of a lower cabinet and examined it closer. He'd missed it on the first search. It was a bullet hole. He reopened the cabinet and found the slug embedded in the plaster backing the cabinet. He'd make sure the CSI team saw it.

"Sheriff Carter said to secure the scene until Morgan arrives. He's going to take the case. CSI won't get here for a few more hours, but Morgan is a half hour away," Joshua said, walking back into the living room.

"Why the fuck would he give the case to Morgan when he knows I've been following the guy?"

"I think you've answered your own question."

Osborne glared at the deputy. "Then we've got a half hour. And you'll keep your mouth shut."

A scratched-up wooden desk sat in the corner of the living room, with a small printer on a stand next to it. There was a router and modem on top of the desk. There was a power cord duct-taped in place but no laptop. Osborne searched through the top desk drawer and found a completely jumbled pile of bills. He picked up a few. They were from the mid-1990's, before Duggan's prison sentence, some from companies no longer in existence.

He looked through the rest of the drawers. Miscellaneous office supplies, all looking cheap and very old, including a half-empty pack of printer paper, yellowed with age.

The last drawer was a different story, with a stack of black and white photographs rubber-banded together in the bottom. He pulled them out and called Joshua over. He undid the rubber band and spread the twelve photos out on top of the desk.

"Erin's girls," Joshua said softly.

"Gracie and Charlotte," Osborne said.

He picked up one of the photographs. It showed the two girls sitting on a park bench with their aunt Lindsey, eating ice cream cones. There were pictures of Erin unloading the girls from the car in front of their school. In a picture taken at a birthday party with an inflated jumping castle, one of the girls was climbing out and crying. There was a close-up of each girl's face.

"Where did he get these pictures?" Joshua said. "He hasn't been to the kids' school, and that's the park over in Lake Delton. His ankle monitor should have gone off."

"Someone else took them. Veronica?" Osborne asked. "It has to be."

He banded the pictures back into a pile and rifled through the rest of the bottom drawer. He found a cheap phone, a brand he didn't recognize.

"It's a burner," Joshua said. "A friend of mine uses a similar phone because it's dirt cheap."

"Does it take pictures?" Osborne said, handing the phone over.

Joshua powered it up. No password protection.

"Hurry. Morgan will be here any minute."

The device had a different number than the women in the park used to contact Duggan, and Osborne wrote it down.

He scrolled through the call history. He counted ten outgoing calls, six incoming calls, all to and from the same number with a local area code, and he added it to his notes.

"This might be Veronica's number," Joshua said.

They should be so lucky.

There were no text messages. There was a camera on the phone, but no pictures had been saved.

"I don't know how to get into the browser history," Joshua said.

"If we've lost Duggan, finding Veronica is going to be near impossible."

"It's Morgan's case now," Joshua said. "Let him worry about it."

"It doesn't work that way. It will always be my case."

They replaced the phone deep in the drawer beneath the photographs and returned to the front porch, waiting for Morgan. A few minutes later, two cars pulled up and parked. Joshua waited outside while Osborne walked Morgan, his partner and two other deputies through the house.

A half hour later, Osborne climbed behind the wheel of the car, and they reversed down the driveway, nearly backing into a gray sedan, who was pulling in behind them.

The same annoying reporter climbed out of the car, along with his camera guy and walked up to Osborne's window.

"Good afternoon, Detective. I understand Duggan's gone missing."

# # #

AUGUST 8th, 6:30 P.M.

BREAKING NEWS – BARABOO NEWS JOURNAL by Richard Fitzpatrick, Reporter

The Sauk County Sheriff's Department as well as Wisconsin State crime lab technicians were called to the home of Stanley Duggan III, a few miles outside of Baraboo.

Mr. Duggan had been recently released from prison after serving twenty years for kidnapping local fourteen-year-old Erin Moore and holding her captive for five months. Dr. Erin Moore-Jackson still lives in the area with her husband and two young daughters.

The whereabouts of Duggan, who had been on ankle monitoring as a condition of his parole, is unknown. Duggan's home is considered an active crime scene. The ankle monitor and blood presumably belonging to Duggan were found in the basement. Sources involved in the investigation report bullet holes in kitchen cabinets. Authorities are not releasing further information currently, and they are not commenting on whether there is an ongoing risk to the community.

Details to follow when they become available.
Follow on Twitter @FitzpatrickRichard14

Chapter Twenty-Six

Erin heard her phone ping repeatedly from the next room as she sat in the upstairs guest bathroom, watching the girls splash in the bathtub. Like usual, they'd made a huge mess with bath bubbles spilling over the side of the tub and various colorful water toys strewn around the room. She sipped her glass of Chardonnay and waited with towels in her arms. There would be grousing when she insisted on rinsing the bubbles out of their hair at the end, but it was still one of their favorite ways to end the day. And hers.

"Erin?" Cody asked from the open doorway. "Did you see Lindsey's text?"

"No. I heard my phone a few times. It was probably her. I think I left it on the bed. I'm sure it can wait."

"Now she sent me one. 'OMG! OMG! Have Erin check her messages. Want me to sit with the girls while you check it out?"

Erin handed the pile of towels to Cody and headed for the bedroom. Five text messages was extreme, even for Lindsey.

"OMG!"

Erin rolled her eyes but kept reading.

"Check out Fitzpatrick's latest news update. Stanley Duggan has disappeared."

"They don't have a lot of details yet, but it said they found blood at his house, and he may have been

murdered."

"He was at his farm, not the half-way house. I thought he was still at the half-way house."

"Is this good news or bad news?"

Erin read the series of text messages three times, then logged into Fitzpatrick's blog. There it was, as her sister had described. Not much in the way of details. Did he really have to include her name every time he wrote about Duggan?

She heard the gurgling of the tub drain and finally the splashing subsided in the next room. This was followed by protests as Cody rinsed out their hair, then wrapped them in towels. The girls dressed in their pajamas came padding down the hallway to the master bedroom, where they climbed onto the bed, giggling and bouncing. Their towel-dried hair stood up in all directions and they beamed. Normally she would try to snap a quick photo, but she was still trying to process what Lindsey had told her.

"What's up with your sister? Did this deserve an OMG?"

Erin nodded and held out her phone. Cody sat on the bench at the foot of the bed and read the news article. He emitted a low whistle.

"What do you think happened?" he asked.

"No idea. I wonder if I should call Osborne. Better yet, Joshua. What time was the blog written? They should have notified me."

"You could call Fitzpatrick," he said.

"That's the last person I'm going to call. Besides, it doesn't sound like he knows much."

"He didn't when he wrote this, but he may know more now."

Erin shook her head emphatically. She wasn't calling the reporter, not when he was trying to make Erin's life part of the story.

"I thought he was supposed to be staying at a halfway house in Baraboo for six months. Isn't that what Osborne told us?" Cody asked.

"He was there less than a week. Joshua said they needed the bed, but I find it hard to believe Duggan was the one they felt most comfortable releasing. How dangerous are the other men at the halfway house if that's the case?"

Charlotte sidled up alongside Erin and reached for the phone. Erin held it over her head and smiled at her daughter.

"I know what OMG means, Mom. It's 'Oh my god!' and Miss Davenport says we aren't supposed to say OMG."

"Miss Davenport is right. Children shouldn't use OMG but sometimes adults will use it in text messages."

"Even Aunt Lindsey?"

"Especially your Aunt Lindsey," Cody said.

"What are you guys talking about?" Gracie asked. "Why should you call a reporter?"

"We're trying to decide if you get a bedtime snack tonight or not," Cody said. "First one to the kitchen decides."

The girls took off running and shrieking down the stairs. Cody followed them out of the room, wincing as he walked.

"Cody?" she called after him.

He appeared back in the bedroom doorway.

"Where were you today?" she asked. "I called a few times late in the morning and you didn't pick up."

"Nothing in particular, running errands. Plus, I caught a meeting up in Tomah." Cody paused and a baffled look clouded his features. "You don't think I had anything to do with this."

"No, of course not. But I think we need to be ready for questions. Osborne is undoubtedly planning to talk to both of us about this."

He nodded.

"I have to be ready for these questions, too."

"Lindsey asked if this was good news or bad news," Cody said.

"And I have no idea."

That night Erin waited for an hour after Cody finally turned off the TV in the family room, where he'd been sleeping for the past few weeks. She quietly climbed out of bed and crept down the stairs to her office. She used the light from her phone and opened the small safe which was hidden in a lower cabinet in the built-in bookcase. All three guns were there, arranged like she'd left them.

She exhaled the breath she hadn't known she had been holding and padded back to bed. She needed to sleep, but a thought stuck in her mind. What if Cody did kill Duggan but returned the incriminating weapon to her gun safe? Wasn't that even worse than the gun being missing? She vowed to change the combination to the safe in the morning.

Chapter Twenty-Seven

"How long are they going to make him stew in there?" Joshua asked.

He and Osborne stood in the semi dark viewing area and studied Cody Jackson, who sat alone in the brightly lit interrogation room. Cody moved from his original seat and now had his back to the viewing window. He slumped forward and rested his forehead on his crossed arms.

Ten minutes later Detective Morgan joined them, a cup of coffee and a clipboard in his hand. He was the shortest officer in the sheriff's department, Napoleon Bonaparte to everyone else behind his back, for his ego as well as his stature. He was twenty years younger than Osborne and held the same title the older man held back when Erin Moore was kidnapped.

"Let's give it another half hour, soften him up a bit," Morgan said.

"Don't be an asshole," Osborne said. "He's a disabled vet with PTSD. Pretty soft target to begin with."

"I heard about the prosthesis, but I also read about his prior arrest for narcotics," Morgan said. "Don't worry. I'll play nice, but you're the one who told me threatened to murder Duggan."

They watched as Morgan entered the room, introduced himself and placed a recorder on the table between them. Cody sat up straight. Osborne wished they could see his face during the interrogation. It was half the value of the interview. There were cameras in all corners, and he'd have to review the footage later.

"Morgan's the last man who should be doing this interview," Osborne said. "Although Cody might respond better to him than me, especially after his recent visit."

"You mean two weeks ago when Cody stopped in here drunk and upset, and you mocked him for not speaking up at the hearing?"

"I know," Osborne said. "I didn't say Morgan was the only asshole."

"Do you think Cody followed through and killed Duggan?"

"I think it's too soon to tell."

"He couldn't even testify at the hearing. Do you think he was emotionally tough enough to take a gun to Duggan's house and murder him? Not to mention, he would have had to move the body from the basement, which is where we found most of the blood. That would have been tough with his prosthesis."

"Adrenaline rush, or maybe drugs. Or there was an accomplice. He could have done it. Plus, the bullet holes were found in the kitchen," Osborne said. He sighed. "It doesn't make a lot of sense, does it?"

"We'll have to wait for the analysis of the state crime lab."

"Quiet. I want to hear his answers."

"Mr. Jackson, can I get you anything to drink? Coffee? A bottle of water?"

"Coffee, please."

Morgan looked up at the window. "Deputy Lippmann, would you mind getting Mr. Jackson a cup of coffee? Oh, and bring a bottle of water, too. Thanks."

"Let Morgan's deputy get him the coffee," Osborne said.

Joshua shook his head and walked out. He returned a minute later with water and coffee, plus sugar and cream packets and a few napkins.

"Hey, Cody, here you go with the coffee. I've got some sugar here."

Cody reached for the cup of coffee and sipped it black. "I meant to thank you for the ride home the other night."

"Serve and protect," Joshua said and smiled at Cody.

Joshua joined Osborne outside the room.

"Where were you yesterday, between the hours of midnight through two in the afternoon?" Morgan asked.

Cody sat up straight, turned around and looked at the one-way glass, then up at the cameras mounted in the corners, and finally back at Morgan.

"Is that when you think Duggan was murdered? I heard about it last night. My sister-in-law follows the news blog."

"Answer the question, Mr. Jackson."

"With my family most of the time. I set my alarm for seven a.m. weekdays. I get the girls up and ready for their summer school. They start at eight-thirty."

"Did you drop them off?"

"No, my wife, Erin drops them off on her way to work."

"So, she was at work yesterday, at the clinic in Lake Delton? I'm sure the clinic can verify that." Morgan made a note on his clipboard.

"No, Thursday's her day off, but she still takes them

to summer school. She runs errands, goes to the gym, things like that."

"Are you employed, Mr. Jackson?"

"Uh, no, I'm not. I worked in construction. When my National Guard Unit got called to Afghanistan, I thought I'd be helping to rebuild. But then after…my leg, I needed to find something else. Still looking, I guess. Thinking of taking online courses and finishing my degree. Accounting or something like that."

"I see. Walk me through your day then. Your wife and daughters leave fairly early in the morning, and they were gone most of the day?"

"What's this about?"

"Did you see your wife at any time after she left to drop off your daughters?"

"Sure, she was home with the girls by four."

"Did you leave your house anytime during the day?"

Cody stared up at the cameras and nodded. Morgan crossed his arms, leaned back in his chair and waited.

"I ran some errands. I ran to pick up some groceries for dinner at the Festival Foods in Baraboo."

"Pretty far out of your way, considering there are grocery stores in Reedsburg."

"They've got the best meat department and Erin insists on free range chicken. Everything's got to be organic," he said quietly. "And I've got the time."

"Did you use a credit card to pay for the groceries?"

"Yes. And I bought gas at the Mobil station a few blocks down the road from the grocery store."

"This accounts for a few hours of your time. What else did you do?"

"I drove up to the VA Hospital in Tomah, right before the grocery store. I attended a support group for vets."

"And they can verify your attendance?"

"No, it's one of the twelve step programs. It's anonymous."

"No sign-in sheet then."

"No, and that's about it. I drove home, worked out in my shop for a while—woodworking. I'm building birdhouses for the school fundraiser next fall."

"Were you driving your 2019 Ford Ranger?"

"No, I've got a Camry sedan and was driving it. I think it's a 2008. It gets better mileage than my truck."

Morgan looked skeptical but said nothing. He sat back with his arms crossed over his chest and looked bored.

"No navigation system or GPS on an old Toyota," Joshua said.

"Interesting Cody has no alibi for most of the day. I wonder if Erin can do any better. I didn't realize she was off every Thursday," Osborne said. "He also asked if that was when Duggan was murdered, not when he went missing."

They turned their attention back to the interrogation room. How long was Morgan going to sit there in silence? Osborne timed it. Just under five minutes. Cody was starting to fidget in the chair and tap his foot under the table. He turned his wedding ring around and around.

"You made a death threat against Stanley Duggan about two weeks ago. Do you remember?"

Cody nodded. "I remember. I had been drinking and I… I was down. Erin and I had a big fight earlier in the day and I was upset. I didn't mean anything by it."

"You mentioned expecting to work on construction in Afghanistan a few minutes ago. Even so, your training for the National Guard included weapons training, am I correct?"

"Sure."

"There is no concealed carry permit in your name. Do you own a firearm, Mr. Jackson?"

"No."

"Are you able to own a gun legally?"

"I suspect you know I can't own a gun."

"What about your wife?"

He nodded. "She does. Three handguns, I think. She does have a concealed carry permit."

"Do you know where your wife keeps these handguns?"

"She carries one with her when she leaves the house. Otherwise, they're locked in a safe in her office, on account of the girls."

"Do you know the combination to the safe?"

Cody hesitated, then admitted he did.

Morgan crushed his empty coffee cup in his hand. A startled Cody partially stood, then settled back into the chair.

"Mr. Jackson, you threatened to kill Stanley Duggan last week. Now he's missing, possibly dead. You can't account for your time on the day of the murder and have access to a gun. Is there anything I'm missing?"

"I'd like to call my attorney now," Cody said.

Osborne slammed his palm against the glass and swore under his breath. "That's the first smart thing to come out of his mouth."

Chapter Twenty-Eight

"Why can't we ever have pancakes? You haven't made pancakes in a hundred years." Charlotte sat at the kitchen table with a napkin tucked into the neck of her pajama top and a fork ready in her hand.

"Two hundred years," chimed in Gracie, not to be outdone by her older sister. She had dressed herself for the day in her sister's soccer uniform.

"I'm quite sure you ate them at your grandma's last time we were in Milwaukee for Thanksgiving. That's less than a year." Erin grabbed a carton of eggs and dish of butter out of the refrigerator, shutting the door with her hip.

"Well, I'm pretty sure it was a hundred years," Charlotte said.

"Sorry, that's not what I'm cooking this morning. Go watch some cartoons. I'll call you when the eggs and potatoes are ready," she said.

Charlotte tossed down her fork, and the girls were out of their chairs and through the door to the family room before she could finish the sentence.

Erin loved Sunday mornings, the only day of the week she didn't set an alarm clock. No patients to see, no school, no dance class. She'd kept the girls off the T-ball and soccer teams that summer, and no one, including the girls missed it. They were still up by eight o'clock, but it was still a break from the weekday routine.

Erin fed fresh oranges into the juicer as the smell of sizzling bacon filled the room. She'd cooked potatoes the night before and was sauteing onions and red peppers to add to the mix. Cooking a hot breakfast was a small thing, but it felt normal and ordinary, at a time when nothing else did.

Erin once tried to make pancakes for the girls and, fortunately, they were too young to remember. It hadn't gone well. She'd mixed the batter from scratch without a hitch and turned out eight neat lightly browned little pancakes. When Cody doused his with maple syrup, it all came back.

She was back in the animal pen in Duggan's barn, and she was cold and hungry. Veronica just shoved a paper plate full of pancakes through a feeding slot and they'd tipped out onto the dirty concrete floor. She'd brushed them off the best she could with her stiff, chilled fingers and tried to eat, since it was possibly the only food she would see all day. They were dripping with syrup, mixed in with the bits of straw and grit from the floor.

Erin had watched her daughters with their pristine, dirt-free pancakes but as soon as the smell of the maple syrup found her, she bolted from the room. The girls didn't notice.

"What time is Lindsey coming?" Cody asked, appearing in the doorway.

"Any minute. She texted. She stopped to pick up some of the cinnamon rolls from Leona's Bakery," Erin said. "I told her there was plenty of food without them."

"I'm not hungry this morning," He disappeared down the hallway.

Cody hadn't joined Erin and the girls for a meal in

weeks, and his clothes were hanging on him. His gait had worsened, and she suspected his prosthesis wasn't fitting properly after the weight loss.

She dumped the spent oranges into the garbage can and filled a glass carafe with the orange juice. She slid it into an empty spot in the refrigerator, in case Lindsey was later than expected.

She heard the whirring of the front gate and spotted her sister's Nissan pull up in front of the house. Erin opened the front door to see her sister standing stiffly with a solemn expression, clutching a large manila envelope tight against her chest. Wordlessly, she followed Erin into the kitchen and hung her purse over the back of a bar stool. Cody had reappeared and was pouring himself a cup of coffee.

"Where are the girls?" Lindsey asked in a low voice.

"Cartoons," Cody said, tilting his head towards the family room.

"Can we go into your office for a minute? I don't want them to hear," Lindsey said.

Erin shut off the burner and left the half-cooked scrambled eggs sit.

"Jesus, Lindsey, you're scaring me. What's up?" Erin asked, shutting the office door behind them.

"I figured I'd bring in your mail, in case you hadn't been out there yet."

"It's Sunday," Cody said.

"I know, I wasn't thinking." She held out the manilla envelope.

It was taped shut with packing tape. Erin flipped it over. The words 'DIE BITCH' were written in black marker on the front of the envelope in tall block letters. It was similar to the writing on the postcards, although the message was considerably darker. There was nothing else written on either side, no stamps. This hadn't been delivered by the US Postal Service.

"Maybe you should put on gloves," Cody said.

"It didn't help the last ten times. I'm not going to bother."

"Don't open it. Call the police. What if it's something dangerous, anthrax or poison, or explosives, or something like that?" Lindsey paced around the small room.

Erin stared at the envelope. Whomever was sending the postcards had sent this, likely a reaction to Duggan's disappearance. She reached for a letter opener and slit the envelope open. She peeked inside, ready to spring back if there was anything but paper inside. There were photographs, a stack of them held together by a rubber band. She dumped them onto the desk blotter, and they all stared in shock.

Finally, Erin picked up the photographs and slipped the rubber band off. She spread the photographs out over the desk, thirteen in all. They were all black and white, and the focus was a little off on several, like someone who didn't quite understand the camera function on their smartphone. In two pictures, the photographer's finger partially filled the field.

Most were pictures of their girls, and they were taken that summer. She recognized the jumping castle from Leo's birthday party in June. Erin had arrived to pick up the girls when Charlotte climbed out of the castle, crying after falling inside. There was a photograph of Lindsey, seated at a picnic bench in City Park, smiling and focused on her cell phone, with her back to the girls who were climbing on the playset behind her. There was a picture of Erin alone, walking to her car in the clinic parking lot, also staring down at her phone. Another showed the expensive condominium complex overlooking Lake Delton, where Alex lived. A photograph of Cody in his truck, sitting in a parking lot, his head hanging forward and his eyes shut, as if he was asleep, or worse.

Each photo had been defaced with a black marker. A knife was drawn ready to enter Lindsey's chest as she played with her phone. A hang noose had been drawn around Erin's neck on the way to her car. A gun pointed at Gracie as she climbed from the jumping castle, and a syringe appeared on the photo of the sleeping Cody, the needle pointed towards his chest.

Cody picked up the picture of Alex's condominium. A border of small hearts encircled the edge of the photograph.

"Where is this?" he asked.

Erin ignored the question. He dropped the picture back onto the desk and closed his eyes.

"You've got to call the police," Lindsey said.

"It hasn't helped in the past," Erin said.

"This is different." Cody picked up the picture of his daughter with a gun pointed at her face. "Please, Erin. This is much more threatening than anything you've ever received. If this is coming from Veronica, she may think you're responsible for whatever happened to Duggan, and you have no idea how far she'll take this."

"You don't know for sure these are coming from Veronica," Lindsey said. "What if they're from Duggan?"

"I don't think so. He was still locked up when the other cards arrived," Erin said. "Who else would be sending them?"

"She can't live too far from here, if she dropped them off herself," Cody said. "The security camera may have caught the car. We might get a plate. She had to drop this off sometime after I got the mail yesterday, which was maybe three o'clock."

"There was a heavy rain last night. That's not going to help with visibility," Erin said.

"Dad. Dad. Mom." Erin had locked the office door, but it didn't deter the girls from knocking. "We're starving. Are you burning the bacon?"

Cody gathered the photos into a pile and shoved them back into the envelope. They exchanged worried looks, but all headed back into the kitchen. Lindsey detoured back to her car for the forgotten baked goods, and Erin poured juice, finished the eggs, and retrieved the bacon from the warming drawer. A few minutes later, the food was all ready and served. The girls chattered away about summer camp, and Erin was relieved they didn't seem to notice the grownups, who had very little to say as they picked at their food.

Lindsey started the Little Mermaid video, an oldie but goodie now that Gracie was no longer frightened of Ursula and her eels. The adults retreated to the office and again locked the door.

Cody brought up the feed from the front door security camera on Erin's laptop. He scrolled back to two in the afternoon to be on the safe side and fast-forwarded through the daylight hours. Nothing. When they hit dusk, around seven at night, the security light with photo sensors over the gate should have come on, but it didn't. The front gate was dark. Minutes after eleven at night, during a torrential downpour of rain, a car pulled up to the front of the gate, turning off their lights before they reached the mailbox. A figure in a dark coat and hood climbed out, darted around to the mailbox, and placed the envelope. They hurried back to the car and drove away. It was about fifteen seconds total. They couldn't tell if it was a man or a woman. It looked like a dark gray car, but they couldn't be sure. They certainly couldn't see a license plate. It wasn't the green Subaru, Erin thought.

"Cody, check the footage from the past week. How long has the security light been out?" Erin asked.

Five minutes later he confirmed it was operational Thursday night, but not since. It went out one night after Duggan disappeared.

"Light bulbs burn out. It could be a coincidence," Lindsey said.

It wasn't, Erin knew. The timing was too perfect.

"We really need to call the police," Cody said.

"Do any of the neighbors have security cameras covering the road?" Lindsey asked. "We know what time the car went by."

"Good idea. I can check. I think it would be best to run over and ask. Maybe the Bennett's to the south, but I'm not optimistic," Cody said.

They all sat in silence, thinking. Someone, presumably Veronica, found a way to take out their security light and left a stack of very threatening photographs. Not only threatening to Erin, but to her entire family and Alex.

"We've got to get the girls out of here," Erin said. "Call your mom. Or one of your sisters. See if they can take them for a couple of days, maybe longer."

"They're going to want to know why. What should I tell them?"

"As little as possible."

Chapter Twenty-Nine

Erin hadn't seen Malcolm in a month, which was shortly before he and his now-fiancée Cheryl rented an apartment on the Chicago north shore. He hadn't been ready, she knew, and while she couldn't discourage him from moving, she did push him to establish with a counselor as soon as he could in Chicago. He'd ignored this recommendation, as he'd done with her suggestion for couples counseling.

He followed her into her office and sat in his usual chair. He was dressed in a blue Chicago Cubs t-shirt and plaid shorts. She'd never seen Malcolm without a cardigan no matter what the weather. She'd once read Mr. Rogers' mother handknit every one of his sweaters. She hoped someone would do the same for Malcolm at least once in his life. Erin offered him a cup of tea like she had on every other visit, and for the first time he accepted.

"We made the move," he said. "It's not as bad as I thought it would be. We've got a first-floor apartment, and I'm relieved I don't have to use an elevator. We're only four blocks from the lake, and I walk to Lincoln Park almost every day with Peabody."

"I'm assuming that's a dog?"

He smiled. "He's a corgi mix, a rescue. I joined a Dungeon and Dragons group who meet in the park and I'm happy I've met some friends."

"That's great to hear. Have you had any success looking for a new job?" Erin scanned through the bio notes to refresh her memory on what he did for a living. Cable service installation—there must be similar jobs in Chicago.

"No, I haven't really looked yet. I've worked full time since I turned eighteen and even worked bagging groceries in high school. It's kind of nice being off for a while."

"Has Cheryl already started graduate school classes?"

"Next week. I'll probably start my job search then."

"How are the two of you getting along?" she asked. "You're obviously spending a lot of time together now that you're both off work."

Malcolm picked up his cup of tea and dipped the teabag in and out repeatedly. An updated version of his foot tapping? He discarded the bag on the saucer she'd provided and took a sip.

"Are you stalling?" she asked.

He bit his lower lip, smiled, and nodded. "We're not fighting. I guess it counts for something, right."

"Sometimes fighting is healthy, if it's done in a constructive way," she said.

"Like I said, I go off to the park in the afternoon. She met some of the students in her graduate program at an orientation, two guys and a girl. They like to go out at night, like Cheryl. It's not every night, but often enough. Then she sleeps in until I'm ready to take Peabody to the park."

"It sounds like you saw more of each other when you were both working full time here," she said.

He agreed.

It had only taken a month for them to carve out parallel lives in Chicago. They were now engaged roommates, and she suspected Cheryl had emotionally moved on to a fellow graduate student. Was theirs any different from her life with Cody? Not much, although they at least shared some responsibility for their daughters, although less every day on his part.

"Have you and Cheryl talked about this, how little time you're spending together?" she asked, knowing the answer.

"I'm figuring once her classes and teaching responsibilities start next week, she won't be going out at night as often. I decided I'll wait to see what happens."

"What might happen instead if you talk to her about your concerns? How do you think she would react?" Erin asked.

"Not yet." He shook his head. "I will at some point."

The alarm chimed and Malcolm stood.

"Do you want to schedule our next appointment? Or if you prefer, I can put together a list of recommended counselors in the Lincoln Park area."

"I'll book online once I know my schedule," he said, and walked out before she could get in another word.

Erin spent the next ten minutes updating her notes. She wondered if Malcolm would accept a job if it interfered with D&D with his new-found friends. She knew all too well the effect long-term unemployment had on a relationship. She suspected she wouldn't be seeing Malcolm again.

Erin rechecked her schedule for the rest of the day and saw her next appointment was a last-minute cancellation. She knew there were patients on a growing waiting list since she'd cut back her hours drastically, and she wondered if Marla even tried to fill the spot. Her stomach grumbled and she thought about the half bagel which passed for breakfast. She wondered if anyone had left snacks out in the breakroom.

Erin signed off the laptop and headed down the hallway. The lights were on, and she heard low voices through the door. She pushed it open to find two of her partners, Jim O'Donnell and Maxine Marquardt, working on a plate of cheese and crackers.

"Did you see the last post?" Jim asked.

He saw her confusion and pointed to the bulletin board, where Fitzpatrick's latest news update had been printed and tacked up. She pulled it down, wadded it up and tossed it into the trash. Erin didn't miss the worried expressions on their faces.

"It sounds like they're not sure if he escaped the ankle monitor or if he's dead," Jim said.

"Let's hope for dead," Erin said, regretting it as soon as she said it.

There was complete silence as she grabbed a paper plate and helped herself to a few pieces of cheddar and crackers.

Maxine finally broke the silence. "Do you want to talk about it?"

Erin bristled at the question. She had come to the lounge for carbs and a break, not an intervention. She knew they meant well, but she most certainly did not want to talk about any of it.

"Sit down, Erin," Jim said. "Your eleven o'clock didn't cancel at the last minute. It was four days ago. I moved one of my patients to late afternoon, and Maxine came in on her day off to meet with us."

She hesitated and glanced at the door. Finally, she

sat.

"You're struggling. We know it's been a rough summer, with Duggan's release, and now this. He's missing and I'm sure that's on your mind," he said.

"You need to realize it's affecting all of our practices, not only yours, and it seems to be getting worse rather than better, even after you cut back your hours," Maxine said. "There have been two more complaints in the past week from the Baraboo Community Clinic, and they're one of our major referrals."

This was not happening, Erin thought. She'd practiced with these psychologists for four years and she assumed they'd have her back. She was not going to cry. She struggled to slow down her breathing. Three seconds in, four seconds out. She had to hold it together, or it would prove their point. She bought time by going to the refrigerator and pulling out a bottle of water.

She sat back down and opened the container, still concentrating on her breathing. Three in, four out.

"I know I've canceled a few appointments this summer, and been late a few times, but I wasn't aware of the complaints from the Baraboo Clinic."

"Nate Lesko said he'd been referring his adolescent girls to you specifically because the families had been pleased with the outcome. He said you saw a fourteen-year-old patient of his twice this month, and then referred her away when you suspected she suffered from an eating disorder," Maxine said. "The family specifically wanted a female therapist. Since I couldn't get her in for two months, they sent her to another group."

"I didn't know you hadn't been able to fit her in. Eating disorders aren't one of my areas of focus and I thought it was better to refer her to you."

"If that's the case, you could have asked Maxine. No, let me reword that. You should have asked her. Lesko has one of the largest adolescent medicine practices in the area, and we can't afford to lose his referrals," Jim said.

"I'm sorry. I'll come to you directly if I need to refer one of his patients." Erin hesitated. "You mentioned a second complaint."

"Stan Bookerman said he'd referred a male patient for his anxiety and depression following a divorce. You saw him for two sessions, then told him you weren't a good match for his needs and canceled his future appointments."

"Do you need the patient's name, or does this ring a bell?" Maxine asked.

"There were extenuating circumstances," Erin said. "Haven't you ever felt that you and a patient were somehow a poor fit, based on your personality differences?"

"Yes, of course, but Stan said it's the fourth time this year you've done it with his or one of his partners' patients. What was the problem in this case?"

She didn't need the patient's name. Michael J. Holloway, a local pharmacist at one of the drugstore chains. It shouldn't have taken her until the second session, but she'd been distracted. Erin knew she couldn't reveal her screening strategy to her partners, but she wasn't about to change it either. After a new patient appointment, she always ran their name through the Wisconsin Circuit Court Database. It was amazing how much information she gleamed.

She didn't care about civil cases or speeding tickets.

Michael J. Holloway's now ex-wife had filed a restraining order during the divorce five years earlier. He may suffer from his anxiety and depression, but she knew about his underlying current of anger.

"We just weren't a good fit. It's hard to be more specific." Erin wondered where this conversation was going. She couldn't lose more hours.

"We think you need to give Bookerman a call and talk to him directly. He's threatening to send his referrals elsewhere."

"I can call him," Erin said. "Next week. Not today."

Maxine and Jim exchanged a long look, then finally nodded.

Erin selected a few more pieces of cheese and crackers and slid them onto her paper plate, trying to demonstrate she was unrattled and still in control. As soon as she reached her office, she locked the door. She tossed the food into the garbage can, curled up on her side on the couch, and wept.

Chapter Thirty

Osborne looked up to see Sheriff Carter standing in the doorway of the breakroom. Joshua quickly gathered up his empty potato chip bag and Mountain Dew bottle and tossed them into the garbage can.

"I hope that's not your breakfast," Carter said. "Your metabolism is going to catch up with you someday, Lippmann. Take my word for it."

"No sir, I've been up for hours."

"I've asked Morgan for an update on the Duggan disappearance. You're welcome to sit in."

They followed Carter back to a small conference room, where Morgan was already waiting with his notebooks and a silver laptop spread out on the table.

"I realize the state crime lab is going to piecemeal their results like always, but what have you got back so far?" Carter asked.

"The blood in the basement is a preliminary match for Duggan's, which we expected, but we'll need to wait for confirmation. The smaller amount of blood smeared on the kitchen table wasn't his."

"Is it in the system?"

"DNA will take weeks." The detective rifled through his notebook. "Bullet holes in one of the kitchen cabinets. We retrieved two bullets from the plaster and we're running them for a ballistics match. That should be back later today."

"Casings?" Osborne asked. He knew there weren't any. He'd done a thorough search before Morgan arrived.

Morgan shook his head. "The shooter must have picked them up."

"This is all you've got?" Carter demanded. "It's been four days."

"We've got an APB out on Duggan, but we suspect he's dead. There was a lot of blood in the basement."

"How the hell did he get the ankle monitor off?"

Morgan shrugged. "The state crime lab is looking into that. They dusted for fingerprints, and we're waiting on that."

"You mentioned you found a burner phone on the premises."

"Yes, a single phone, and we were able to track it down. It was purchased at that Walmart right off the highway on a busy Saturday morning. We looked at their security tapes, and it was a zoo there like you'd expect. We didn't see Duggan in the footage, and it should have set off his ankle alarm if he'd gone that far, but we also didn't clearly identify the time of purchase. The phone was part of a two-pack, and we don't know where the second phone is."

"All the calls were made to a single number, which was not part of the original two-pack he purchased. It appears the second phone is either turned off or possibly destroyed. We haven't been able to find any more information on the missing phone, but we do know Duggan had been contacting women in the area with a burner different from the one we recovered."

"Contacting women? You mean he was dating around? Already?" Carter asked. "Incredible."

"We know of at least three women, and one he met through a dating site," Osborne interjected. "We spoke to two of them. I can get Morgan their pictures if he wants to go back through the Walmart security tapes." Osborne knew it would be a waste of time, but it would be Morgan's time, not his own.

"Please tell me it wasn't through Tinder. Let's assume Duggan is seriously wounded or dead. Any suspects? I saw you brought in Cody Jackson. Anything there?" Carter asked.

"I don't think so," said Morgan. "Although we'll see when the fingerprint results come back. It's interesting neither Jackson nor his wife Erin can account for where they were most of the day. He's unemployed and Thursday is her day off. Same goes for Erin's sister."

"I understand Erin's alibi for the afternoon was the more interesting of the two."

Morgan chuckled. "She didn't give that up easily, as you can imagine. Apparently, she's got a standing…" He searched for the word. "Appointment. She kept every other Thursday appointments with Alex Folk for the past year. He's got a condo in Lake Delton, overlooking the water."

"Folk is the developer who keeps suing the Dells zoning commission, worth millions I've heard," Osborne said.

"Isn't he married?" Carter asked.

"Apparently his wife thinks so," Morgan said. "She lives in Madison, teaches at UW. We were able to catch Folk at his condo for an interview. He backs up Erin's story and says she was with him from one to three the day of the murder. He was livid that she gave us his name."

"Let me know what else you find. I'm going to try to salvage what's left of my vacation day and get in eighteen holes." He stood to go.

"Wait, Sheriff," Morgan said. "Two more things you need to know."

"Shoot," Carter said.

"We found Duggan's laptop. It was hidden in his bedroom, shoved between the mattress and bed frame. No password protection, same as his phone," Morgan said. "It was full of porn, most of it your run of the mill stuff. A little S&M. You know. But we found a small file of child porn as well, young girls, some boys. Maybe five or six years old." Morgan powered up the laptop and turned it around for Carter's benefit.

Carter sat back down, took reading glasses out of his breast pocket and looked at the images. He shook his head and closed the laptop.

"Any evidence Duggan took any of the pictures?" Carter asked.

"He didn't own a digital camera. There was a low-quality camera on his phone but no images on it. He likely downloaded these."

Osborne was infuriated Morgan was burying the lead, the stack of photos of Erin's girls. He and Joshua had missed the laptop in their search of the house, but there wasn't enough time for a thorough search.

"One other thing." Morgan gloved up and removed the stack of photographs of Erin's daughters, which they had found in the bottom drawer of the desk. He sorted the twelve photos in three rows.

"We found these hidden in a drawer. The two little girls are Erin's daughters, Grace and Charlotte."

Carter gloved up and picked up each photograph and

studied it.

"They dusted these for prints?"

Morgan nodded. "Results are pending, but it looks like the only one who handled them was Duggan."

"But that's impossible, because Duggan's ankle monitor never signaled he'd gone beyond his five-mile leash," Joshua said. "We know where some of these were taken."

He pointed to the photo of Erin loading the girls into her car.

"Heritage Learning Academy in Lake Delton. Twenty-three miles out of range. And the picture on the swing set is City Park in Reedsburg. Out of range."

Osborne cursed under his breath. Lippmann needed to think before shooting off his mouth.

"You've seen these photos already, haven't you? How else would you know exactly how many miles away? You were ordered to secure the crime scene until I arrived, but you searched the house, didn't you?" Morgan said.

A flush crept across Joshua's cheeks as he realized his mistake. Carter sat back and shook his head.

"I'll deal with that matter later. It appears someone is taking pictures of Erin's daughters and giving them to Duggan." Carter pushed the open laptop towards Osborne. "These child porn photos on the laptop. You've had the most contact with the Moore family. Are any of these photos of her girls?"

Joshua and Osborne slowly scrolled through the photos. The images were repulsive, and Osborne felt a bitter taste rising in the back of his throat. There were little girls the same age as Erin's, but the faces were distinctly different. He held up the photos of Gracie and

Charlotte to the laptop screen and shook his head.

"No, thankfully," Osborne said.

"How did Erin and her husband react to this news, that Duggan had recent pictures of the girls?" Carter asked.

"We haven't told her," Morgan said. He turned to Osborne. "You want to get involved in this case, go ahead. Stay the fuck away from my crime scene, but you can let Erin and her husband know about the pictures. Get back to us after you do."

It would be a difficult conversation, but Osborne didn't mind. He was back on the case which was all that mattered.

Chapter Thirty-One

August 13th
BREAKING NEWS – BARABOO NEWS-JOURNAL
by Richard Fitzpatrick, Reporter

The Sauk County Sheriff's Department has released no further information concerning the whereabouts of Stanley Duggan III, who was discovered to have escaped his ankle monitor five days prior.

Of note, on searching Duggan's home, where fourteen-year-old Erin Moore was held hostage twenty-one years ago, a laptop belonging to Duggan which contained pornography including images of children was found. In addition, recent photographs of Dr. Erin Moore-Jackson's young daughters Charlotte and Grace Jackson as well as her extended family were also in Duggan's possession. His ankle monitor, which was a condition of parole, was left behind.

The Sauk County Sheriff's Department did not return calls for comment. At this time, I was unable to reach Dr. Erin Moore-Jackson for comments. Information was obtained from anonymous sources close to the Moore-Jackson family and the investigation.

Additional information will be reported as it becomes available.

Chapter Thirty-Two

"Erin, I have no idea how Fitzpatrick found out Duggan had photographs of your daughters," Osborne said. "I'm as furious as you are."

That was impossible. Erin was seething, and the muscles in her forearms ached from clenching her fists. Her kidnapper had photos of Gracie and Charlotte, recent photos. These were her daughters.

"And the child pornography. There was child porn on his laptop," she said, then lowered her voice. "I had a right to know."

Erin crossed her arms and paced in front of her clinic office window. She checked her watch. Her next patient was due in fifteen minutes, and she'd canceled on him once this month already. She'd rearranged her schedule too many times since Duggan's release. She couldn't ask again, especially after the break room ambush the prior day.

"It's still early in our crime investigation, which may involve a dangerous parolee on the run or possibly a murder. You do not have a right to know everything we find at the scene. That includes the photos of your kids," he said. "But we should have kept it away from the press."

"It's your fault a dangerous parolee isn't still sitting in prison, isn't it? And I disagree. I have every right to know about the pictures of my girls."

Osborne took a deep breath and exhaled. "You and your husband are still considered people of interest in this investigation. Even your sister. That shouldn't surprise you."

"You seriously consider us suspects?"

"I'm going to stick with 'persons of interest' until we know more. The three of you, more than anyone, had a motive for wanting him dead, and none one of you can account for your time the day he disappeared," he said.

"I still think you should have let us know about those pictures," she said. "Do you have any idea where Fitzpatrick got his information?"

"Not yet, but he released his Breaking News report last night. I thought I'd talk to you first. The sheriff isn't going to be any happier about this leak than we are. We'll get to the bottom of it."

Erin sat down behind her desk and clutched her head in her hands.

"We're trying to move the girls out of town until it's safer," she said. "Cody's parents would be our first choice, but his dad is having health problems."

"There's no reason to think your girls are in any danger."

Erin looked up at him. Was he short-sighted or lying to her? She wanted to ask it out loud. She turned to her messenger bag and pulled out the manilla envelope of marked-up photographs. She slammed it down on her desk.

"These were shoved into my mailbox at home Saturday night. We could see the car stopping on our security footage, but it was during an absolute downpour. We couldn't see any details about the driver or the car. Our security light, which normally would have lit up this area, was out. That's suspicious, too."

Osborne took the envelope and sat down. He took out a pair of latex gloves and pulled out the rubber-banded stack of photographs. He went through them one by one, flipping each over. Nothing on the back. The final photograph showed him sitting in an unmarked police car with his deputy, who was holding a camera to the open window, taking a picture of Duggan as he met one of his ladies in the park. A red clown nose had been drawn on both of their faces.

"You should have called to report this," he said softly.

"Because that's worked well for me in the past?" she asked.

"At least we know for sure Duggan wasn't the one taking the pictures. These are the same photos we found at the crime scene, except for this one."

He held up the last photo of himself and Joshua. "The set at Duggan's house weren't marked up like this."

"These must have been taken by Veronica. No one else had any reason to do this," she said.

"I'm going to speak to Fitzpatrick," he said.

"You think he might have taken these pictures?"

"No, look at how amateurish these are. These were not taken with a professional camera, or even a good phone camera. But he's getting his information from somewhere."

Erin's desk phone rang, a signal her patient was waiting.

"I'm sorry but that's all the time I have," she said.

"One other thing. I'll make it quick," he said. "I know you have a valid concealed carry permit, and your husband mentioned you do carry a gun in your purse. He said you own three handguns."

"Perfectly legal," she said, hoping he hadn't seen the sign at every entrance to the clinic banning firearms. She was breaking clinic policy, not state law.

"Would you be willing to allow us to compare the ballistics from your guns, all three of them, to the evidence from the crime scene?" he asked.

"Why would I do that?" she asked.

"It would go a long way in terms of eliminating you and your husband as persons of interest."

"I suggest you look elsewhere. We didn't have anything to do with his disappearance. Now I'm asking you to leave."

"Interesting you won't cooperate, since it's in your interest as well for us to find Duggan if he's alive, and his killer if he's not." He shoved the photographs back into the envelope. "I'm going to take these for now."

Erin said nothing as he exited.

The patient would need to wait a few more minutes. Erin sat back in her chair. It was a reasonable request to compare ballistics. She knew she didn't shoot Duggan, as much as he deserved it. She wouldn't have missed, for one thing. If she had been there, the police would never have found a laptop or pictures of her daughters left behind. She would have searched his place and taken everything.

But what if it had been Cody? He knew where her weapons and ammunition were kept, and he knew the combination to the safe. She had checked and all three handguns were there, but this didn't mean he hadn't borrowed one. His military training included firearms.

Osborne had made a polite request. The next time it wouldn't be as courteous, probably a search warrant. She didn't know if Cody could shoot a man, even someone deserving like Duggan. She could have shot Duggan without hesitation. But she didn't, and if her husband had, she was going to have his back. She would dispose of the guns. She would purchase a new handgun and get rid of the others.

Chapter Thirty-Three

Erin reluctantly agreed Betsy could take the girls for ice cream after summer school and go to a nearby playground for an hour. Her last patient had called and rescheduled for the following week, and she finished her charting earlier than expected. She'd missed the ice cream but thought she could at least join them at the park and push her daughters on the swings.

She parked at the curb at the far end of the playground and climbed out of her car. There were a dozen vehicles in the adjacent parking lot, including her sitter's dark blue Honda. She spotted Betsy sitting on a park bench in the deep shade of a large maple tree, her attention focused on her phone. She watched as the girl posed for a selfie and texted away, wondering how long it had been since the sitter had looked up.

The playground was packed with children, mostly around the same age as Charlotte and Gracie, although she saw a few young mothers helicoptering behind their wobbly toddlers.

Betsy finally looked up from her phone as Erin approached and quickly tucked it into her pocket.

"Hey, Erin. You're here early."

Erin sat down on the bench and turned her attention to the playground. She saw Charlotte trying to climb up the slide in the wrong direction, even though Erin warned her it was unsafe. But where was Gracie?

"Gracie?" she called out.

Erin stood and jogged towards the playset, the sitter close at her heels.

"She was here a second ago," Betsy said.

Erin hurried towards Charlotte and scooped her off the slide. She stood the startled little girl on the ground and hugged her tightly.

"Where's your sister?" she asked, loosening her grip.

"I don't know," she answered, straining to break free.

Erin released her and looked wildly around her. There was a short climbing wall on the south end of the playground, and she ran to it. It would be like her daughter to hide behind it. But Gracie wasn't there.

Erin spotted a woman she recognized as the mother of Gracie's classmate and hurried towards her. What was her name?

"Sorry, but have you seen Gracie? She's in your daughter's class."

"Erin, how are you? I haven't seen Gracie, but we've only been here ten minutes," the woman answered. "Are you all right?"

Erin ignored the question and turned back towards the playground. Ten minutes–was her daughter been missing that long and Betsy hadn't noticed? Erin clenched her fists and called her daughter's name as loud as she could. She barely recognized the high-pitched wail emanating from her mouth, as she struggled to hold back tears.

She spotted a dilapidated white van parked half a block down from the far end of the playground. There were no businesses in the area. What was a windowless van doing next to a park? She broke into a run in its direction and watched in horror as it pulled away from the curb. She whipped out her phone and tried to capture a picture of the license plate, but it was too far away. Erin swore and turned back to the playground.

By then other parents joined in the search.

"Erin, she's fine," Betsy called.

Erin whirled to see the sitter standing in the doorway of the women's restroom, beckoning for her to come. Charlotte stood by Betsy's side, holding her hand.

Betsy lowered her voice when Erin reached them. "Gracie's inside. She had an accident, and her pants are wet. She was too embarrassed to come out, but she's fine."

Erin's shoulders slumped with relief. She brushed away tears and went in. Gracie had locked herself in the third stall and was on the verge of crying but was unhurt. Erin asked Betsy to wait inside with her daughter while she retrieved a change of clothes from her car.

Gracie, who was even more of a germaphobe than Erin, was reluctant to change her clothes in the bathroom stall, but finally saw there was no choice. Erin and the girls headed home.

The anger came later, after the girls were bathed and in their pajamas. She would need to fire Betsy, but first she needed to find a replacement. Lindsey couldn't (or wouldn't) pick up the girls every day. Cody had been on better behavior for the past week, but who knew how long it would last. She couldn't quit her job or cut back on her hours any further. They didn't have enough savings to cover the shortfall forever. One more screwup from Betsy, and she'd have to consider giving Cody one more chance.

Erin tucked the girls into her bed that night and remembered she needed to run a quick load of laundry. She retrieved the plastic bag containing her daughter's urine-soaked shorts and tossed a few other items of clothing into the washer.

She heard her phone ring in the adjacent kitchen and let it go to voicemail. Fifteen minutes later she checked the message.

Cody had been taken to the St. Claire Emergency Room with a drug overdose.

Chapter Thirty-Four

"Pick up, pick up," Erin phoned Lindsey, then Betsy, but there was no answer. She didn't leave a message. She didn't have the luxury of waiting for a returned call.

There was nowhere she could drop the girls off. She didn't know their friends' parents well enough, and she had only talked to her own neighbors a handful of times since the girls were born. She roused the girls from their beds and helped them change out of their pajamas. They protested and whined but followed her down to the kitchen, and fortunately they didn't ask any questions. She gave them each a juice box and led them to her SUV. Her eyes darted to the rear-view mirror as she pulled onto the road. They were already sound asleep.

There was little traffic that time of night and she made it to St. Claire's in fifteen minutes. She woke the girls, who were surprised to be in front of the emergency room entrance.

"Why are we at the hospital?" Charlotte asked.

"Your dad is here," Erin said. "I'm sure he'll be fine, but he needs to get a checkup before he comes home."

Gracie began to wail, and Charlotte looked miserable, her hair sticking out in all directions. The nurse who phoned Erin hadn't given her any information regarding Cody's condition other than it was drug related. She would have told her if he was dead, wouldn't she? Erin had no idea what to expect inside. She scooped up Gracie and took Charlotte's hand. The automatic doors whooshed open, and they hurried in.

Erin settled the girls in the waiting room as far away from other patients as she could. Gracie's wails dwindled to whimpers as she stared around the brightly lit room. The nurse at the triage desk took Erin's name. Erin imagined what she was thinking. What kind of mother would bring her little children to the emergency room late at night when their father overdoses? Someone with no other choice. The nurse told her to take a seat and the doctor would be out to talk to her in a few minutes.

"Is he going to be all right? At least tell me that much," Erin said.

"Have a seat, please," the nurse repeated, and turned away to take a phone call.

She wasn't going to sit down until she had an answer. She drew in a deep breath and exhaled loudly, waiting for the woman to turn around.

"Erin?"

She whirled around to see Richard Fitzpatrick standing ten feet behind her.

"What are you doing here?" she asked. How could the night get any worse? Not only was Cody possibly dead or dying from a drug overdose, but it would now be reported in the next news article.

"I'm here to check on Cody, same as you," he said.

"How did you even know he was here?" she asked.

The triage nurse interrupted. "Mrs. Jackson, the doctor said you could come back to your husband's room."

Erin looked from the nurse to the reporter, then to her girls who by now were eerily quiet, leaning up against each other and watching her.

"Can the girls come back with me?"

"No, I'm sorry. If you'd prefer, I can ask the doctor to come here to talk to you, but I know he's busy, so it would be a while."

"I'll sit and watch them," Fitzpatrick said. He didn't wait for an answer and crossed the room toward her daughters. He veered towards a child-size table in the corner and picked up two picture books which he handed to the girls. They took the books and seemed to relax. What choice did she have? Even Fitzpatrick wouldn't stoop to pumping half-awake children for information, would he?

"What should I tell the doctor, Mrs. Jackson?"

"It's Dr. Moore-Jackson," Erin said. "I'm coming."

She followed the nurse through secure doors into the emergency room proper. They passed multiple rooms with curtains drawn until they reached the last.

"Go on in," the nurse said. "I'll let Dr. Buntrock know you're here."

Erin knocked on the door frame, then pushed the curtains aside and entered. Cody was in a semi-upright position on the ER bed, dressed in a hospital gown. There was a nasal cannula in place, an IV in his arm and was connected to a heart monitor. A thin cotton blanket was pulled up to the middle of his chest. His face was pale and drawn, which accentuated the dark circles under his eyes. But he was alive.

"Cody, I'm here," she said.

He opened his eyes and turned his head towards her, nodded and shut them again. She moved closer and reached for his hand.

"Don't," he said, pulling away. Tears trickled down

his cheeks and he wiped them away with the edge of the gown. "I wasn't sure you'd come."

Before Erin could respond, the ER doctor swept the curtains aside and entered, his eyes fixed on the iPad in his hand. He was stocky and in his late forties, gray-haired and dressed in dark blue scrubs underneath a pristine white coat. His name was embroidered on the pocket as Myron Buntrock, MD. He ignored Erin initially and went to the monitor.

"How are you feeling?" he asked Cody.

"Better. I'd like to go home."

The doctor turned towards Erin and introduced himself. "Your husband was unresponsive when the EMTs brought him in, even after they'd given him Narcan. He responded quickly to a second dose and oxygen here and looks much better."

He turned to Cody. "I'm going to admit you for observation. It will likely be for just one night, but I'm concerned about your oxygenation level. You're at 85% saturation, and someone your age should be in the upper 90's. Are you a smoker?"

"No. Can't you just give me another dose of the meds and let me go?"

He shook his head. "That won't help. Your respiratory rate is already normal. In fact, I'm concerned you may have pulmonary complications related to the medication. There have been cases of adult respiratory distress syndrome, which limits how much oxygen your lungs can exchange. We'll get a chest x-ray before you go up to the floor, and probably a repeat in the morning."

Cody leaned back into the pillow and stared at the ceiling. Erin was relieved he didn't refuse or threaten to sign out against medical advice.

"The full toxicology panel won't be back until tomorrow. We've been seeing an uptick in overdoses in this area over the past several months related to Oxycodone laced with Fentanyl. There have been three deaths in the past few weeks in Madison."

"I'm sure there was no Fentanyl," Cody said quietly.

"I checked your electronic health record, and I can't see that any physician has prescribed Oxycodone for you. If you're buying it on the streets, you have absolutely no idea what you're taking."

Cody closed his eyes and remained silent.

Buntrock turned to Erin. "Registration wants you to stop on your way out for insurance information. He's being assigned to one of our hospitalists, Dr. Gerber, who'll likely discharge him in the morning. Any questions?"

"Does this get reported to the police?" Erin asked.

Cody sat forward and looked at the doctor. It was clear he hadn't considered this risk. He was still on probation for drug charges and his freedom might be in jeopardy.

"He was brought in by the EMTs, and a police officer was the first responder at the scene, so they're aware. Your husband is lucky to be alive." Dr. Buntrock took one more look at the monitor and left.

"Who's watching the girls?" Cody asked.

"Fitzpatrick's sitting with them in the waiting room. I had no other choice. I have no idea why he's here."

"I was with Fitzpatrick. He called 911 and saved my life."

"Is he supplying you with the drugs?" she asked.

"Of course not. He's just a friend."

"Damn it, Cody. Where are you getting the Oxy?"

Erin stared at her husband, who couldn't meet her gaze.

He dropped his chin to his chest and said nothing else. They sat in silence while the x-ray tech wheeled in a portable x-ray machine and told Erin she would have to step out.

She found her way back to the waiting room, where Fitzpatrick sat cross-legged on the floor with her girls. There were empty bags of cookies and candy wrappers from the vending machine stacked high and each girl was holding a can of root beer. Erin cringed at the sight, wondering how many infected people had coughed or even vomited on the waiting room floor. She was surprised Gracie hadn't picked up on this. They'd have to shower before going back to bed.

Fitzpatrick climbed to his feet and met Erin. They stepped away from the girls.

"How is he doing?"

"They're going to keep him overnight, but they expect he'll make a full recovery and come home tomorrow."

Fitzpatrick let out a long exhale and looked back at the girls.

"You were with Cody when he was taking the drugs." It wasn't a question. Cody had told her he had called 911.

"We were supposed to meet up for coffee, and I ran a few minutes late. When I got there, he was slumped in his pickup in front of the café, and I called for help."

"Why were you meeting with my husband?" she asked.

He said nothing.

"You can't write about this. I'll get a lawyer and stop you." It was an obvious bluff. They both knew it.

He'd have the blog out there before morning and there wasn't anything she could do to stop it.

Fitzpatrick turned and walked towards the exit. She followed, trying to get ahead of him.

"You can't do this!"

He broke into a run once he was outside the automatic doors, heading towards his car. She started to follow until she heard Gracie wailing behind her. She turned to see both of her daughters huddled together on the sidewalk outside the Emergency Room entrance, and she let him get away.

Chapter Thirty-Five

"Should I assume this is about my Tuesday morning news report?" Fitzpatrick asked. He accepted a cup of coffee from Joshua and took a seat in the interrogation room. "And before you ask, I do not consent to your recording this conversation."

"You want this off the record? I'll agree to that, but it goes both ways," Osborne said.

"I will admit I regret providing the children's names, given their ages, and at my editor's suggestion this information has been removed from the online version. Was there anything incorrect in my report?"

Not really, Osborne thought, which made it even more frustrating. The laptop had not even been fully evaluated, although they'd found the porn immediately. It had been in a folder labeled Porn.

The photos of the Moore-Jackson family were still being tested for fingerprints, once it was determined the printer they found in Duggan's house wasn't operational. Someone else had taken the photos since the locations didn't set off the ankle monitor alarm. As much as Sheriff Carter wanted to believe Veronica had never existed, Osborne knew better. Duggan had an accomplice and he or she was still in the game.

"I've tried to interview Erin several times, and she's been uncooperative to the extreme that I wonder about her stability," the reporter continued.

"How is it mentally unstable to want privacy?" Joshua asked. "I wouldn't talk to you either, if I were her."

"Fortunately, her family members have been a little more forthcoming. Like it or not, Duggan's disappearance immediately after his release on parole is legitimate news."

"Again, she has a right to her privacy," Joshua said.

"Does she though? I'm not sure I agree." Fitzpatrick said. "Again, I shouldn't have mentioned the daughters' names."

"Who is your source?" Osborne clenched his fists. He wanted to pound the fucking table, but it wasn't going to do any good. It would also probably end up in the next Breaking News.

"You know better than to ask that question."

"You mention sources close to the family. Erin and her family members were not informed of the findings at the crime scene."

"Of course not, because I'm assuming they're all suspects. I know you believe Duggan is dead and not just missing." Fitzpatrick said. "And those photos of the children up the ante, don't they? What parent would want a pedophile having pictures of their daughters?"

The logic was circular, and Osborne knew it was intentional. Erin and Cody hadn't known about the photos of their girls until someone dropped them off at their house, a few days before Fitzpatrick's blog. Even then, they hadn't known Duggan possessed copies.

"You didn't find out about the porn and photos from anyone in Erin's family," Joshua said. "You couldn't have."

"That's correct. There are other sources, as I clearly

stated in the article."

"You're suggesting someone from the sheriff's department," Osborne said.

"I suggested nothing of the sort, but I'll leave the detecting up to you. But I think we're finished here."

"We're finished when I say we're finished," Osborne said.

Fitzpatrick laughed and stood.

"Gentleman," Fitzpatrick said, and he left.

The two men sat in silence. Osborne had overplayed his hand. He knew it, Fitzpatrick knew it, and Joshua had better know enough to keep his mouth shut, or he'd learn quickly.

"That went well," Joshua said. He stood and walked towards the doorway.

"He didn't deny the information came from someone in this department, did he? Carter is livid. He wants me to find the leak."

"From this department or possibly someone in the State Crime Lab." Joshua said.

Osborne nodded. He'd considered it.

"You don't think Erin or her husband killed Duggan, do you?" Joshua asked. "Assuming he's dead."

"I hadn't until yesterday. Erin refused to allow ballistics testing on the three handguns she owns. She's got a concealed carry permit. Fitzpatrick is right. I'd want to murder anyone who threatened my daughters. Who else has such a strong motive?"

"I was thinking about the photograph of you sitting in the car, taking pictures of Duggan and the women in the square."

"You think someone killed him because he didn't ask for a second date?"

"No, I'm serious. We're assuming his accomplice Veronica took the picture, and likely the rest of them, right? How would she feel about Duggan dating, especially if she'd hung around for twenty years waiting for his release?"

Osborne had wondered about that briefly, after seeing the photograph. He wondered if the photographer had been tracking Duggan or following them.

"I think we should consider whether it could be someone else from the community. There were reports of a white van sitting by the playground over on Beecher Street the past few weeks. Locals called it in to complain. Maybe it was some concerned parent. Or a concerned cop with misgivings about Duggan's release in the first place," Joshua said.

Osborne sat in stunned silence. Yes, he'd had regrets and second thoughts, especially when he'd seen Duggan's gym setup in his barn. The man was not the frail, sickly seventy-eight-year-old his attorneys had claimed. Osborne admitted this to himself. Still, did this rookie deputy think he would commit murder? He felt his face redden and he glared at his underling.

Joshua stood up and headed for the door.

"Wait, Lippmann."

The younger man stopped and turned, avoiding eye contact.

"I have a friend at the State Crime Lab. I know what you've done. You won't get away with it."

Chapter Thirty-Six

Alex stood in the doorway with his arms crossed and stared at Erin like she'd been scraped from the bottom of his shoe. Soft jazz emanated from the room behind him, as it always did when she arrived. Was he expecting her, or was he really ending it like this? After two years? She felt a flush creep into her cheeks, and she waited. Finally, he stepped aside and motioned for her to enter.

"It's been a shitty day," she said. "Do you mind if I pour myself a glass of wine?"

He said nothing but walked into the kitchen and returned with a glass of white wine for her and a can of beer for himself. Erin opened the French doors to the balcony, which looked down over the lake. He followed her outside and they sat. She usually found the swaying branches in the trees overhanging the balcony and the distant hum of power boats on the other side of the lake peaceful, but no one was relaxing that day.

"I regret I had to give the detective your name, but they demanded to know where I spent the day."

"You were only here two hours, maybe a little longer. You didn't gain much by giving me up. You spent most of the day elsewhere."

She nodded. He was right. Now the Sauk County Sheriff's Department knew they were having an affair. She wouldn't tell him about the photograph of his condominium marked up with a border of hearts.

Detectives Osborne and Morgan weren't the only ones who knew about Alex. If the photographs were taken by Veronica, and who else could have done it, she had followed Erin and she then guessed about their arrangement.

"They've questioned Cody and me twice each, which is ridiculous. It's only because they have no other suspects."

"If this gets back to my wife…" He put the beer down on the side table and shook his head as if there was nothing else to say.

"I'm sorry, Alex, but I had to tell them something."

"On the contrary, you didn't. I wasn't going to lie to them and tell them you were here all day."

"I never asked you to lie," she said.

"An alibi for two hours wasn't going to help you. If you didn't kill the man, which I'm assuming is true, then they aren't going to find any evidence to implicate you. You put my marriage at risk, and it didn't accomplish a damn thing," he said.

"What about my marriage?" she asked. "This is more likely to get back to Cody than it is to your wife down in Madison."

"I don't give a fuck about you and Cody. You've been talking about leaving him as long as I've known you.

"I'm sorry. That's all I can say."

"It's not just the sheriff's department. That reporter you complain about, Fitzpatrick. He cornered me in a restaurant having lunch, thankfully alone and not with a client, and asked about you. He asked if we were having an affair. I don't know how he tracked me down."

Shit. How had Fitzpatrick found out? And if he

knew, could he have been behind the picture of Alex's condo?

Erin didn't need her psychology degree to read his body language. He may have let her into his home, but he wasn't listening to her, not really. He sat rigid in the chair, arms still crossed over his chest, and he stared up into the trees. She'd screwed up. Alex was right. Since she hadn't murdered Duggan, she didn't have to worry. Still, she wished he'd been shot on her long office day, when she was a solid alibi, and not on a Thursday. She briefly wondered if it could have been intentional on someone's part, to frame her for his murder or disappearance.

"I suppose I should go," she said and drained the last of her wine.

A half hour later, she searched the room for her second shoe. She found it in the hallway. She hadn't remembered removing her shoes on the way to the bedroom, but things had progressed quickly. Angry sex, she discovered, was even more intense than makeup sex. She went into his bathroom and urinated. She'd be sore for a week.

Erin took a seat at the kitchen island. Alex set out a plate of olives and small squares of cheese, and he had poured her a second glass of wine.

"Peace offering?" he said.

She picked up an olive and popped it into her mouth.

"Sorry if I got a little rough in there," he said.

"You're a little rough on a good day," she said.

"I've never heard you complain."

She smiled, and he leaned over the island, and kissed her.

"Why did you come by today without texting?" he

asked.

"I wasn't sure you would answer, or I thought you'd say no."

He nodded. "That's probably true."

"Would you like to hear about my shitty day?" she asked.

"Only if it ends with another trip to the bedroom," he said.

She smiled but it faded quickly.

"The practice administrator stopped in my office yesterday after my last patient and suggested I strongly consider a temporary leave of absence."

"On what grounds?" he asked.

"I'll admit, I've had to cancel some appointments over the summer, which is not like me. It's been undeniably hard to concentrate with Duggan out there. And it doesn't help when the detective keeps stopping by my office unannounced." She didn't tell him about Cody's visit and the blowup where he announced she was having an affair within ear range of staff and a patient.

"I think you should follow the administrator's advice. Take a few months off. What would be the downside?"

Erin felt the muscles tightening in her neck and upper back. He was being unreasonably cavalier about her career. She had been working for years to build a psychology practice, and it was falling apart through no fault of her own. She would have to start over, since it was likely her partners would take on her current patients.

Alex also didn't have to worry about money. She'd seen a picture of his house just outside of Madison with one hundred feet of sand beach on Lake Mendota, and she knew he had vacation homes in Aspen and South Beach, not to mention the lakefront condominium where she now stood. Erin needed to keep practicing.

"I take it more than one client has complained," he said.

She nodded. "But I can turn it around."

"Even with Duggan missing? They don't know for sure he's dead, do they? What about this woman you talk about, Veronica? She hasn't gone away, has she?"

"No. You could try to be a little supportive here, Alex," she said.

"Being supportive is overrated. I'm being realistic, which some people appreciate. What do you plan to do?"

"Nothing right now. It's officially a suggestion at this point. I'm going to get my act together and keep working."

"You think it'll be that easy?" he asked.

"They've taken so much away from me, from my family. They're not going to take away my practice."

He nodded. She debated telling him about Cody's recent drug overdose, another narrative inexplicably involving Richard Fitzpatrick. She decided he would be even less sympathetic since she chose to stay married to a drug addict.

"All right, I listened." Alex reached over and unbuttoned her blouse.

She leaned in and kissed him. At some point she'd have to tell him about the photos. Fitzpatrick and Osborne weren't the only ones who knew about Alex.

Chapter Thirty-Seven

In her rush to get to school pickup Wednesday afternoon, Erin left half of her clinic notes unfinished. She'd jotted down her own shorthand notes on each patient, but she still needed to complete them in the electronic health record before Monday per clinic policy. She didn't need one more complaint from the practice manager who was particularly persnickety about record completion. Erin couldn't afford to add fuel to the fire.

The clinic was closed on Sundays, and she used her ID badge to enter through the front door. She was surprised to see the hallway door to the office suites was wide open and the overhead light on. Could the cleaning crew who came through Sunday mornings have forgotten? She would shut the lights off on her way out and spare them the practice manager's wrath.

As Erin headed back towards her office, she heard the side door of the clinic slam shut. She froze and listened. A car engine roared to life and peeled out of the back parking lot. Erin turned and ran to the side door in time to see the taillights pull onto the street. It hadn't been another green Subaru. She was certain of that. It had been a nondescript gray sedan.

They'd used the side door, which meant they had a key to enter, and not an ID badge, like she had used.

Erin turned and walked back down the hallway to the break room and grabbed a bottle of water from the refrigerator. Who had left through the rarely used side door and why were they in such a hurry? She made a mental list of who had keys to access to the building, besides the cleaning crew, the practice manager and maybe one of the senior psychologists. Everyone else used their ID badges to enter. She stood in the hallway outside her office and listened to the near complete silence.

She'd heard one person leave, but what if there was still someone else in the building? She heard the soft hum of the central air unit outside the clinic but nothing else. No voices from behind the closed office doors. No footsteps.

"Is anyone there?" she called out.

There was no response.

Erin cleared her throat and repeated the question louder. She reached into her purse and pulled out the gun. She concentrated on slowing her breathing, as she did on the firing range before shooting. She was overreacting, she knew. It was likely one of the other clinicians there for the same reason she was, who'd left without realizing she'd come into the building. She'd get logged into the computer, complete the notes, and get the hell out of there.

She found her office door was unlocked. Erin had locked it on Wednesday afternoon, hadn't she? She had been in a hurry to get to the school, but the cleaning crew would have been through anyway and left it locked. She scanned the corners of the room, reassured she was alone. She deposited her purse into the visitor's chair, shut the door behind her and double-checked to make sure it was locked. Finally, she slipped the gun back into her purse. Erin rolled her shoulders to relax the tight muscles in her neck and upper back and sat behind the desk.

An oversize white envelope rested in the middle of her keyboard. She knew with certainty it hadn't been there on Wednesday. More pictures of her family? Additional threats?

Her plans to move the girls out of town had fallen through. Cody's sister was traveling, and his father was in and out of the hospital with kidney infections. On her side, there was only Lindsey.

Erin picked up the envelope and judged its weight. It was thin and light, likely only a single sheet of paper. She'd given up on fingerprints a long time ago. She sliced open the edge of the envelope with her letter opener and took out a single sheet. It was standard copy machine paper, folded into quarters to resemble a greeting card. A handwritten message on the cover in black ink contained a quotation from C. S. Lewis, who she knew wrote the Narnia books she had loved as a child. She wasn't familiar with the brief quote.

"The death of a loved one is an amputation."

Did this imply Duggan was dead, and not just missing? She wasn't sure. She opened the handmade card and read the message inside.

"Erin:
An eye for an eye. A tooth for a tooth.
A sister for a sister.
A lover for a lover.
And there's nothing you can do to stop me.
V."

This was the first of the many cards Erin received over the years to bear a signature, even if it was only the letter 'V,' and it also contained the most handwriting.

Maybe she should have been more careful where she handled it. She read the message aloud. She understood the concept of a tooth for a tooth, a lover for a lover, but she had no idea why Veronica would threaten her sister.

"And there's nothing you can do to stop me."

Apparently, there wasn't. How had she managed to get into her locked clinic, and into her personal office? There were no security cameras for reasons of patient confidentiality, but she wondered if adjacent businesses could have caught the car pulling away. Veronica had no way of knowing she would be stopping in. She almost never came in on Sundays. What would she have done if Erin walked in and caught her in the act, rather than hearing her run out the side door? Did Veronica know it was Erin arriving at the clinic, or had she taken off running when she heard the door open?

She went to her purse and pulled out her gun once again, and she called Osborne.

He arrived nearly an hour later, about the same time as her practice manager. Neither of them regarded this as an emergency. She peeked between the blinds and saw them conversing in the parking lot, both looking unhappy to be there on a Sunday afternoon. Erin slipped the gun back into her purse and unlocked her office door.

Osborne gloved up and examined the card, which she'd placed back in the envelope and positioned on her keyboard as she'd found it. He'd examined the side door through which the suspect had exited, and presumably entered. There were no scratch marks to suggest that the door had been picked. Jerrod Gates, the practice manager, reassured Osborne that only the cleaning crew, one of the senior partners and he as practice manager had a key. Everyone else including the other psychologists and office staff entered by swiping their ID cards.

"And no one should have been here on a Sunday, including Dr. Moore-Jackson," Gates said. He went through the building and verified the other offices were all locked and every computer was powered down.

Erin followed Gates into his small office at the back of the clinic. He sat down behind his desk and massaged his temples.

"I only came in to finish a few of my clinic notes from Wednesday, that's all. I wanted to start the week completely caught up."

"The clinic was open and accessible Thursday, Friday and Saturday morning. I don't appreciate having to come in on a Sunday afternoon because you haven't followed policy."

"Aren't you concerned someone broke into the clinic? Isn't that a more significant issue than my coming in to finish up my notes?" His attitude was unreasonable, even inexplicable. She was certain he'd picked up on Osborne's skepticism when Erin described what transpired. Osborne didn't believe her, but how could Gates doubt her story? Neither one seemed particularly concerned about the threatening card.

Osborne appeared in the doorway.

"Does anything else appear to be disturbed?" Osborne asked.

"Not as far as I can tell," Gates said. "Thank you for coming."

"I'll write up the incident and follow up tomorrow, when I'm on duty. I may have some other questions."

"I'll be available," Gates said.

"Questions for both of you," Osborne said, looking at Erin.

She nodded and he left.

"Do you mind if I finish up those notes as long as I'm here?" she asked.

He scowled and shook his head, then asked for her ID badge and tucked it into the top drawer of his desk.

Erin was officially on a leave of absence.

Chapter Thirty-Eight

"You could have accessed these records without hiring me, Erin. They are all a matter of public record." Attorney Martha Snyder escorted Erin and Lindsey into her inner office and shut the door.

"How is Cody these days?" Snyder asked.

"All right, some days are harder than others," Erin answered, figuring the attorney was asking out of politeness rather than true concern. Snyder had been his defense attorney during his conviction for drug charges a few years earlier, and she wouldn't be happy to hear he was using again. Erin immediately regretted not choosing another attorney for the job, even if it meant a few weeks' delay.

"Tell him I said hi," she said. "I'm assuming he knows you're here."

Erin smiled and nodded. She would tell Cody, of course. At some point. Same thing.

Snyder passed over a file folder with twenty-some sheets of paper.

"Most of this is empty paper. Stanley Duggan had just a few individuals listed on his approved visitors list. Wisconsin allows prisoners to list up to sixteen. I'm not sure if it includes immediate family. In his case, it doesn't matter. You can see in his first year he had one female visitor. Her name and whatever information they collected is in there. Then I see the detective involved in the original arrest was a frequent visitor. Of course, he didn't have to be on the approved list. I counted over thirty visits he made over the years."

"Thirty visits?" Erin was surprised. Was Osborne as haunted by what happened twenty-one years ago as she was? Or had he developed a relationship with Duggan during the trial, which might explain why he'd supported his release at the hearing?

"And that's it?" Lindsey asked. "He's had one single visitor other than the cops in twenty years?"

"As far as these records show," Snyder said. "Like I said, you could have saved yourself some money.

"We've got to identify the female visitor," Erin said.

"Since it was only the one, the clerk at the prison agreed to make a copy of the ID she provided at the time. That's in the folder as well. They probably wouldn't have made the copy for you. I guess hiring me wasn't a total waste."

"Thank you," Erin said.

Erin tore open the envelope and flipped through the pages until she came across the copy of the woman's driver's license. It was a copy of a twenty-year-old copy, but it was clear enough. There was no resemblance to the Veronica she remembered. She replaced the papers in the folder and stood.

"Wait, one more thing," Snyder said. "I have another connection in the Department of Corrections. Someone I dated back in law school, believe it or not. You've both heard the term 'follow the money,' right?"

They nodded.

"Family members and friends, anyone in fact, can send money to inmates' accounts, which makes life much easier during incarceration. They can buy snacks and books in the prison commissary, although I suspect most of it goes for cigarettes, drugs, or protection. And cell phones, of course."

"It isn't part of the public record?" Lindsey asked.

Snyder shook her head no. "There were seven women depositing money in Duggan's account while he was at Columbia. Two of them have given him thousands of dollars over the years, and that doesn't include the care packages they may have sent."

"Were you able to get the names?" Erin asked.

Snyder slid a paper across the top of her desk. "This didn't come from me. But I can tell you there isn't any Veronica or anything similar on the list."

"What about the female visitor, Trudy Bell?"

"She's not on the list."

"I don't suppose they keep track of mail," Erin said.

Snyder shook her head. "They monitor incoming mail and check it for contraband, pull it if there's something suspicious. Outgoing mail is the same."

"No list?" Erin asked.

"No list. But since Duggan received no visitors, he must have been communicating with these women by mail. Or telephone. He had a generously funded prepaid calling account, which meant he could call out freely, but no one could call in."

"I don't suppose…"

Snyder laughed. "No, I don't have a list of his phone calls. My friend bent the rules to get a list of his sugar mamas."

"Somebody footed the legal bills for his parole hearing," Erin said. "I wonder if it could have been one of these women."

"It's possible, and before you ask, I have no

connections at Beres, Scott and Mulcahy. I can't get that information."

"I think this is a good place to start," Erin said, and she held up the folder.

They climbed in the car and Erin started the engine, turning the air conditioner to the maximum setting.

"I don't see how this is going to be helpful," Lindsey said. "You knew Duggan was seeing different women since he's been out. Osborne showed you some of their pictures. Didn't he tell you one of them had been sending him money?"

Erin nodded. "I'm more interested in who's missing from the visitors list."

Lindsey looked confused.

"Richard Fitzpatrick. He lied when he said he'd interviewed Duggan in prison. Then where is he getting his information?"

They sat in silence. Erin ran through a mental inventory of the facts Fitzpatrick claimed were directly from Duggan and realized there weren't that many.

"Where to next?" Lindsey asked.

"An electronics store," Erin said. "We're going to buy a GPS tracker. It's time we find out what Fitzpatrick is up to."

She was surprised at the variety of tracking devices available at all different price points. Apparently, trust was in short supply. She'd opted for the longest battery life unit in her price range. It was motion-activated and would track for thirty hours of driving time. She slid her credit card into the slot at checkout, and it was refused. She tried twice more with the same result. Embarrassed, she pulled out her personal backup card knowing she would be making the minimum payment, likely for months to come until she was working full-time again.

Erin hadn't seen any evidence Cody had been going on shopping sprees. Was he taking out cash advances on the card often enough to max out the credit line? Was that how he was paying for his drugs? She clenched the steering wheel tight and said nothing on the drive home. Lindsey had the good sense not to comment.

Don't overreact, she told herself, at least until you know the truth. It's possible it was a glitch, or the card was somehow demagnetized, or some other innocent explanation.

As soon as she got home, she barricaded herself in her office, opened the laptop and logged into the credit card account. They were nearly a thousand dollars over their credit limit. The charge history showed cash withdrawals every few days for the past month. The balance had been near zero last month and now approached seven thousand dollars. She clenched her fists and banged them on the desk. How could he be so irresponsible?

Cody hadn't come home the prior night, which was when he'd made his latest ATM withdrawal. He still didn't know she was now officially on leave of absence. She understood addiction, as a psychologist, but it didn't make it any easier. She brushed away a tear of anger before rejoining her sister in the kitchen.

Once there was an adequate charge on the tracking device, she and Lindsey drove to the newspaper office and saw Fitzpatrick's car was still in the lot. No more delays. Erin watched the front entrance in case the reporter exited, while Lindsey snuck behind his car and placed the tracker in the right wheel well. They were back on the street in a matter of minutes. There were security cameras pointed at the parking lot, but it was unlikely they were continually monitored. No one would be looking at the footage unless a car was stolen or vandalized. At least that's what Erin hoped.

Cody was waiting at the house and pacing in the kitchen when they arrived. He was pale and perspiring heavily. She wondered if he tried to take out more cash and been refused.

"Osborne stopped by," he said. "You didn't tell me there was another letter."

"It was left at the clinic yesterday, and you were out when I got home," she said. "And didn't come home last night.

"He showed me what it said. He had a snapshot of it on his phone. You didn't think it was important enough to mention?"

He was right. This one involved both Cody and Lindsey. They deserved to know.

She also needed to tell Betsy she'd be losing her job now that Erin was on leave of absence. She pulled her phone out of her purse and brought up the screenshot she had taken.

"The death of a loved one is an amputation," Erin read aloud. She mentioned the poet's name and his connection to the Narnia series.

She scrolled to the inside message and passed the phone to Cody and Lindsey. They both sat in stunned silence.

"The girls are safe," Cody said. "As long as they're at school, I mean."

"She doesn't even mention the girls," Erin said.

"No, but she's threatening me, isn't she?" Lindsey asked.

"I don't remember enough about Veronica to know if she had a sister. It's possible," Erin said. "But this makes no sense. It's unfair enough that she blames me for Duggan's disappearance or death. That's who she must be referring to as her lover. But what in the hell did I ever do to her sister?"

"If she blames you for Duggan's disappearance, at least it means they're not a team anymore. He didn't escape to be with Veronica," Lindsey said.

"She's never going to leave us in peace," Cody said, and he continued to pace. "I don't think I can do this anymore."

Erin told him about the meeting with the attorney and emphasized the fact Fitzpatrick never interviewed Duggan at the prison like he'd claimed. She also told him about the GPS device she'd planted on his car.

His agitation intensified. It wasn't the right time to confront him about the cash withdrawals and she didn't want to have that conversation in front of her sister. If he didn't know she had frozen the joint account, he would find out soon enough.

"I'm going to find a meeting," he said.

He grabbed his phone and car keys and was out the door to the garage before she could respond.

"Do you think he is going to a meeting like he said, or is he meeting his drug dealer?" Lindsey asked. "He looks as bad as he did back when…you know."

She didn't need to finish the sentence. Erin remembered all too well the nightmare of returning from work to find her unconscious husband behind the wheel of his car in the garage, with their three-month-old baby screaming alone in the house. Her first thought had been carbon monoxide. The reality was as deadly.

"Maybe you should have put a tracker on his car, too." Lindsey picked up her sister's phone and examined the verse again. "Is Osborne going to do anything about this? I feel like I've got a big target painted on my back. You live in this house with a locking gate and a perimeter fence, a high-end alarm system and you've got a handgun in your purse everywhere you go. What about me?"

"I'm sorry, Lindsey. I never expected you would get sucked into this."

"I've got a cheap-ass lock on my apartment door and my car is in a poorly lit parking lot behind my building."

Erin let her vent. It wasn't fair. None of it.

"You're welcome to move in here until this is resolved. The girls would love it."

"What about Cody?"

"I've asked him to move out. I know he's initially going to be staying with a friend in Wisconsin Dells. He's expecting to be out by the weekend."

"How did the girls take that?"

Erin winced. "We haven't told them yet." The girls would be upset, but Lindsey's presence might soften the blow.

Lindsey nodded and accepted the offer.

"She mentions your sister which is clear enough. When Veronica mentions your lover and threatens him, do you think she means Cody or Alex?"

Erin wondered the same thing.

Chapter Thirty-Nine

Joshua saw the note on his desk when he returned from lunch. He was wanted in Sheriff Carter's office at one p.m. He looked at his watch and sighed. He was already ten minutes late. He took the stairs two at a time to the third floor. He wasn't sure what Carter wanted, but he knew Osborne was behind it. They hadn't had a civil conversation since the day of the waterpark fiasco.

The deputy staffing the desk outside Carter's office waved him in. He knocked and pushed open the door.

"Deputy, thank you for coming. Pull up a chair," Carter said, pointedly looking at his watch. He was seated behind a large oak desk with a single file folder on top.

Joshua was not surprised to see Osborne sitting in one of the guest chairs. He'd been expecting this, but thought it would be between him and Osborne, a showdown rather than an execution. He took the seat next to Osborne's but adjusted it to partially facing them both.

"Could you explain this request?" Carter slid the folder towards him.

He knew what it was before he opened the folder, although he didn't yet know the results. He studied the report. It compared the two bullets removed from the wall in Duggan's kitchen with a ballistics report from Osborne's service weapon from a justified police shooting two years prior, shortly before he'd been assigned to work under the detective. The report officially eliminated Osborne's Glock 17 as the weapon involved.

"Deputy?"

They all sat in silence for a minute. He stole a sideway glance at Osborne, who was leaning back in his chair, arms crossed, and his face redder than he ever imagined possible.

"I was concerned," he began, debating how much gasoline he could afford to throw on the fire. "As you're aware, Detective Osborne attended Duggan's parole hearing and spoke up in favor of Duggan's release into the community."

Osborne's face darkened considerably.

"I knew you both attended the hearing. But why in the hell would you have taken that position?" Carter asked, now staring at Osborne. "Why would you intentionally increase the chances of his returning to this community?"

Osborne was now the one squirming, Joshua noted with some satisfaction. It seemed Carter hadn't known, even though the reporter wrote about it in his blog.

"His health had deteriorated, and he served twenty years," he said quietly. He glared at the deputy.

"And we see how well this turned out. He's either dead or in the wind, and that's on you, Osborne," Carter said. "Jesus H. Christ."

Joshua continued. The damage was done. "Duggan has been seen in his white van at local playgrounds and sitting outside the library. I know Detective Osborne was worried, especially since he played a part in the man getting parole. We even spent several days tracking

Duggan."

Osborne said nothing but continued to glower in his direction.

"I thought it would be beneficial to exclude Detective Osborne's gun as the involved weapon to better proceed with the investigation."

The three men sat in silence. Joshua handed back the ballistics report and avoided eye contact with Osborne.

"Did you discuss this with anyone?" Carter asked.

"No, sir."

"You're suspended without pay for one week for insubordination. Please turn in your badge and service weapon. You're dismissed."

He stood to leave.

"Deputy, you will be reassigned to work in the jail division on return."

He looked back as he left, to see Osborne openly smirk in his direction.

Chapter Forty

Erin had always been an avid crime fiction reader, but for the first time she understood how truly mind-numbingly boring a stakeout could be. In the novels, characters brought along snacks, a water bottle, audiobooks, a bottle for urine, if you possessed that sort of plumbing. Caffeine, caffeine, and more caffeine.

Her leave of absence from work made the surveillance much easier, although she prayed it was short-lived. They had some savings but hadn't been able to add to the cushion since Cody stopped working, which was now entering its second year. Erin sat in Burke's Coffee Shop across the street from the courthouse and a half block down from the newspaper office, waiting for the GPS monitor they'd stuck on Fitzpatrick's car to do something, anything. He'd driven from his apartment over a plumbing supply store on the south side of town to the newspaper office nearly four hours ago. Luckily, the GPS only triggered when there was movement. Otherwise, she'd be changing out the batteries continually.

She had followed him most of the prior day, from the YMCA where he spent a worthless twenty-four minutes, to a diner, and then on to a pet supply store, where he'd carried out a large bag of dry food. She hadn't been aware he owned a pet, but she knew almost nothing about his personal life. The man spent an inordinate amount of time alone in his apartment. She almost felt a twinge of sympathy— almost. She had peed in more Kwik Trips the past two days than her entire life.

Erin swapped cars with Lindsey, who was only too happy to commandeer her Volvo SUV for a couple of days and let Erin use her nondescript gray Nissan sedan. She spent ten minutes on the phone with Cody finalizing his plans for moving out later in the week.

At 2:23 in the afternoon, her phone pinged. Fitzpatrick was on the move. Finally. She followed him north for fifteen miles, all the way to Wisconsin Dells, where he pulled into the parking lot of a medium-sized office building on the outskirts of town. It was Alex's building, although he only occupied one of the larger suites on the ground floor. What the hell was the reporter doing?

There were a half-dozen other tenants listed on the sign in front of the building, but this was too big of a coincidence. He was there trying to interview Alex for a second time, who would be furious about the further invasion of his privacy, especially in front of his office staff. Erin had reluctantly given up Alex as part of her alibi the day Duggan disappeared, but how did the reporter discover his name? Detective Morgan would never have shared her alibi with the press. There must be a leak in the sheriff's office. There was no other way possible. In the end, it made no sense.

Even if one of Morgan's deputies leaked it to Fitzpatrick, which seemed unlikely, they couldn't have given the information to Veronica. It didn't explain how she had known about Alex; she had included a photo of his condominium in that last packet of pictures. Was Veronica following her and if so, for how long? She ducked lower in the car and scanned the parking lot. Could she be watching her now?

She stewed in the car for a half hour, until Fitzpatrick finally came out. She stayed low in the driver's seat until he pulled away, then she followed.

She hung back a safe distance as he headed south on Highway 12 out of town. He turned off the highway and meandered on intersecting small roads until he pulled into a grass-covered parking lot. A small wooden sign marked the site as the Mound Man Park. She read about it a year ago in a local interest blog site. It was an ancient effigy mound, and no one knew who built it or what it represented. A county road had inadvertently been built across the thighs of the giant creature, and the legs and feet were part of an active farmyard on the opposite side of the road.

Erin parked fifty yards short of the entrance to the site and was still too visible. She tried to dip the car into the ditch, but not so deep she'd need a tow truck to get out. It wasn't four-wheel drive like her SUV. She ducked into the scrub woods along the roadside, heading east towards the park.

Fitzpatrick's car was parked next to an older gray four door, like the one Erin was driving. She couldn't tell the make from this distance, but it obviously wasn't the green Subaru. She thought about the gray car which had sped away from the clinic after leaving the threatening card on her desk. Could this be it? There were millions of similar cars. She pulled out her iPhone and snapped a picture of the vehicles side by side. Useless, she knew. No license plates visible.

She crouched in the deep brush to the west and slowly moved towards the park. Fitzpatrick climbed out of his car and approached a woman dressed in a long gray flowing dress, who stood in front of the information placard. He flailed his arms into the air, yelling loudly, although Erin couldn't make out the words. The woman whirled to face him, and it became a shouting match.

Erin snapped another photo, still too far away. She enlarged the woman's face, but it became grainier, and she couldn't make out her features. Erin crept on her hands and knees in the ditch to get closer, but she knew she wasn't completely out of sight. Her hand sunk into a pool of mud, and she wiped away what she could on the tall grass, finally drying her hand on her jeans. She slapped at the flies buzzing about her face. Why hadn't bug spray been on the stakeout list?

Erin couldn't make out the conversation, but clearly, they were fighting. The woman stormed back to her car, backed out of the park and peeled off to the east. Erin still couldn't catch a license plate. She swore and stayed in the ditch. It rained the night before and she could feel the moisture seeping in through her pants. What would Fitzpatrick do at this point? Would he follow her?

He strode back to his own car, climbed in and headed west, back towards town. She lay flat in the ditch, hoping he wouldn't spot her as he passed. He parked alongside. Erin wondered how long he would wait. Thirty minutes. He waited a full thirty minutes, while she batted away biting horseflies. Finally, she gave up, stood, and walked back to Lindsey's car.

"I saw you in the ditch when I drove by and wondered how long you were going to lay there," he said. "What the fuck are you doing here?"

"I might ask you the same," she said, wishing she'd told Lindsey where she was heading.

"You've been following me," he said.

"Who was the woman?" she asked. "Veronica?"

Fitzpatrick shook his head derisively. "As far as I know, no one other than you even believes she exists."

"Who was the woman?" she asked again.

"A confidential source. I'm a reporter. It's part of doing business," he said. "She has nothing to do with the Duggan case."

"I don't believe you," Erin said.

"I don't give a rat's ass about what you believe. How did you know I would be here?"

She said nothing.

Fitzpatrick took out his phone and aimed the flashlight under the car, searching around the underside of the bumper and wheel wells. A minute later, he found the magnetic GPS Lindsey had attached to the passenger rear wheel well. He pulled it out, threw it to the ground and stomped on it, grinding it into the pavement. He then scooped up the pieces and placed them in the trunk of his car.

"I'm going to the police. You have no right to place a tracker on my car. Detective Osborne already wonders about your stability, and this has certainly crossed a line," he said.

"Wait, Fitzpatrick," she said. "Please! You know as well as I do Veronica is real. She's been sending me threatening messages over and over. For years, decades. But recently these have been extremely specific threats. I got a message a few days ago saying she's going to kill Cody or my sister. She clearly thinks I had something to do with Duggan's disappearance."

"Show me," he said, looking startled.

She brought up images on her phone of the outside

of the greeting card, as well as the message. The signoff was V.

A concerned expression flickered across his face, but it was gone in a millisecond. She wondered if she imagined it.

"You could have written this yourself. This proves nothing."

"Why would I make this up? Or make up Veronica, for that matter?"

"You're the psychologist. Maybe you can answer that," he said. "And even if she exists, and this warning is from her, it doesn't give you the right to stalk me."

"I wasn't stalking you."

"Leave me the fuck alone. I'll report you to the police if you try to follow me again."

He hopped into his car and sped away.

She hadn't asked him about his visit to Alex's office, afraid she wasn't going to like the answer.

Chapter Forty-One

Erin's contact with Cody's friends was limited since the girls were born. Only a handful attended their wedding years ago, and the visits dwindled over the years. She had never met Gunther, who arrived to help Cody load up his boxes and suitcase, as well as a few pieces of furniture into the back of his pickup truck. The men carried out the double bed frame from their spare bedroom and a small dresser and chair, and Erin helped with the heavier items like the mattress. She noticed Cody was doing his best to carry his share of the load, although he still winced as he lifted anything heavier than a small box.

Gunther was polite but eerily quiet. He was dressed in a heavy metal band t-shirt and cutoff jeans. There were visible scars on both of his forearms, but nothing looked fresh. Like most of Cody's current friends, they'd met in recovery meetings. She bit her lip and said nothing. He had offered Cody his spare bedroom temporarily until he found his own apartment and she was grateful.

"I'm going to see how long Gunther will put up with a houseguest," Cody said, while his friend was out in the back of the truck rearranging the load. "I priced a studio apartment and it's going to cost nearly a thousand a month with utilities. Add on cable and the internet for a few hundred more."

"We can afford it," Erin said. "I'll be back to work

in a few more weeks. This will be temporary."

"What part of this is temporary, Erin? Me moving out of the house, or you losing your job?" he asked. "I'm sure you've made up your mind about my leaving, but you have no idea when they're going to let you come back to the clinic."

He was right, on both accounts. Cody wouldn't be moving back home, not unless he went into inpatient rehab first. And as far as returning to the clinic, she didn't have an answer. When Erin temporarily surrendered her practice, there had been no discussion of an endpoint. She hadn't told Cody about her sleepless hours reliving the moment of turning in her clinic ID, debating whether she should have refused to take the leave of absence, wondering if she should still hire a lawyer which she probably couldn't afford, and whether she couldn't afford not to hire one.

"I'm optimistic," she said.

Neither of them believed that. Optimism had never been her forte.

Cody looked tired and disheveled as he carried boxes down to the front door. She'd heard him up most of the night, finishing his packing. His hair was long overdue for a haircut and hung limp and greasy down to his shoulders. He'd changed into a clean polo shirt and khakis, but badly needed a shower and shave.

As they'd agreed, he'd confined his packed boxes to the guest bedroom where he had been sleeping, and the girls hadn't realized he was packing. Cody would get moved into Guenther's apartment, then return in the late afternoon after the girls were home from summer school. They would do this by the book, parents jointly announcing their decision to separate, and both emphasizing they would still be active in their lives. Erin's throat tightened thinking about it.

"I'd be happy to bring the girls there as soon as you're settled in. Then they can see where you're living and meet Guenther."

"You'll drop them off, or would this be a supervised visit?" Cody asked.

She didn't answer.

"That's probably not a good idea," Guenther said.

Erin turned. She thought he was still out in the driveway with the truck. She hoped he hadn't heard Cody's comment about trying to stay as long as possible.

"This isn't the type of place to bring kids, little girls especially," Guenther said. He opened the refrigerator and helped himself to a can of beer.

"What do you mean? It seemed decent enough," Cody said. "You've even got a pool."

"It's one of the few buildings in the county that accepts registered sex offenders. Yeah, it's a nice apartment and it's clean, but…" He popped the top and drank thirstily.

"Got it," Erin said. Her mouth went dry, and she backed up a few steps away from this man. How could Cody have thought this was acceptable, or hadn't he known? Gracie and Charlotte would not be visiting, and Cody needed to find his own apartment as soon as possible. She would also get Gunther's last name from Cody when he came back later in the afternoon and run him through the Wisconsin Circuit Court access site to find out if he was a registered sex offender. Is that how he ended up at that complex?

"We'll head out then," Cody said.

"Are you going to manage to unload the mattress

and dresser?" Erin asked. No way in hell was she going to volunteer to follow them to that apartment building.

"We'll be okay on my end. Always a couple of guys hanging around without much to do," Guenther said.

Cody would fit right in.

"What time are you coming back?" Erin asked. "We agreed we would talk to the girls together."

"I'll be here around five."

Cody didn't show up at five or respond to her texts or phone calls. At seven she stopped trying. She needed the girls to see Cody moving out as a mutual decision, even though it hadn't been, not by a long shot. She knew that. Erin also wanted to know Guenther's last name. Cody hadn't given her the address of the new apartment. Fortunately, she had bought a three-pack of GPS monitors the day before. After the girls were tucked in bed, she opened her laptop and searched. She located his truck on the outskirts of Mauston, a nearby small town.

She should have done this a long time ago.

Chapter Forty-Two

"Did you know about the GPS tracker? Your wife is batshit crazy. You should have called her off, or at least warned me," Fitzpatrick said. "How long has this been going on?"

"I'm sorry, man. I thought things would get better after Duggan was dead. That's what they think, isn't it? They believe he's dead and hasn't escaped?" Cody climbed down from his seat atop the picnic bench and paced. "But everything is worse."

"That's because your wife is making it worse," Fitzpatrick said.

"No, those photographs messed with her mind. Mine, too, if you want the truth. Whoever's behind this has gotten way too close to our girls."

They silenced their conversation as a couple walking two Corgis passed them on the park path. It was early morning, earlier than Fitzpatrick liked, and a cooler morning than usual for late August. The dew was still shimmering and damp on the grass. His Converses were soaked through, and his feet were cold. They started down the wood chip path which meandered through the small park.

"Why is Erin convinced I know who's sending this shit?" Fitzpatrick asked.

"It's your Breaking News alerts. Lindsey started watching for them, and now Erin checks. It would help if you stopped reporting on Duggan's disappearance," he said.

"You do realize that's my job, right?" Fitzpatrick lifted his shoe and stared in disgust at the Corgi poop he'd ground into the treads. The fucking mongrels had no business being in a park. "Besides, Erin's mental health is her own responsibility, isn't it? It's not like she's been treating you particularly well."

Cody told him about moving in with a friend and Erin's ultimatum about his entering rehab. Fitzpatrick knew the man needed help before he overdosed and died and felt an unexpected twinge of guilt that he hoped Cody would hold out a little bit longer. He was surprised Erin would want to be alone in such a big house with her daughters, considering Veronica and possibly Duggan were still out there. Fitzpatrick found a stick and leaned against a tree to scrape the animal shit from the bottom of his shoe.

"All right, stop mentioning Erin's kidnapping then. She doesn't need to read about her past trauma every couple of days. That's old news. And the girls, they're off limits. You published their names."

"I removed their names from the piece."

"I know," Cody said. "But it was too late."

This was going nowhere. He wasn't going to stop reporting on the Duggan murder or any salacious tidbit he learned about Erin Moore-Jackson. The number of hits on the site had increased exponentially since Duggan's release from prison and took another leap when he disappeared. But now he needed information from Cody to keep the story fresh, and his increased vulnerability now Erin had tossed him to the curb could only work in his favor.

They circled back to the picnic table near the parking lot.

"I should report your wife for tagging my car with the GPS," Fitzpatrick said. "I'm curious. Shouldn't she have been seeing patients Wednesday? I thought Thursday was her day off."

"No, she's always had Thursdays off, but..." He hesitated.

Fitzpatrick slid a small envelope out of his shirt pocket and put it on the picnic table, his hand cupped over and partially concealing the packet. Come on, Cody, reach for it.

"Erin's taking some time off work. This whole thing has been too stressful," Cody finished. "And now this latest threat, a homemade card she received. I don't think she could work if she wanted to."

"Sorry to hear that. You're saying this wasn't her choice to take this time off?"

"They made her turn in her work ID and keys," he said.

"She showed me a picture on her phone yesterday when I confronted her about the GPS. A handmade card she said someone left at her desk. It got me wondering about the wording, of course," Fitzpatrick said.

"What about it?"

"The note mentions her sister and her lover. Does it mean you or Alex Folk, the developer?"

"Is that who...?" Cody's face reddened, unable to finish the question.

Anger or shame? Likely a little of both. Would Cody even know who Folk was? His name had been in the local news for multiple controversial building projects over the past ten years, but how closely did an unemployed stoner like Cody follow business headlines?

"The developer. I'm sure you've seen his name in the paper before."

Cody nodded. "I didn't know who she was seeing. She denied it when I asked."

"The good news is there's only a fifty-fifty chance the greeting card was referring to you." He doubted if Erin had regarded Cody as her lover for a very long time.

Cody sat back down at the picnic table and lowered his head into his hands. Fitzpatrick slid the small packet across the table. Cody snatched it up before he could change his mind.

"If our relationship is going to continue, and I hope it does, I'm going to need more information than you've been giving me. Think about that."

"I can't. Erin is very fragile right now. And now she's kicked me out…"

"I promise everything you tell me is off the record. You know I'm good at my word. After your AA meeting in Tomah, at the coffee shop, you told me about why Erin came back to the area after she finished school. Have you seen anything about that in my blog?"

"No."

"It helps if I understand what happened back then. That's what I'm interested in, as a journalist, more than anything. It's not going to end up in the News-Journal. This is just between us," he said.

Fitzpatrick wasn't lying, not technically, not that he cared about the truth. The dirt he was collecting on Erin would help round out his chapters for the true crime book. No way did he plan to share the juiciest information with the News-Journal readers.

"What do you need to know?"

He spoke so softly, the reporter had to lean forward to hear.

"Erin is successful with her career, married with a family. It seems like she's learned to deal with the past, at least until Duggan was released. Do you see anything in her day-to-day life before this to indicate she still struggles with what happened twenty years ago?" He pulled a notebook and pen from his messenger bag.

Cody smiled ruefully and shook his head. "I don't even know where to begin."

"Try harder." Fitzpatrick slid a second packet of pills a third of the way across the picnic table.

"I'll start with the obvious. You've seen the security gate around the perimeter of our property."

"Yes, and the security cameras. You're not telling me anything I don't know." Fitzpatrick reached out and pulled the packet of drugs a few inches farther from Cody.

Cody swore under his breath.

"I don't know what you want."

"Are there any triggers your wife might have? Anything that brings back strong memories of Duggan or the woman?"

"Food, I guess. Erin doesn't have an eating disorder or anything like that, but there are a few foods she won't cook or even let me cook. Brownies, chocolate chip cookies. And pancakes. Never ever pancakes."

"They remind her of Duggan and Veronica?"

"Erin was a little on the heavy side back when…she was taken. Not fat, but heavy. Duggan used to tell her how disgusting she was and tried to force her to eat raw vegetables instead of normal food. As soon as he left, the woman would pull out the bag of cookies and brownies and heaping piles of pancakes. She told Erin she would slit her throat if she ever became thin enough for Duggan."

"They were playing cruel mind games about food?"

"Even now, Erin gets nauseated if we're out for breakfast somewhere and there's the smell of maple syrup."

"I remember she lost a lot of weight during the five months."

Cody nodded. "I didn't know her back then, but that's what I've heard."

"One could conclude Veronica lost the battle over the food."

"I suppose."

"Duggan was never charged with sexual assault. That surprised a lot of us covering the trial," Fitzpatrick said.

"She never said, but if she was assaulted, it was likely Veronica," Cody said quietly.

"Are you sure?" he asked.

"I'm not sure, but I suspect so. Like I said, Erin would never talk about it." Cody said, and he grabbed the second packet off the table and headed towards his truck.

Fitzpatrick smiled as he stood, brushed a few pine needles from the seat of his pants, and headed down the pathway to the parking lot, debating what to throw in the blog and what to keep for the book.

It had been worth it, dog shit and all.

# # #

August 24, 3 p.m.

BREAKING NEWS – BARABOO NEWS-JOURNAL by Richard Fitzpatrick, Reporter

Sauk County Sheriff's Department reports no progress in locating Stanley Duggan III, missing from his home outside Baraboo three weeks prior. Bullet casings and blood found at the home suggests Duggan may have been injured or even killed. Department detectives admit questioning Dr. Erin Moore-Jackson and her husband Cody Jackson in the disappearance, and both remain persons of interest. Dr. Moore-Jackson had been kidnapped as a teenager by Mr. Duggan, who was recently released from prison.

Efforts to contact Dr. Moore-Jackson for comment at her home in Reedsburg were unsuccessful. Confidential source at Meadowview Counseling Center in Lake Delton reports Dr. Moore-Jackson is no longer in practice at that site.

Mr. Cody Jackson, now a resident of Mauston, declined to comment.

Details to follow as they become available.

Chapter Forty-Three

Fitzpatrick opened the small plastic bag and dumped the broken fragments of the GPS unit on the detective's desk.

"What's this?" Osborne asked. He poked through the pieces, spreading them apart.

"The remains of a GPS tracker which I found on my car yesterday. I went to a park to meet a confidential news source about an entirely different story and caught Erin Moore-Jackson hiding in the bushes, spying on me."

"She placed this tracker on your car? Are you sure?"

"I found it in one of the rear wheel wells and she admitted she had placed it."

"Did she say why?"

"It's obvious, isn't it? I'm doing my job, reporting on Duggan's disappearance and she wants to know my sources," Fitzpatrick said. "She seems to have some illusion that I can take her to Veronica or Duggan."

"Giving up her little girls' names wasn't part of your job. How did you know there were pictures of her daughters at Duggan's house?"

"We're off topic here. She illegally placed a GPS tracker on my personal vehicle."

Osborne scraped the electronic remnants into his wastebasket. He would have done the same thing in Erin's situation.

"Do you want to press charges?"

The reporter shut his mouth for the first time since coming into the office. He pulled a bottle of water out of his messenger bag and took a long swallow.

"I don't want to make things more difficult for her."

"If that were true, you wouldn't be airing her business in those articles of yours. There was nothing newsworthy about her husband moving out of the house, yet you mentioned it. That's definitely making her life more stressful. If you don't want to press charges, why are you here?" Osborne asked.

"I don't want to endanger her job. I've heard she's been asked to take a leave of absence from her practice. She's not dealing well with Duggan's release and disappearance. I'm frankly worried about her."

Bullshit, he thought. Erin's actions were borderline unstable, he agreed with the reporter, but who wouldn't react the same way. He suspected Fitzpatrick would regard anything Erin did to retaliate as fodder for another story.

"She got another note of some kind signed with the letter 'V,' and it threatened retaliation for the loss of her lover and sister," Fitzpatrick said. "She showed me a screenshot she had taken on her phone."

"We're aware. And we also knew about the stack of photos you mentioned in your article.

"I know she carries a gun, and I'm worried about what she might do," he said.

"You could consider a restraining order," Osborne said. "The judge may not grant it unless she specifically threatened to harm you."

The reporter shook his head vigorously.

What game was he playing? Reporting Erin for placing the GPS but refusing to take the next step? What did Fitzpatrick hope to gain by coming in? Was he hoping Osborne would slip up and give him his next lead? No chance in hell.

"I'd like to avoid a restraining order. It could hurt her career permanently. And I have held back information to protect Erin. I should get some credit for that."

"For instance?"

"The News-Journal is not a gossip rag. It's a small-town newspaper, but we care about the truth. I could have reported Erin is having an illicit affair with a local developer, for example."

"Don't." It wasn't a request. "Are you trying to destroy that woman?"

Osborne stood up from his desk and walked over to the reporter. When he'd assisted Duggan in getting parole, he had intended to bring down Veronica. Any pain he caused the Moore-Jackson family would pale compared to their relief when she was captured. But it hadn't happened.

Osborne had been keeping watch over Erin's home ever since he'd witnessed Duggan lifting weights in his barn nearly a month ago, parking just down the road for a few hours after the lights went off inside the house. He didn't do it every night, but often enough he was exhausted. He hadn't felt any relief when Duggan disappeared. Now she was alone in the house at night with the little girls, and Fitzpatrick included that information in his latest news update.

Erin Moore's actions spoke of pain and desperation, and it worried him more that she was starting to fight back, with the GPS. He knew she'd been visiting the local gun range several times a week. What was she prepared to do next? Osborne blamed himself, and he had no idea how to stop her.

Chapter Forty-Four

"Why do you keep checking that news site when you know it's going to upset you?" Alex reached out and tugged Erin's phone from her hands. They were sitting in his bed, leaning back against down pillows.

"I read it because everyone else in town does," she said. "I hear the little digs at the school when I go to pick up the girls. They had one of his news stories printed out and tacked up in the clinic breakroom."

Erin held out her hand and he returned the phone. She compromised and tossed it onto a nearby chair.

"He had no right to report that Cody moved out. That's not legitimate news. And now everyone also knows I'm taking a leave of absence from work. The way he worded it, 'not currently practicing at this site,' makes it sound permanent. Meadowview has arranged for Marquardt and O'Donnell to see my patients until I come back, but I'll certainly lose some of them permanently, especially if this drags out."

"Have you thought about seeing a therapist yourself? It might help you gain some perspective on this whole mess to keep it from lasting forever," he said. "Your clinic supervisor would also see it as a positive step on your part."

She nodded. She wasn't going to argue about a therapist. That wasn't what she needed right now. She needed Veronica and Duggan to be captured and put behind bars. She needed Fitzpatrick to run out of angles or interest in her story and disappear. At least he hadn't mentioned Cody's recent hospital stay with the overdose, even though he'd been with Cody that night. Was it because he was somehow responsible? Her husband had denied it.

She still hadn't told Alex about the latest threat, which was the original purpose of this visit. He deserved to know, not that she minded the detour to the bedroom.

"Alex, I told you about the last piece of mail I received. It was about a week ago, a homemade card from Veronica."

"You mentioned it," he said. "You were at the clinic on a Sunday."

She again reached for her phone and opened the photo album. She showed him the front of the card, with the quote from C.S. Lewis. He scrolled to the next image. The inside message, mentioning a lover and a sister. They sat in silence.

"You're suggesting this is about me?" he asked. His voice was measured and noticeably quiet. "She blames you for Duggan's death, if that's what happened, and she's going to retaliate by hurting me?"

"I'm saying I don't know. She could be referring to Cody."

"How does she even know about me?" he asked.

"It's a small town. You're a big fish. I certainly never told anyone until I needed an alibi, but I get the feeling it's out there. Cody knew I was seeing someone. Lindsey knew. And now Detective Morgan and I'm assuming others in the sheriff's department."

"There's no way she would know my home address, even if what you say is true," he said.

Erin reached out for her phone and scrolled to an earlier album showing the thirteen photos delivered to her mailbox on that rainy night, marked up in red and black pen. She brought up the image of Alex's condominium complex, with the border of red hearts.

"I told you about those pictures of the girls I'd received. This was in the pack."

He studied it, nodded, and handed back her phone.

"You received these more than a week ago, didn't you?" he asked. "She must have followed you here."

She nodded.

"You saw how easy it was to put a tracker on the reporter's car. Did you think to check your own?"

Why hadn't she, after seeing how easy it was to track the reporter and Cody? Was that how Veronica tracked her to Alex's condo?

"You recognized this as a possible threat to my life, yet you waited to let me know." It was a statement, not a question.

She said nothing.

"I'm going to shower. I want you gone by the time I finish," he said, quietly. He climbed out of bed, walked into the bathroom, and shut the door behind him.

Erin quickly dressed and hunted around for her shoes. She wouldn't leave until she asked him about Fitzpatrick's visit to his office days earlier. She carried both of their empty wine glasses into the kitchen and gave hers a partial refill. She heard music emanating from the bedroom suite which usually meant a longer shower.

Erin eyed his tidy desk up against the living room wall. There were a few sheets of paper neatly stacked on top which proved to be notices of upcoming local building committee meetings related to his latest projects. She opened the top drawer and found an orderly selection of pens and staplers, and scissors, as neat as her own collection at home. The second drawer was more of a mess and contained odds and ends, a package of unopened thumb drives, earbuds with tangled cords, and a small stack of business cards. The top card read "Richard J. Fitzpatrick, Baraboo News-Journal. She picked up the card and flipped it over. There was a handwritten phone number which she guessed was the reporter's cell phone.

    She hadn't been sure what she was looking for. The business card didn't prove Alex was cooperating with the reporter. It was true Fitzpatrick revealed events about the kidnapping she had only shared with Alex and a therapist who was long retired and living in Florida. She was fairly certain she had never discussed it with the police years, although it was a long time ago, and she had been very fragile. Could she be wrong?

    Fitzpatrick knew she was on a leave of absence from her job, and he knew Cody moved out. Alex knew those facts, but so did Cody and Lindsey. What possible motivation would Alex have to cooperate with the reporter? Was he being blackmailed? His cooperation for Fitzpatrick's silence about their affair? It was possible.

    "Can I help you find something?"

    She whirled to see Alex standing in the doorway, wrapped in a towel, Bruce Springsteen still playing quietly in the background. She'd been engrossed in her search and didn't notice he'd turned down the music.

    "I asked you to leave, but instead…?" His calm voice belied the flash of fury in his eyes.

    Erin slowly shut the drawer and turned to face him.

"I think I found what I was looking for." She held out the business card. "Richard Fitzpatrick visited your office last week, didn't he? Is that when he gave you his business card?"

Alex continued to stare. She held his gaze and he finally turned away.

"So, what if he did? He's a reporter. Surely, you've seen the writeups about the newly proposed convention center near the heart of the Dells."

"Are you sure that's all you talked about?"

"You're convinced every conversation is about you, aren't you? I hate to disappoint you, but this was about zoning and board approval. Not about you."

She walked to the kitchen island and set down her wine glass.

"It's time for you to get the fuck out of my house."

Erin grabbed her purse and walked towards the door.

"And don't contact me ever again."

Tears of anger stung her eyes as she walked out into the parking lot. What had she expected? He was right. He never would have spoken to Fitzpatrick about their relationship. He never would have dished on the bits and pieces of information about her kidnapping she'd shared. Also, she made sure Cody and Lindsey knew of the threat Veronica alluded to in the recent card. Why had she waited to tell Alex?

She scanned the lot and adjacent road for suspicious cars and saw nothing, then climbed into her car and sped away. She'd check for GPS units as soon as she got home.

She would not soon forget the look of rage and disdain on Alex's face.

# # #

She was halfway home when her phone rang, the familiar ringtone she'd assigned to the Heritage Learning Academy. Had something happened to one of her daughters? She clenched the steering wheel tighter and noted the time. The summer program ended nearly forty minutes earlier. The girls should be home with Lindsey by now.

"This is Dr. Moore-Jackson," she said. "Is everything all right?"

"This is Janet Cooper from the summer school office. Your daughters are sitting here with me. They said their aunt was supposed to pick them up this afternoon, yet here they are."

Erin checked the time again. "There must have been a mix-up. I can be there in twenty minutes."

She tried Lindsey's phone, and it went immediately to voicemail. Where was she? She knew her sister had planned a lunch date in Madison with an old boyfriend from university, but she still should have been back in town two hours ago. Unless, Erin thought, the lunch turned into a bedroom romp. She could hardly blame her sister, considering how she had spent her own afternoon, but she should have called.

On the drive, she tried Lindsey's number repeatedly, always going to voicemail. She left three messages and hung up. Erin vacillated between anger and unease. Her sister knew she was counting on her today. Would she have shucked off all the responsibilities for sex, even exceptional sex? She remembered with guilt luxuriating in the cool cotton sheets with Alex two hours earlier. Why hadn't she picked up her daughters herself? Had she also put Alex ahead of her girls?

When she arrived at the school, she found the girls

sitting side by side in the school office, holding their backpacks in their laps.

"I'm very sorry about this mix-up," Erin said.

Janet Cooper sat behind her desk and took off her reading glasses. She pulled a slightly tattered tissue from her dress pocket and wiped the lenses, then reached for an envelope and handed it to Erin. Her name was written on the front, and it was sealed.

"I suggest you wait until you're at home to open this," she said.

Erin nodded, apologized again, and led the girls to the car. The girls quietly climbed into their car seats, and Gracie started to cry.

"Mom, she was super mad at us," Charlotte said. "She made us sit there and do nothing. I asked her for paper to draw on and she yelled at me."

Erin sighed and started the car. Did the woman really have to take it out on her daughters? "She wasn't angry with you—she was angry with me."

"But it was Aunt Lindsey who was supposed to pick us up today."

"Sorry to put you in this situation, girls. I promise it will be all right."

Erin eyed the envelope next to her purse. She opened it and withdrew the single sheet of paper on official school stationery, a letter addressed to her and Cody.

The girls were suspended from the summer school program starting immediately. Fortunately, there was only a week and a half left. It wouldn't be a big deal, and Gracie would likely welcome the change. Erin checked the rearview mirror and was relieved her daughter had stopped crying.

Erin stared at the second paragraph and shook her head with disbelief. The headmaster requests an in-person meeting with her and Cody on Friday morning to discuss their daughters' enrollment in the fall semester. They wouldn't kick the girls out over a few late school pickups, would they? She thought about the unopened billing statements from Heritage sitting buried in her to-be-paid pile at home, likely past due. She knew there was usually a waiting list for enrollment. Had the school filled their spots?

She shifted the car into gear and headed home. She tried Lindsey's cell phone one last time. The school drama would have to wait. She needed to find her sister.

Chapter Forty-Five

When they arrived home, the security gate was wide open, and Cody's truck was parked in front of the garage. He was sitting on the front steps scrolling through his phone and he stood when she pulled into the driveway.

The girls jumped from the car and ran to Cody, who scooped them up one by one and spun them around. Erin grabbed their backpacks from the back seat and paused. A distinct floral smell wafted up from Gracie's bag. Gardenias? Erin stiffened. She unzipped the bag and examined the contents. There were a couple of small travel size hand sanitizers, and she wondered if one was leaking. She opened them one by one—no gardenia fragrance. She pulled out her daughter's sweater, closed her eyes, and inhaled. Had she imagined it? She dumped the backpack out onto the floor of the car and went through item by item. Nothing.

She held the backpack itself up to her face. There it was, just a hint of gardenia fragrance. The same scent Veronica had worn. On her daughter's backpack. It made no sense.

She shoved her daughter's possessions back into the bag. She'd ask Gracie later. She joined her family at the front door.

"Did you catch any fish, Daddy?" Charlotte asked. "You said you would take me fishing next time you went. You promised."

"I don't like fishing," Gracie said. "You have to touch worms."

Cody looked up at Erin, puzzled, then caught on.

"Sorry, Charlotte, they weren't biting. I didn't catch a single fish," he said.

Erin opened the front door and dropped the backpacks on a bench.

"There's time for cartoons before dinner if you hurry," she said.

The girls whooped with delight and scampered past their dad into the house. Erin shut the door behind them. They would speak out of hearing range.

Cody put up his hands as if he was surrendering. "Look, I know you're upset but let me explain."

"We agreed we would talk to them on Friday, together," she said, keeping her voice low.

"I know, and I apologize, but a friend from my support group needed me to sit with him at the hospital. He'd tried to cut his wrists. One was deep enough they had to call in a hand specialist from Madison."

Erin shivered involuntarily, wondering if this was true or if he knew it would be a great story. He could have at least called or texted. She studied her husband. He was wearing a neatly pressed button-down shirt and clean blue jeans. He'd shaved and washed his hair since she'd seen him last. His eyes were clear, and his voice was steady.

"Let's talk to them now, after dinner. I'm assuming I'm welcome to stay for dinner," he said.

"We're going to have to take a raincheck on that. I'm worried about Lindsey. She was supposed to pick up the girls after school today and never showed up. She's not answering her cell and it's been…" She checked her watch. "It's almost two hours."

"We're talking about your sister, right?" Cody smiled and opened the front door. "Isn't she late more often than not?"

"Let's stay out here and talk for a few minutes," she said.

Cody nodded, shut the door, and sat on the bench. He stretched his legs out and rubbed his knees.

"I mean, being late is kind of her thing, isn't it? Isn't that why we haven't used her very often for childcare in the past? She was making you late for work" he said.

"This feels different," Erin said. "She was worried about her own safety after that last note from Veronica, and she even asked to stay with us for a while, since the house is much more secure than her apartment." Erin remembered the security gate and opened the app on her phone to close it.

Cody pulled out his phone and dialed Lindsey. Same thing, right to voicemail.

"Also, I think someone has been tracking my car. I think that's how they got some of those photos they'd marked up."

She pulled out her cell phone and activated the camera. She searched the underside of her car for a GPS device, just as she'd seen Fitzpatrick do, finding the small black device in less than a minute. It was the same brand as the one she had placed on the reporter's car a few days earlier, but a cheaper model, and was stuck in the front driver's side wheel well. Whomever placed it must have read the same website she had used.

Cody followed her into the kitchen, where she found a small screwdriver and removed the battery. She wondered if the police had some way of tracing the owner. She didn't want to destroy it, like Fitzpatrick had done, but she needed to disarm it.

"That's how she followed you, to get those pictures?" Cody asked.

"Probably," she said. "If it was Veronica."

"Duggan couldn't have taken them. He was still in prison when the kids went to that birthday party. And you've been seeing that developer for a long time, haven't you? I'm curious. How long have you been seeing him?"

"Can we not do this? Not right now," she said.

"All right, you tell me when the time is right. You seem to be the one calling the shots."

"I promise we'll talk about Alex. I owe you that. But right now, I'm worried about Lindsey. She still isn't responding."

"Did you try the Find My Friends app?" he asked.

Erin had installed the phone app a few years earlier and insisted anyone who picked up the girls from school or drove them anywhere used it. This included Lindsey and Cody, as well as every babysitter with a driver's license. It hadn't made Erin overly popular with their last couple of sitters.

She opened the app and brought up Lindsey's information. "Location Not Available."

Impossible. Lindsey never turned off her phone. Would she have let the battery run down to nothing? Not likely, especially when driving out of town, and she had a phone charger in her car. Erin tried again with the same result. She wondered if she was doing something wrong. She searched for Cody's phone, and it identified its location as feet from her own.

"I know about the GPS," Cody said softly.

Erin wasn't sure she'd heard him.

"On my truck. I left it there. I knew it was you."

Erin's face reddened. Shortly after Cody got out of rehab, a friend of hers suggested she place a GPS on his car. She'd checked on him intermittently, especially the first few years and she'd switched it out for a newer model when she'd purchased the unit for Fitzpatrick's car, wondering if his meetings at the Tomah VA were excuses to meet with his dealer.

"I don't blame you. You were right not to trust me. I'm fucked up again, I know. I've tried to stop," he said. "But you didn't have a reason to spy on your sister. Did you put a GPS on Lindsey's car, too?"

She nodded and studied Cody's face. He looked defeated in a way she'd never seen before, even when he was at lowest after his arrest. Had she done this? Or had she contributed?

"Cody…"

"Let's find Lindsey," he said. "The rest of this can wait one more day."

She followed him into the house and retrieved her laptop from her office. She logged into the GPS tracking program and waited. A location pinged in less than a minute. The car was parked on the edge of Wisconsin Dells at the Amtrak station. That made no sense. Lindsey had been excited about her lunch date in Madison. The train ran to Milwaukee in one direction, and Minneapolis in the other. It went nowhere near Madison.

There was no logical reason for her car to be at the Amtrak station.

Lindsey called Betsy who agreed to come watch the girls. She threw together peanut butter and jelly sandwiches and put out a plate of cookies, unsure how long they'd be gone. They were out the door the minute Betsy arrived.

Erin parked in the first empty spot at the train station, and they climbed out. They had no trouble locating Lindsey's car in the small parking lot.

"That's hers, isn't it?" Cody asked. "But the license plate is missing."

Erin studied the sedan. Both front and back plates had been removed. The doors were locked. She peered in and recognized her sister's bright red travel cup. Her daughters' car seats were belted into place in the back seat, and between them one of Gracie's stuffed animals was face down.

"We've got to call the police," Erin said.

"Let's check the station first."

They hurried into the small one-story brick building and checked the schedule. There were a few people sitting on benches, staying cool in the air conditioning while waiting for the daily train from Milwaukee, due at 5:49 p.m., which was minutes away. The unmanned station hours were posted as 4:45 until 6:45 p.m., with an employee showing up only long enough to unlock and lock the station. There was no one to ask if Lindsey had purchased a ticket on the noon train to Milwaukee.

They took a seat on an empty oak bench and Erin again tried Lindsey's number. The next five minutes stretched into an eternity. Finally, they heard the clanging warning signals as the nearby gates closed and the whistle from the approaching train. Erin hurried out to the platform, then waited for Cody to catch up. There were more passengers than she'd expected, and it took longer to unload than she had patience for. Finally, the last stragglers carrying their shopping bags and suitcases found their cars and the parking lot was close to empty. They hadn't missed her. Lindsey's car sat nearly alone in the lot.

They debated waiting an hour longer until the Amtrak employee came to lock the station but decided against it.

Erin needed to face the facts. Veronica hadn't come for Cody or Alex. She'd come for Lindsey.

Chapter Forty-Six

Erin and Cody climbed back into the SUV and debated their next step.

"We can't call 911. It's not that kind of emergency," Cody said.

"Should we call the county sheriff or the Wisconsin Dells police?" Erin asked. "She was probably taken near her apartment since she was going there to change her clothes on her way to Madison. Her apartment is in Sauk County, but her car is in the Dells and I'm not sure which county it's in."

"If we call the Sauk County sheriff, they at least know what's been going on with Duggan, but that means possibly having to deal with Osborne," he said. "What about his deputy, Joshua? He's more likely to help. Did you save his number when he texted?"

Erin scrolled through her contact list.

"Found it," she said.

He picked up on the second ring and recognized her number, calling her by name. Erin put him on speaker phone, fighting back tears.

"Joshua, we need your help. Tonight. It's an emergency. My sister Lindsey's has been taken and she's in extreme danger."

"What do you mean, taken? Do you mean you just can't find her, or did you see someone physically kidnap her?"

Erin started at the beginning and told him about the handmade card promising revenge for a lover or sister. She described how Lindsey had plans in Madison but expected to be back to pick up her daughters after school, and now her car was abandoned at the Wisconsin Dells train station. Her phone was off, and Lindsey never turned off her phone, even when she should.

An audible sigh came through the speaker.

"I understand you're overly concerned, but Lindsey is an adult. As unlikely as that seems to you, she may have left of her own accord. It's only been a couple of hours, right? The sheriff's department won't start a missing persons investigation at this point."

"Even with the threatening note?"

"I couldn't help you, even if I wanted to. I'm officially on suspension right now. I get my badge and gun back tomorrow," Joshua said.

"Why were you suspended?" Cody asked.

"Let's just say Osborne and I didn't see eye to eye on some aspects of the Duggan investigation. I'm being reassigned to work the county lockup starting next month."

"Sorry to hear that. Do you think I should call Osborne?" she asked. It was the last thing she wanted to do.

"You have nothing to lose, and I can give you his cell number. But I'll be surprised if he does anything until she's been missing forty-eight hours. He may even tell you it's out of his jurisdiction because of where her car was found. He'll likely suggest she parked her car and took a train out of town voluntarily."

"Shouldn't they base the missing report jurisdiction on where she lives? Her apartment is in Baraboo."

"Give Osborne a try."

"Would it be better calling the general information number at the sheriff's office?" she asked.

"When they hear your name, they're going to run it through him either way," he answered. "Even if he's not on duty tonight."

Erin made a note of Osborne's cell phone number, thanked him, and hung up. The deputy had been the only sympathetic ear she'd encountered in the sheriff's department, and he'd be reassigned in another week.

"Look, it's the Amtrak agent coming to lock up," Cody said, pointing to a small elderly man in a blue uniform heading into the station.

They hopped out of the car and hurried to the door. The man was emptying the garbage cans into a large, wheeled bin and looked up, startled as they approached.

"The station's closing in five minutes, folks. There won't be another train coming through until noon tomorrow."

"Can you help us?" Erin asked. "My sister's car is parked here in your lot, and we need to know if she climbed on your noon train."

"Sorry, can't help you with that. I stop by to open and lock up, but the station is unmanned other than that. We don't even sell tickets here."

"What about security cameras?" Cody asked.

Erin and Cody peered up into the high corners of the room. A single security camera was pointed at the entrance.

"That one up there, and then there's another one outside pointed down at the platform," the agent said.

"We need to see the footage from today. It's an emergency. We think my sister is in danger," Erin said.

"From nine-thirty this morning until five p.m."

"The recordings are in a remote location. I have no idea where, and that's way above my paygrade. Sorry, and I hope your sister is okay."

"There must be a number I can call," Erin insisted.

"I can give you the number for Amtrak customer service," he said.

Erin took the number, and they walked back outside. She studied the roofline of the building and spotted the second security camera. It covered the platform, but very little of the parking lot. Whomever drove Lindsey's car there, whether it was her sister or someone else, would probably have avoided the camera.

Back in the car, Erin tried to get through to Amtrak security. She was placed on hold and transferred four times. Thirty minutes later she reached someone knowledgeable about the security camera footage at various Amtrak stations.

The news was disappointing but not surprising. Yes, the footage was available, but they only responded to formal requests from law enforcement agencies.

She hung up without another word. They sat in silence. She wondered where her sister was being held, assuming she was still alive. Erin should have protected her. This was her fault. She fought back the tears, dialed Osborne, and left a message on his voicemail. She emphasized the urgency of the situation and hung up. They were halfway home when he called back. She pulled into the parking lot of a closed gift shop and answered.

"Erin, tell me what's going on."

"I'm putting you on speaker phone. I'm in the car with Cody," she said.

"Your message said this is about your sister Lindsey."

"Yes, you remember the last piece of mail I received from Veronica?" she asked.

"Which you're assuming came from Veronica, but yes, I remember," he said.

"She threatened my sister or my lover."

"I remember wondering if she was referring to your husband or your developer, to be honest." He cleared his throat. "Sorry, Cody. I know you're listening."

Cody said nothing but Erin knew this had to sting.

"She left my house this morning to drive to Madison to meet a friend. She was supposed to be back to pick up my girls after summer school and she never showed up."

"I'm assuming you've tried to call her."

Did he really ask if they thought to call her? Erin took a deep breath.

"A hundred times. It goes right to voicemail. I think her phone is turned off, which isn't like her. And we found her car parked at the Amtrak station in the Dells."

There was a long silence at the other end.

"Fitzpatrick dropped by a couple of days ago with a smashed-up GPS unit. He declined to press charges. Is that how were you able to locate your sister's car so quickly?"

It was Erin's turn to be silent.

"You placed a GPS on her car, too, didn't you?" Osborne asked. "I'm assuming you did it without her permission."

"Yes, and I'm glad I did. We need to find her before it's too late."

"Are you at home? I can send an officer over to take your statement, but they aren't going to do anything this soon. There's no evidence she was snatched up. She could have taken a train somewhere or met up with a friend and used the train station lot as a safe place to leave the car," Osborne said. "Maybe she was hungry for privacy and knew you'd been tracking her car."

"Can you at least make a request for the security video from the Amtrak station? They have a camera outside the building, although it doesn't likely cover the entire parking lot."

"She'd have to be considered a missing person to make that request."

"She could be dead by the time forty-eight hours is up," Erin said. "Please help me find her."

"Do you want me to send an officer by your house or not?"

"Not if he won't help," Cody said.

Erin disconnected the call. She gripped the steering wheel tightly and her knuckles ached. Veronica had Lindsey. She was sure of it. At least the girls were still safe at home with Betsy, behind a locked gate.

"Let's go to her apartment," Cody said. "You've got a key, right?"

She nodded.

"We know she was taken after she left our house, and her apartment would be the logical place. You thought she was going to stop to change her clothes. It's not like they could stop her car on the highway. She needed to be parked. Let's see if anything looks suspicious," Cody said.

Erin nodded, put the car in gear and spun gravel exiting the parking lot. She drove fifteen minutes to Lindsey's apartment, which was in an older apartment complex on the outskirts of Baraboo. They parked in the guest parking behind the last building from the road. The door to the apartment foyer was unlocked, but she used the fob her sister had given her to pass through the inner door and a key to enter the apartment itself.

"No one could have gotten up here without their own fob, unless Lindsey brought them up." Cody stepped into the living room and looked around.

"They could have forced her up here at gunpoint or tied her up and taken it from her. Or even just waited and followed some other resident in."

They hastily searched the one-bedroom apartment. It didn't take long. There was an empty coffee cup in the sink, but otherwise it was as tidy as Erin's own kitchen. No evidence of a struggle. No upturned furniture or books knocked from their shelves. A half-completed jigsaw puzzle occupied most of the small dining room table, and a closed laptop sat next to it.

"This didn't help," Cody said. "Maybe we should head home. Whoever has Lindsey may have left a message for us there."

"I know who has her. It's Veronica. It has to be," Erin said.

"Let's go home," he repeated.

Cody headed towards the apartment door. She flipped off the lights and followed him down the hallway to the elevator. It had been hours since he'd taken anything. She could tell by the size of his pupils and his increasing limp. His hand shook as he reached out for the elevator button. They rode down in silence.

Erin stopped short after they exited the elevator. She grabbed Cody's arm and looked around to make sure no one was close enough to hear.

"What if Lindsey's apartment had been tossed when

we got here? Nothing actually broken, but we tip over a chair and a lamp, throw the pillows around."

"But it wasn't," Cody said.

"Then we could call the Baraboo Police Department, instead of the county sheriff. They'd have to take her disappearance seriously."

Cody looked at her, shook his head and left the lobby.

"We should think about it," Erin said, once they were seated back in her SUV.

"I'm not going to file a false police report, or let you file one. I'm still under court supervision. I'll do anything in my power to help you find Lindsey, but not that."

Cody's hands shook visibly as he buckled his seatbelt. He was sober and straight, and she wondered how long it would last.

Chapter Forty-Seven

It was nearly eight p.m. when they reached home. Erin hopped out of the car and ran to the mailbox, hoping for something that would lead them to Lindsey. There was a bill from the electric company and a sportswear catalog. She threw them in the back seat of the car in frustration. She searched for a note or package left at the security gate. There was nothing.

A single porch light shone in the early darkness of the evening. A bolt of lightning flashed across the sky and a slow steady rain began to fall. Erin maneuvered around Betsy's car and Cody's truck in the driveway and parked in the garage.

They walked into the kitchen. Betsy was sitting at the island with her laptop open, and she muted the music when they entered.

"Where are the girls?"

"They both fell asleep watching a video. I covered them up and left them on the couch in the family room."

Erin thanked her and gave her a handful of cash. She watched the car pull out of the driveway and shut the gate. It hadn't protected her sister, because one couldn't live forever behind a locked security gate, not forever.

Erin plugged her phone into the charger and saw it registered eleven percent. She tried Lindsey's number again, with the same response.

"Try Fitzpatrick," Cody said.

"What good would that do?" she asked.

"You think he's involved in this somehow. How could it hurt?"

"I don't think I've got his cell number." She searched her contact list and shook her head. She wished she had grabbed the card from Alex's desk, or at least taken a screenshot of it, but that was when he walked in on her. She debated calling him to ask for the number but thought it was unlikely he would answer. "Maybe if I call the newspaper, they'll give it to me."

Cody pulled out his own phone, dialed the reporter, and handed his phone to Erin. She stared at him, and he looked away. The reporter answered after a few rings.

"Cody, you shouldn't be calling me," Fitzpatrick said.

# # #

"No, he definitely should not be calling you," Erin said.

There was a long silence at the other end.

"Is this Erin?" he asked quietly.

Why did Cody have the reporter's cell phone number? Why would he call Fitzpatrick? What was going on? She glared at her husband, who refused to make eye contact. She'd get the answer out of him later and doubted she would like it, but at that moment she needed to focus on finding her sister.

"Don't hang up," she said. "Yes, it's Erin. I…we need your help. Please."

"I'll give you thirty seconds," he said.

"You remember that note I showed you, in the effigy park?"

"Where you followed me after illegally bugging my car? I remember."

"It's happened. She's taken Lindsey, my sister," Erin said. "Sometime this morning. She's missing, and the police won't do anything for forty-eight hours. She could be dead by then."

"Slow down. How do you know she's been kidnapped? Maybe she took off for the day, maybe even the weekend. Isn't this something she's done in the past?"

"Yes, but this is different," Erin answered. "She was supposed to pick up my girls after school and she never showed up. We found her car at the Amtrak station. And before you ask, yes, I did put a tracker on her car, and I'm glad I did."

There was a long silence. Erin waited, hoping he hadn't disconnected.

"I'm sorry, but I'm not sure how I can help," he said.

"You know more than you're saying. You knew about those photos of my girls at Duggan's house even before I did. And those comments in your last blog about food deprivation during my kidnapping. Where did you get that information? I checked the visitation records at the prison. You never interviewed Duggan. You lied about that, and I want to know what else you're lying about."

"If I knew anything about your sister's whereabouts, I would tell you, but I don't. I need to protect my confidential sources for the rest of it."

"You were with a woman at the park. Was it Veronica?" she asked.

"No, it was a source of mine. Nothing to do with Duggan or your family. Put Cody back on," he said.

Erin's shoulders slumped. Another dead end. She was failing her sister. What would she tell Charlotte and

Gracie? She handed the phone to her husband.

"Get him to tell you," she whispered, her eyes tearing in frustration.

# # #

Cody took the phone and stepped into the dining room.

"It's me this time," he said.

"If your wife ever calls me again, I can guarantee your probation will be revoked. I've got the photos to fuck you up and I won't hesitate to do it."

Fitzpatrick hung up. Cody hung his head in silence.

# # #

This hadn't been part of the plan. Fitzpatrick tried her burner phone repeatedly for hours, and finally at four in the morning she answered.

"What have you done?" Fitzpatrick said, hoping he wasn't too late to stop her.

"Don't talk to me in that tone of voice or I'll hang up," she said. "I don't know what you're talking about."

"I'm talking about Lindsey Moore. Please tell me she's still alive," he said.

Chapter Forty-Eight

Cody had a pot of coffee brewing when Erin dragged herself down the stairs the next morning. She hadn't slept much during the night, but must have fallen asleep at some point, remembering fragments of a nightmare where she and Lindsey were both caged in Duggan's barn on a freezing day, and Veronica gave them one jacket to fight over. She'd woken up gasping for air, shivering and shaking as if the cold was real, and she wasn't sure she'd dozed off again after that.

It was early Tuesday morning, and she knew they'd have trouble getting help from the police until sometime the next day. Too much could happen by then.

Erin poured a cup and sat down at the kitchen table opposite Cody. His eyes were watery and bloodshot, and the dark circles underneath matched her own when she'd looked in the mirror that morning. She suspected he'd slept even less if that was possible. He wore an old t-shirt and gym shorts, spattered with dried paint, having moved most of his clothes to Gunther's apartment.

She watched as Cody stirred three heaping spoonful's of sugar into his coffee and tapped his foot rapidly under the table. He was sweating despite the cool temperature in the room. Erin needed his help, and he was clearly trying to keep it together. Briefly, she wondered if he might function better with a little bit of Oxycontin in his system rather than going through withdrawal, but it was the last thing she could suggest.

"I'm clean, if that's what you're wondering," he said.

"I'm hoping you're feeling all right, that's all," she said. "You look like you're…struggling."

"You know, when that last note came about the death of a loved one being similar to an amputation, I thought it might be my only chance to get rid of Alex Folk, once and for all," he said. "I didn't think it meant me, especially when there was a picture of his condominium building. She had to mean Folk. I admit I hoped she'd follow through and kill the bastard."

Erin started to speak, but he held up his hand.

"I truly wanted him dead, even though I knew it wasn't going to make things any better between us," he said. "What does that say about me? But now she's taken Lindsey."

He left out a single sob and clenched his eyes tight. A tear snaked down his cheek.

"I'm sorry about Alex. It was such a mistake, and we broke up last time I saw him. But I won't apologize for not trusting you. You've been keeping narcotics in this house with our girls."

"You expect forgiveness for betraying our marriage vows, but you won't cut me some slack over my addiction?"

"You brought dangerous drugs into our home. That's where I draw the line. My affair didn't put the girls in jeopardy. And I'm not expecting your forgiveness."

He gave a brief mirthless chuckle. "You were right not to trust me. If you only knew how right…" He sat up taller and wiped the tear from his cheek. "We need to focus on finding Lindsey. The rest of this shit is going to have to wait."

She nodded in agreement. "What do we know for sure about Veronica?"

They sat in silence. They knew very little.

"She lives locally. She's dropped things off in our mailbox and at your work. We can assume she has to be within driving distance," Cody said.

"She never visited him at Columbia. He only had the one visitor way back at the beginning of his sentence, and they did a thorough ID check at the prison. They required a photo ID, and it wasn't her. Didn't look anything like her."

"Could it have been some relative?"

"Possibly. But more likely it was one of Duggan's groupies. Prisoners like him receive a lot of letters from women, and one may have arranged for a visit." She went into her office and retrieved the folder of Duggan's visitors. "It was a few months into his sentence when this woman, Trudy Bell, saw him."

She pushed the copy of Bell's ID across the table.

"It doesn't look anything like her." Erin was certain.

"What about the woman Fitzpatrick met at the park, when he found your tracker?"

"I don't think so, but I didn't get close enough to be sure."

"Is there an address listed for the visitor?"

"There was, but whoever copied this blacked it out with a marker. But I've got a date of birth. May 14, 1959. She'd have been about forty back then. That's what I guessed Veronica was, although a fourteen-year-old isn't the best judge of age," she said. "Everyone over thirty looked old to me."

Erin went back into her office and brought out her laptop. She Googled Trudy Bell, Wisconsin and came back with nothing.

"Lindsey mentioned looking up boyfriends in some court database. Try that."

"It wouldn't have gone back twenty years, but I can try. Maybe she received a speeding ticket or something more recent." She typed in the necessary information. "Nothing. Maybe she's from another state. Or an exceptionally good driver."

"Or dead," Cody said. "That card targeted lovers and sisters. Try Veronica Bell. Maybe they were related."

"Or lovers," Erin added.

Nothing to lose. Erin typed in the name and came up with no matching responses.

She typed in Stanley Duggan and a long entry came up, detailing his parole hearing. It listed his original address in the town of Baraboo. She had driven by the old farmhouse occasionally over the past ten years. A few times she even cutting the lock from the chain and driving up the driveway, wondering who was replacing the broken locks. She noted with satisfaction the porch was beginning to droop, and shingles had blown off the roof in various storms. It had taken all the self-control she could muster on more than one occasion not to torch the house and barn.

What about Trudy Bell? If she'd been local, her name might come up in a search of property records. She poured herself a second cup of coffee yawned.

"This could take a while, but what if this woman, his visitor, owns a house in the area. I should be able to find it in the search of county records."

"Want me to start breakfast?"

She shook her head. She'd need to eat at some point, but she had no appetite and suspected Cody didn't either. They both jumped when her cell phone rang. It was the generic ringtone, not Lindsey's. The phone ID read Joshua Lippmann.

She snatched up the phone and answered, "Yes?"

"Erin, it's me, Joshua," he said. "I'm checking in, hoping you've heard something from your sister."

"Nothing at all. Her phone still goes right to voicemail. We even ran over to her apartment last night and checked it out."

"Nothing out of place?" he asked.

"Not that we could tell. Is your suspension over?" she asked.

"Yes. This morning I got back my badge and service weapon, which is a relief. I'm assigned to the investigation for one more week, then off to work at the county jail."

"I'm sorry this happened to you," she said.

"I'm hoping it's temporary. Be sure to call in and report Lindsey missing first thing in the morning. Call Osborne directly. He can't ignore this."

"I appreciate your help," she said. "I'll let you know if anything changes."

Cody busied himself making food neither of them would taste. The girls were sleeping in later than usual, and they would make do with cereal and fruit.

She made a note of possible counties in terms of distance from Baraboo and Duggan's place. She'd start with Sauk County and work concentrically through the seven adjoining counties. She'd search every damn county in Wisconsin if she had to. Hopefully, Trudy Bell or the real target Veronica, who may or may not be related, owned property somewhere in the state.

Cody delivered a plate of scrambled eggs and rye toast, and she ate, surprising herself and finishing every morsel. She thanked him and poured more coffee.

"I texted Betsy and she's available later this morning to babysit," Erin said. "I didn't tell her what was going on. I don't want her to worry the girls."

Cody dropped a plate while loading the dishwasher and it broke apart into large fragments. He hurried towards the broom closet and stepped on a shard. He hobbled over to the chair and sat, blood dripping from the bottom of his foot onto the floor. Erin grabbed a roll of paper towels and ripped off a fistful of sheets. Cody held these up to his foot while she cleaned up the mess. Once the bleeding let up, they examined the cut. Erin retrieved tweezers from the downstairs bathroom and extracted an inch long ceramic sliver from the wound, which again started oozing and dripping. She wrapped a tight bandage around the cut. Cody limped into the family room and lay down on the couch, elevating his foot.

Erin inspected the floor for any remaining glass, then finished loading the dishwasher. It was past eight and there was still no sign of either girl. She climbed the stairs and peeked into their rooms. Both were sitting on Gracie's bed playing a game of Candyland. She tiptoed away, figuring they would come downstairs when they were ready.

Erin returned to her laptop in the kitchen and started in on the rest of the counties. Three hours later, as she approached the bottom of her list, she got a hit in Juneau County. There was a sixty-two-acre property in the

Township of Lemonweir, ten miles outside of Mauston. She was familiar with Mauston, where Cody had recently moved, but never heard of Lemonweir. The owner was listed as Trudy F. Bell, with an address on 21st Street. She copied it into the search engine, and saw it was deeply rural and isolated. The property value was listed at only seventy thousand dollars in the tax records, even with the acreage, and the description included a trailer, a small barn and a few sheds. She tried to find a street-view of the property but came up empty.

Tax records showed no one paid the property taxes for the prior two years, and she wondered how long it took for a tax lien and auction of property in Wisconsin. That seemed like a short window for an eviction and home seizure, but she wondered if the home was abandoned.

She copied down the address and called into the next room to tell Cody what she'd found.

"Search for Veronica Bell, same county."

Nothing.

"This could be his visitor. Trudy is not a very common name. She lives in the right area," she said.

"Even if she is, it doesn't mean she has any connection to Veronica. She might be someone who got carried away watching the news years ago, who knew about your kidnapping and Duggan's arrest. She might have been a trial junkie who was thrilled to meet him in person."

"Right now, that's all we've got," she said.

Cody returned to the kitchen and sat. "We started with the question, what do we know about Veronica? Maybe we should also ask what we know about Fitzpatrick."

Erin nodded and considered the question. She'd considered him a nuisance twenty years ago, and over the past few months she'd come to think of him as a tormentor, nearly as bad as Veronica. But who was Richard Fitzpatrick and what did they know about him?

"He's worked at the same newspaper for a long time. My parents loved him back then, while I was missing and after I'd been released. They think he helped break the case," Erin said. "I didn't like him, even back then, but my parents wanted me to answer all his questions after I was rescued. I know he won some sort of prize for his reporting."

"No disrespect to your parents, but I don't think that means we should trust him," Cody said. "We know he lied about seeing Duggan in prison."

"We don't know how he knows about those photographs, both from Duggan's house and those marked-up pictures someone dropped off in our mailbox."

"Christ, Erin," he said softly. Cody covered his face with his hands, and when he finally dropped them down to the table, tears coursed down his face and his shoulder shook with sobs.

She looked up from her laptop and waited. Five minutes later he was silent. Finally, he sat up and swiped at his eyes with a napkin.

"Some of that's on me. I talked to him a few times," he said. "More than a few times. I'm sorry. I let him know how upset you were about those pictures, but I swear he already knew about them. He told me he's got a contact in the sheriff's department, which is how he found out about the porn and pictures of the girls at Duggan's house."

"I suspected it was either you or Lindsey. I'm afraid I can guess what kind of leverage he's been using."

He nodded, his face contorted with shame and pain. "He's got a large supply of Oxy. I have no idea where he gets it, but he's been trading it for…access. But that's over. I can go to more groups. I can get this straightened out on my own once this is over."

Erin had heard this before.

"It would help if I could move back home," he said.

She shook her head. She wasn't going to endanger her daughters.

"I would never do anything to hurt our girls."

"You're not moving back into this house until you've gone through inpatient rehab. This isn't up for debate."

"Fuck you, Erin. This is my home, too, and my girls."

"Can we discuss this later? We've got to think about Lindsey."

Cody took a deep breath and stared out the kitchen window.

"Let's go pay Trudy a visit," she said. "Please, Cody. I can't do this alone."

He said nothing.

She texted Betsy and received no reply. She'd try back again in a half hour. The girl promised she'd be available.

Cody headed for the guest room to get cleaned up. Erin called down the girls who finished bowls of cereal in front of the family room television while Erin showered and dressed. A text pinged through.

"Sorry, but I can't watch the girls today. On the way to Minneapolis with Trevor."

Erin frowned and rubbed the back of her neck. Betsy had promised and she had counted on it. She ran through a mental list of other potential sitters and came up empty.

She heard a door slam while she was dressing, followed by the security gate opening. When she returned to the kitchen, Cody and his truck were gone. She walked outside and bent down to examine a small heap of plastic and electronic components in the middle of the driveway, the remains of a GPS tracker.

Chapter Forty-Nine

Erin scooped up the pieces of plastic and metal and threw them into the kitchen garbage. In the family room, the girls had abandoned their tablets and were starting a Disney video. She didn't care how many hours of cartoons they watched that day or possibly ever again.

Her sister was missing and almost certainly in danger, no matter what Osborne thought. Cody felt justified abandoning her since she'd forced him to move out, but how could he abandon Lindsey, who had done nothing to him? Her sister hadn't treated him with suspicion or kicked him out of his own home. Lindsey also hadn't picked him up from the hospital after his latest drug overdose. She hadn't climbed out of bed long after everyone was asleep to search the house, every little nook and cranny, looking for his stash, night after night, since she suspected he was using again.

Erin yawned and rubbed her eyes. She hadn't slept through the night since first learning Duggan was up for early release, and it was only getting worse. She prayed he was dead but there was no proof. She feared there would never be any proof. And what if Lindsey was never found?

It was her own damn fault, Erin knew. If she'd been strong enough to testify at the parole hearing, it would have made a difference. If she'd been in the room, Osborne wouldn't have had the balls to openly support

Duggan's release, not if he had to look her in the eye as he testified. This was on her, and her sister was in imminent danger and might already be dead. Erin wondered if she could live with that outcome. And did it mean she or one of her daughters was next?

Erin pulled out her cell and tried Lindsey's number. She now heard the recording announcing the voicemail was full. How many messages had she left? She dialed Cody and he declined the call, not even giving her a chance to leave a message. She understood his anger with her, but this wasn't about Erin. It was about rescuing Lindsey.

She ran down the list of who she could call. She had already talked to Joshua and as much as he wanted to help, his hands were tied. Calling Osborne would be a complete waste of time until the next day, and she worried he wouldn't even take it seriously after forty-eight hours.

Cody's parents and sister lived in Milwaukee, but she knew his dad was still recovering from his surgery. They would also question why the plea for help was coming from their daughter-in-law and not their son.

She considered her partners at work. They were sympathetic if not supportive, up until the point they banned her from the building. Erin scrolled through the contact list in her phone, mostly contact numbers of the mothers of her children's friends. That didn't mean they were her friends. She struggled to remember many of their first names.

Erin pulled up the submitted applications for babysitters and scrolled through the information on the girls she'd interviewed and rejected. Their perceived flaws seemed insignificant now. How ridiculous she had been. Did it matter if one had a GED and not an actual high school diploma, or if another had two speeding tickets in the last five years? She would have left her daughters with Cody, who almost certainly had a stash of Oxycontin somewhere on his person. Hell, she would have left them with Osborne. They'd be traumatized when she returned, but they'd be alive.

Erin started phoning. She left voicemails with three mothers of her daughters' classmates, two of them single moms who might be more sympathetic to her plight. She left a message with the high school dropout and two of the other women she'd turned down to watch the girls.

She had never had a huge network of friends in high school or college, but there were always a few she could count on, even in graduate school. Her high school classmates knew her past, and, in some ways, that made it easier. She never disclosed the details of the kidnapping to anyone in college, but by the end of her junior year, somehow, they'd all found out. Copies of old newspaper articles appeared on the bulletin board in her dormitory, including a picture of her taken on the day of her rescue, a shell-shocked expression on her face, covered in filth and wearing ragged clothing, as she was led away from the prison in Duggan's basement.

She'd spent her senior year in an apartment off campus living in avoidance, disregarding all social invites, and ignoring the more persistent friends when they'd pounded on her door. It was so much easier than explaining. Why did they think they deserved the details of the worst time of her life?

The same thing happened halfway through her doctorate program, although she'd gained a little perspective by then. She'd maintained her two closest friendships even after the big reveal, probably because they knew not to push too hard for information. They were psychology graduate students, after all. But it hadn't taken many years for the contacts to dwindle to Christmas cards with pictures of their respective families. It didn't matter, since they both lived states away.

By midafternoon, Erin still hadn't heard back from any of the potential babysitters. She briefly considered taking the girls along to check on the Lemonweir address of Trudy Bell. It would be limited to a quick drive-by, and if she saw anything suspicious from the safety of the car, she could call Osborne.

She again brought up the images from Google maps. It was a wooded area with a gravel driveway leading into the trees. She'd need to get out of the car or drive up the private road and she couldn't do either. Erin couldn't endanger her daughters, even if it was Lindsey's life at stake.

She jerked to attention when her phone rang. She'd dozed off sitting at the kitchen island, her head resting on her arms. How long had she been sleeping? The caller ID read Glenda Albright, little Leo's mother. Her hands trembled as she answered.

"Hey, Erin, I got your message. Sorry it took a while to call back. We just got back from the waterpark. It was perfect weather, and the kids had a great time."

It was all Erin could do to let Glenda finish her sentence.

"I've got a family emergency and I need your help," Erin said, knowing she should have rehearsed her story. She'd had hours and she certainly couldn't tell this stranger her sister was in danger. "My sister has been hospitalized in Madison and I need to run down to see her tonight. Is there any way I could drop off the girls? It should only be for a few hours."

"Oh, I don't know, Erin. It's not good timing. Leo's already sound asleep on the couch. He runs around like a little energetic bunny at these parks, then totally collapses the minute he's in his car seat."

"Please, it's an emergency," Erin said. "There's no one else I can ask." She bit her lip until she could taste blood, wondering what she would do if this woman refused to help.

"Cody's not available?"

Erin inhaled and chose her words carefully.

"He doesn't live here anymore, and I haven't been able to reach him. I've been trying all day. Usually, my sister is the one I would fall back on, but…" Erin's throat tightened and she bit her lip harder to stave off the tears.

"Oh, Erin, I didn't know. Go ahead and bring the girls over. It might be hotdogs for dinner, but I'll get them fed."

Erin found her voice to thank the woman and hung up. She packed a backpack for each girl, containing pajamas, a toothbrush and a favorite stuffed animal. The girls were excited to see Leo, who stood half-asleep on the front porch with his mother when she arrived. She waved as the girls ran up the walk and pulled away from the curb. Glenda wouldn't see they'd come prepared to spend the night until she was miles down the road.

She pulled over a half mile away, her hands shaking on the steering wheel. The girls were out of danger, and safer in the Albright's home than they would be with Betsy at their own house.

Erin knew what her next step was, to locate the

home of Trudy Bell, and to find out what if anything the woman knew about Duggan and Veronica. It could easily be a dead end or a long-abandoned property.

She tried Cody's phone once again. She'd been blocked. She tried texting and got the same reply. She was on her own.

If she failed, her sister would likely die. Erin had to act. She thought about her two innocent daughters, happily playing at Leo's house. What if Erin didn't make it back? Who would Glenda call? She didn't have Cody's number and eventually she'd have to call the police. If something happened to her tonight, how would Cody manage to take care of the girls when he couldn't even take care of himself? Would he rise to the occasion knowing there was no other choice if he wanted to keep his daughters out of the foster care system, or would the added stress of Erin's demise send him further down an already slippery slope? She suspected the latter.

Erin opened her contact list and texted the information for Cody's parents to Glenda Albright. Just in case.

Chapter Fifty

The sun was low in the sky by the time she arrived at the address, and it was darker still with the heavy cloud cover, which nearly obscured the rising full moon. It was a desolate country road, peppered with potholes and stretches where the asphalt was long gone. The heavy morning rain still stood in puddles reflecting Erin's headlights. She slowed as she approached an opening in the trees, a gravel driveway, with no address sign or mailbox.

She drove a mile past the property in each direction noting the addresses marked on the few identifiable driveways, then turned back to the unmarked gravel road. A rusted metal pole stood which may have once held up a mailbox, now long gone. If Trudy still lived here, she wasn't encouraging mail delivery.

Erin drove twenty feet down the driveway and cut the headlights. She climbed out of the car and examined the driveway ahead. The sparse gravel gave way to packed dirt and mud. There were clearly visible car tracks ahead, which appeared fresh. Someone, possibly Trudy Bell, had driven here since the morning rain. She turned the brightness down on her cell phone flashlight setting. Should she walk down the driveway or climb back into the car?

She had no idea how far back the trailer and sheds were. The property tax listing described a sixty-two-acre plot of land. She had no frame of reference as to how big that was, especially since she had no idea of the shape of the property. What if the trailer was at the far end?

She climbed into the car and reset the trip meter to zero. She turned the automatic headlights off and was left with the dim LED running lights. There was barely enough light to follow the path of the driveway, and she hit a few potholes deep enough to scrape the bottom of her car. The driveway gradually sloped downward, and the puddles were deeper as she went down the incline.

This was ridiculous. Erin knew nothing about Trudy Bell, not even if she had ever lived at this address. She might find an abandoned empty trailer or possibly scare the hell out of some elderly lady watching game show reruns on a humid summer night.

She'd also read about a growing problem with meth labs in rural areas of Wisconsin, and the occasional fires or explosions in dilapidated trailers in the middle of the woods, she imagined in a setting like this. She braked and rolled down her car window, and she sniffed the night air. The earthy smell of decaying leaves wafted in, along with the residual odor as proof a skunk was in the neighborhood. There was no telltale smell of ammonia or cat pee, which she'd read were typical of a meth lab, but maybe the smell was confined to the inside of the building.

Erin swatted away a mosquito from her forearm and rolled the car windows up. She hoped there was still a can of insect repellant in a travel box in the back of the SUV. She might be doing some hiking.

She studied her odometer as she slowly forged ahead, the dim light barely illuminating the path ahead. She was nearly a quarter of a mile down the twisty drive before she came to a tall, rusty chain-link fence, with a sturdy padlock on the gate. She turned off the running lights and climbed out of the car, shutting the door far enough that the interior lights dimmed.

Fifty feet past the gate, she made out the outline of a single wide trailer, with two cars parked in front. The porch light was turned off, but enough light filtered from inside the trailer that she could see one of them was the same general size and shape as Fitzpatrick's. She couldn't make out the color and it was a common car silhouette.

Trudy Bell, or whomever lived on the property, couldn't have fenced in the entire acreage. She pulled out her cell phone and had no bars, and she realized she had been going steadily downhill since the main road.

Erin opened the glove compartment. She pulled out her Smith and Wesson and tucked it into her waistband. She took out her compact baby Glock and slipped it into her sock, covering it with her pant leg. She lifted the back hatch of the SUV where she retrieved a pair of compact binoculars, which she hung around her neck, and doused herself generously with bug spray. She set out to see how far the fence went.

Forty minutes later she had encircled the entire fence line and returned to her car, hot and sweaty from the exertion. Her shoes were caked in mud, and she scraped the largest clumps off with a stick. The fencing material looked old and rusted in spots but there were no gaping holes and she had nothing to cut through. There was no way other than to climb over the fence.

This wasn't some innocuous elderly lady living in a trailer in the woods, that much she knew. The fence around the entire perimeter and locked gate eliminated any semblance of innocence. The possibility of a meth lab moved higher on her list. It would also be an ideal place to hold a woman captive. Erin debated her options. She could wait until one of the cars left and follow, but it might be too late for Lindsey if she was in fact being held in the trailer. She wasn't leaving until she found out if her sister was inside.

Erin knew she needed a backup. She was armed, but what was she walking into? It would have been different if Cody were with her, with his military background, and if he'd been clean. She would at least try Osborne again. She was certain she had crossed over into the next county based on the tax records, but Osborne knew the situation.

She again checked her phone and there were zero bars. She tried to connect a call, but nothing happened. She headed back towards the car, backed out the entire length of the driveway and still barely had a half bar. She drove two miles in the direction she had come from, onto higher ground and possibly nearer to a signal tower. Osborne picked up on the first ring.

"Detective, it's Erin again and I need your help right away. I think I've found where my sister is being held, but it's too dangerous for me to go in alone."

Erin heard a long, loud sigh on the other end.

"Where are you?" he asked.

"Here's the location of the property," she said. "It's not well-marked."

He repeated the address for verification. She hoped he was writing it down.

"That's in Juneau County, out of my jurisdiction. What makes you think Lindsey is being held there?" he asked.

She described tracking down the prison visitor's log

and finding a single woman visitor in the twenty years, near the beginning of his sentence, and finally tracking down a property owned by that visitor.

"Do you think this Trudy is your Veronica?" he asked.

"No, but they might know each other, or even be family," she said. It sounded lame when she said it out loud.

"You were very young when the trial took place, and of course you couldn't sit in the courtroom except on the day you testified, but Stanley Duggan attracted a lot of women. The gallery had ten or fifteen women there every single day hoping to catch his eye. It's much more likely this Trudy was one of them. You said you got a copy of her ID. That's not an open record, and I'm curious how you managed that. But you admit she looks nothing like Veronica."

"Why can't you at least check it out?"

"I know you're worried about your sister, and I'll admit I'm getting concerned you still haven't heard from her. I'm out at an accident site on the highway. Four cars involved and it's a mess. At least one fatality and we're waiting for Flight for Life for two passengers. There's nothing I can do right now. Call me first thing in the morning and we'll fill out a missing person's report."

The phone went dead. Erin swore aloud and slumped forward, resting her forehead on the steering wheel. She briefly closed her eyes and forced herself to take a series of deep breaths. She lifted her phone and tried Cody's number. This time it went to voicemail, and she left a short message. Erin was on her own.

She put the car in gear and retraced her route down the long driveway, this time parking farther away from the gate. She needed the element of surprise. If she could see their cars, they likely could see hers. An outside light high on a pole had been turned on, and now lit up the area in front of the trailer, including the cars. She was increasingly doubtful one of them belonged to Fitzpatrick. Why would he be parked out in the woods by this dilapidated trailer? She remembered Cody used Fitzpatrick as his supplier, but it seemed unlikely this was where he came for his drug purchases.

She approached the fence wishing she had worn shoes with more pointed toes than her running shoes. She checked that both of her guns were securely strapped in and started to climb. She managed to scale to the top, swing her leg over, and made it partially down the other side before her grip slipped and she plopped unceremoniously onto the mixture of mud and gravel.

She studied the chain-link fence and gate from the inside. It wasn't as decorative as the wooden gate and fence surrounding her property, but it was still a challenge to breach. Her enclosure at home was to keep intruders out. She wondered if this fence had been built to keep someone in.

The area around the cars and entrance to the trailer was now too well-lit to approach directly.

She needed more information. If this were a drug lab, she would silently creep back to her car and drive away, whether Fitzpatrick was there or not. She didn't care where he bought his supply. Erin edged along the inside of the fence until she was well past the trailer. She wasn't been able to see the back of the structure at all from outside the fence, and it was possible she could get a glimpse of the inside with her binoculars. She stayed well within the tree line planning a wide circle around the structure. She made out the silhouette of a small shed halfway between the building and where she stood.

Light shone through two windows at the back of the trailer, but the shades were drawn. She lifted the binoculars to her eyes and studied the windows, looking for any significant holes. A shadow moved back and forth across the shades, as if someone was pacing. There were several smaller windows which were unlit, and she suspected they were the bedroom or bathroom windows. She needed to get closer.

Erin continued her circle around the trailer, flinching at the snap of every twig, certain they could hear inside. She stepped carefully over crumbled dead logs, the waft of the rotting wood even stronger than the insect spray she had doused herself in. There was a new smell, initially sickly sweet but as she got closer, it became stronger, rank, and nauseous. Erin covered her mouth and nose with her hand and stepped up her pace to get away from the odor.

Her shoe caught on a root or log buried in the plant debris, and she tripped forward, landing in the wet ground cover and mud. She slowly climbed back to her feet, checking that she hadn't lost either gun or her binoculars. She wiped the mud from her palms onto her jeans. The stench was now overpowering. She turned on her cell phone flashlight and examined the ground behind her.

Two gleaming white shafts rose from the mat of rotting leaves, one wider than the other. Erin approached and bent down for a closer look. They were bones, picked clean of all soft tissues. She picked up a large stick and dug around the base. Beneath the surface, protected from the animals, there were still remnants of muscle and skin attached to the bones, and shreds of blue jean material stained a dark brown. While the foot and ankle had been cleanly severed and removed, she recognized what she was seeing. It was the tibia and fibula of a man's lower leg, likely connected to the rest of the body.

Erin turned and hastily stepped away from the body of Stanley Duggan before she vomited onto the ground.

Chapter Fifty-One

Duggan was dead. He wasn't on the run or hiding out. Instead, the man was partially buried on this property, which based on tax records belonged to his only female visitor during his twenty years of incarceration. Erin got far enough away from the body that she could tolerate the smell of rot. Her breathing eased up, and she leaned up against the stump of an old tree to clear her head.

He had been buried in a shallow grave in the woods behind this decrepit house trailer. Trudy Bell was not one of the fawning fans at Duggan's trial. This had to tie into Veronica, but why would she kill Duggan? And if she was the one to kill him, why would she vow to avenge his death? Isn't that what the last card threatened? Nothing made sense.

Osborne would be forced to come when she told him she had uncovered a body. All she needed to do was to hike back to the gate, climb over and drive back to where she could get a cell phone signal. This was all the information she needed.

She made a wide circle around the burial site and again walked slowly, as silently as she could manage back to the gate. She confirmed she still had both guns and her binoculars and started to climb. Again, it was difficult finding a foothold with her rounded shoe toes, but she was swinging her leg over the top of the fence when she heard it. A single gunshot from the direction of the trailer.

Erin froze, one leg in the air, her hands clamped tightly on the top of the chain link fence. She strained to hear, but no shouting or other noise came from the trailer. Had they just shot Lindsey? She couldn't leave now. Lindsey could be dead before she got back. She dropped back onto the ground and turned. She needed to find out if her sister was in the trailer, and if she was still alive.

Erin crept towards the trailer and parked cars, walking through the brush and scrub trees close to the driveway, crouching low to stay out of sight. Once she was closer, she took out her cell phone and snapped a photo of both cars. The SUV's license plate matched Fitzpatrick's. He was a dirtbag supplying her husband with drugs and seemed hellbent on torturing her with his news releases, but it still seemed unlikely he was involved in Lindsey's kidnapping. Could he have uncovered Veronica's whereabouts and be here to negotiate Lindsey's release? He had sounded genuinely upset when she'd informed him her sister was missing.

She heard low voices coming from the trailer, then music, which she suspected was coming from a television. She crept around the back of the trailer where the tightly drawn shades concealed the living room. Erin found a scrub pine which had managed to take root feet from the trailer, and climbed three feet higher, the pine needles scratching at her face. It was high enough to see into the trailer through a small rent in the shade, and she saw Lindsey duct-taped to a kitchen chair, her head hanging forward. Erin held her breath and watched.

Was she alive? There was no visible blood, but she could only see her sister's head and shoulders. She could have a gaping bullet wound in the middle of her chest and she'd miss it from this vantage point.

Erin debated again whether she should climb back over the fence and drive for help. If Lindsey were still alive, help might arrive too late. She climbed down from the tree, pulled out her Smith and Wesson and inched her way up a small set of stairs to a backdoor. Pine needles and forest debris covered the steps, suggesting the door hadn't been used in a long time. The screen door opened with a slight squeak. She stood perfectly still, waiting to see if there was a response from within the trailer. After another minute, she tried to turn the doorknob. It was locked. She had nothing to pick the lock with, even if she knew how, which she didn't. She could fire her gun into the mechanism, like she'd seen on so many television shows, but she'd lose any element of surprise. She checked her phone once more. Still no bars.

She slunk down the stairs and crept around the far side of the trailer, keeping to the shadows. It would be Fitzpatrick and Veronica in the trailer, and at least one of them was armed. There was no choice. She sneaked towards the front steps, unable to avoid stepping into the light.

"Stop right there," a male voice behind her said. It was Fitzpatrick. "Reach back with your left hand and give me the phone."

She froze, then did as he asked. She heard her phone slam into the ground followed by multiple stomps and the sound of breaking glass.

"Now the gun—drop it."

She did. Erin now had her answer to one of her questions. Fitzpatrick wasn't there to help.

Cynthia Rice

"We've been expecting you. Both hands on top of your head. There's someone who's dying to meet you."

Chapter Fifty-Two

The trailer door swung open, and in walked Erin Moore, all grown up but with the same asinine look of terror on her face as the last time Veronica had seen her, her hands in the air and Fitzpatrick following with a gun held to the small of her back. She'd seen Erin from afar many times over the years, but never this up close. She whooped with pleasure. It was like Christmas morning and Santa had dumped his entire fucking bag of toys down her chimney.

"That was her at the backdoor, trying the knob. I told you it wasn't the squirrels. I caught her sneaking around the back of the trailer."

"You're right. The second GPS unit did the trick."

He forced Erin farther into the small living room and set her Smith and Wesson on the kitchen counter.

"Search her. She may have a second gun. Remember she goes to a shooting range all the time." She crossed the room, took the gun from Fitzpatrick, and pointed it at Erin's chest. "I hope this doesn't go off, dear. I haven't got the steadiest hands these days."

"Lindsey," Erin called out. "Lindsey, look at me."

Sure enough, Lindsey's right eye flickered open a smidge. The left was swollen shut and heavily bruised. She didn't lift her head off her chest or answer her sister, and she would have fallen forward onto the floor if she hadn't been securely duct taped to the chair. Duct tape and W2. You could fix everything with one or the other.

"Don't worry about her. I gave her a sedative, quite a bit of it. I'm impressed she's still breathing."

She snorted at Erin's shocked expression. This was going to be entertaining. She wished Stanley was there to share the fun.

Fitzpatrick went through Erin's sweatshirt pockets and found nothing. He pulled the binoculars off her chest and tossed them onto the counter next to Lindsey's phone and wallet. Finally, he found the second smaller gun tucked into her sock, which joined the other items.

"Put her over on the couch," Veronica said. "Tape up her hands."

He shoved Erin towards the couch, and she sat. Fitzpatrick bound her wrists in front of her with duct tape.

"How did you find this place?" Veronica was delighted Erin had shown up, but she worried she might have tipped off the cops.

"It wasn't that hard," Erin said. "The sheriff's department will be here any minute."

"Bullshit," Veronica said. And it was. If the cops were on their way, Erin would have waited for them. "We knew you were close by. You think you're smart, don't you? Did you ever think there might be two GPS units on your car?"

Lindsey gagged, then started to vomit. Fitzpatrick jumped back to avoid the splatter. Then she lurched forward and tipped over her chair, landing face first on the old carpet.

"Help her," Erin cried. "She's going to choke."

Erin rushed forward and struggled with her bound wrists but managed to turn her sister and the chair on the side and then supported her head as she continued to vomit. Too bad about the smell and the carpet, but this was otherwise quite entertaining. She and Stanley should have taken both the girls two decades ago. They hadn't thought it out properly.

"Lindsey, it's me," she said.

Lindsey finally stopped retching, but her breathing was loud, and she coughed and gasped for air. She probably aspirated some of the puke when she tipped onto the floor. Veronica hoped it would clear. A quick death for either of the Moore girls, even one as gruesome as choking on her own vomit, hadn't been part of the plan.

"Can I have a towel?" Erin asked. "Please."

Fitzpatrick stepped into the kitchen, ripped off a half dozen squares of paper towel and brought them back. She dabbed away the crud from her sister's face and shifted the whole chair, sister and all, a half foot closer to the door, so her head was no longer resting in the largest pool of vomit. She was surprisingly strong, even with her hands bound. Not the powerless little girl she had been.

"You need to call an ambulance or let me take her to the hospital. She's going to die if she doesn't get help."

"Erin," Veronica said, soothingly, "she was always going to die. From the minute I tazed her at her apartment building yesterday morning and tossed her in my trunk. She knew it, too. Screaming like a little bitch, crying, begging for mercy. Mercy. Like the judge gave my Stanley twenty-one years ago, throwing him in prison. Mercy, like you gave him when you killed him three weeks ago."

"We don't know he's dead," Fitzpatrick said.

Veronica said nothing. She knew Stanley was dead. He never would have taken off and left her behind, not in a million years, not after those phone calls. She felt her pocket for her burner phone.

"I didn't kill him," Erin said. "I have no idea who killed him, but I swear it wasn't me."

"Of course, that's what you would say, ain't it?" she asked.

"But it's true."

"I seen you going to the shooting range." She held out Erin's gun. "This looks pretty new."

"I bought the gun for protection, not to commit murder."

Lindsey started another coughing fit and Erin knelt beside her again.

"Get her chair sitting upright." Veronica motioned for Fitzpatrick to help.

They struggled with the weight but finally got Lindsey and her chair upright. Fitzpatrick looked down, clearly grossed out over the slime on his hands from touching her clothing. He ran over to the kitchen sink, squirted dish lotion on his hand and scrubbed and scrubbed. The man would have never made it on a farm.

"If you were smart, you'd make a run for it," Erin said. "My husband drove to call the police. They'll be here any minute. You've got time to run. But not much."

"Did you see him out there?" she asked Fitzpatrick.

"No, but the gate's locked. She managed to climb over, but there's no way he could have made it, not with that leg of his."

"Between his bad leg and his drug-addled brain, he won't make it too far. He's not going to get a cell signal around here. Too far from the nearest tower and we're in a valley. Made for shitty farmland, I can tell you." She turned to Fitzpatrick. "Maybe you should go out and look for him."

"He drives just fine." Erin made a show of cocking her head. "Is that a siren I hear in the distance?"

Veronica responded by viciously pistol-whipping Lindsey in the back of the head. Erin gasped and suddenly wasn't so smart-assed. She moved to stand protective-like next to her sister, staring at Veronica, paler by the second. She wouldn't be able to protect Lindsey from what was about to happen, and it would gut her. Little Erin finally realized who was in control and it wasn't either of the Moore girls. Or Fitzpatrick for that matter.

Veronica had been invisible most of her life, one of those women who gets passed over for her turn at the bakery counter even when she was holding the next little paper number. Until she met Stanley, that is. He'd made her feel seen and valued, until a few months into the kidnapping, when he hadn't, when he'd started looking at Erin like he used to look at her. But she got even and eventually even forgave him, once he was in prison. After all, she helped put him there. You didn't cross Veronica and get away with it.

She motioned for Erin to go back to the couch and this time she did what she was told without shooting off her mouth. Fitzpatrick went out the door and was gone for ten minutes. When he returned, he held up a set of keys which included a fob.

Erin gasped.

"Cody's not going to get far without his car keys. I found them in the dirt on the other side of the fence. Her car is parked fifty yards down the driveway and his truck is right behind it. No sign of him though. Even if he tries to hike out, he'll never make it far enough to get a phone signal."

"After we're finished here, you need to go find him. You can use his truck. It's too bad because I was hoping we could…" Veronica smiled at Erin. "Hoping we could take our time."

Erin shuddered and her grin broadened.

Veronica was pleased Lindsey was a little more alert. The girl's breathing was still rough, but she was breathing. She opened her one good eye and looked around the room. She saw Erin sitting on the couch, and they stared at each other, but had the sense to keep their mouths shut, or at least Erin did. Lindsey began to weep quietly. It would be much better now that Lindsey was awake. It would make it much harder on her sister.

"Watch them," Veronica said.

She went into the kitchen and rummaged under the kitchen sink looking for a plastic bag. Not one of those flimsy Walgreen bags which always had a tear somewhere big enough to let in a little air. No, she wanted one of the thick yellow Family Mart grocery store bags, with nice handles made to be tied around someone's neck. She grabbed a boning knife out of the knife block and made her way back into the living room. Veronica had never boned a damn thing in her life, which made it the sharpest knife in the kitchen.

Erin's eyes widened, even if her sister was still too dazed to appreciate the moment.

"I didn't kill Stanley, I swear," Erin said. "I didn't want him dead."

"Sure, honey, I believe you," Veronica said. "I'm

sure there were no hard feelings about what happened to you."

She walked behind Lindsey, who was now alert enough to realize she was about to die. Veronica pulled the yellow plastic bag down over her head but left plenty of room around the neck. The bag occasionally sucked up against Lindsey's mouth, but she was able to blow it away. Her breathing became faster, and she shook her head back and forth to try to dislodge the bag. She was panicking but there was plenty of air circulating her head, for now. Just wait because it was going to get worse.

"Don't, please," Erin said. "You don't want her, you want me. Let her go."

Veronica took the boning knife and made a superficial cut on Lindsey's right arm extending from the upper forearm to the wrist. The girl screamed and struggled with the tape, but it held firm. Her breathing grew more ragged. Veronica followed with a similar cut on her left. A thin trickle of blood formed along the edges, and there was a steady drip down her hand onto the floor. She'd gone in a bit deeper than she planned. She'd have to recarpet the whole damn trailer by the time she was finished. Puke and now blood. It smelled of cat piss anyway. Not much of a loss.

"Stop, please." Erin began to shake and shake. She was whiter than Veronica thought possible, and her forehead was drenched with sweat. She started rocking back and forth like a lunatic, moaning and drawing her knees up to her chest, and then she suddenly dropped to the floor and lay still.

"Fucking A," Fitzpatrick said. "Is she unconscious?"

"Yeah, I seem to recall she did that a lot. I thought she would have outgrown it by now." She yanked the plastic bag off Lindsey's head. They'd have to wait it out.

Chapter Fifty-Three

Cody limped up to the gate and looked beyond at the parked cars and trailer. He saw Erin slink towards the front of the trailer, and he watched helplessly as a man approached her from behind and aimed a gun at her back. He pulled out his binoculars and focused in on the man's face and swore under his breath when he saw it was Fitzpatrick. What was he doing out here at this Trudy Bell's property? Erin had been right not to trust him. Maybe Cody would have figured that out if he hadn't been relying on the man for his next fix.

After he'd stormed out of the house, Cody drove around town for hours, ignoring Erin's calls. When he'd finally listened to her voicemail, he realized how much danger she was in. He'd driven to their home to stop her, but it was too late. She was gone and so were the girls. She wouldn't have taken their daughters along, would she? There was no note on the kitchen counter, where they always left any important messages. He checked the gun safe and found two were missing.

He pulled a Glock from his pocket, the gun Erin had left behind, knowing he couldn't shoot Fitzpatrick from this distance. It was too dark, too far, and he had always been a lousy shot. He hadn't been going to the shooting range like Erin and couldn't even legally be holding the gun. Cody froze, unwilling to move in case a snapped twig or sound of his shoes on the gravel carried. He watched in horror as Erin and Fitzpatrick disappeared into the trailer.

He sized up the fence and knew he wasn't going to make it over. His boots were too wide to find a toehold and he didn't have the necessary flexibility with his prosthesis. The padlock looked new, and he debated trying to shoot through the mechanism. Finally, he limped back to his truck, falling twice when his foot became entangled in tree roots.

Once he reached his truck, he pulled out his cell phone and tried for a signal. There was a faint wisp of a single bar, better than before. He tried sending a 911 call. Nothing. He reached for the truck keys, and they were gone. He searched every pocket, came up with his wallet, gun, a small envelope of pills and his phone. The key fob was gone.

He needed to turn around. He must have dropped them when he fell. He activated the flashlight function on his cell phone and traced his footsteps back to the fence. He dimmed the light, realizing Erin might be in even more danger if he was captured. He kicked at clumps of leaves along the side of the path, straining to see a glint of metal from his key fob. He should have checked his pockets as soon as he had fallen. How had he been so careless?

After fifteen minutes of searching, he gave up. Cody sat down on the ground and wept. Erin had been courageous enough to confront Lindsey's kidnappers alone, and he should have been there by her side. His stump throbbed and he was exhausted. He pulled out the small packet of Oxycontin from his pants and shook two of the small pink tablets into his palm. He would only take two. He couldn't help Erin unless he had the pain under control. Just two, he told himself. He swallowed them dry without difficulty. It had come with practice.

Fifteen minutes later, he brushed away his remaining tears and climbed to his feet. He reassured himself the phone, gun and pills were safely stowed, took one more look around for the keys and headed back towards the vehicles.

He opened the back hatch of his wife's SUV, searching for anything he could use to call for help, but found nothing other than Erin's tennis bag and a pile of kids' books awaiting return to the library.

Cody passed his truck and kicked at a tire, then started the slow uphill hike back to the main road, where he stood, praying for a passing vehicle. He gave up after a half hour. He hadn't seen a single car. It was probably at least three miles to the nearest intersection, and that hadn't been a very busy road either. He couldn't make three miles, even with the Oxy on board.

He tried his phone again, and there was a partial bar, minimally larger than it had been back in the woods, but still not enough to place a call. He tried texting his new roommate, but it wouldn't send. He'd need higher ground to get a stronger signal and he wondered how far he would have to walk. It was too dark to see if there was a hill in either direction.

If he couldn't drive to higher ground, he'd have to climb. There were oaks and pines lining the driveway as well as the main road. He picked one with plenty of low branches and started his ascent. He was able to get a good hand grip to pull himself up, foot by foot, doing the heavy lifting with his arms and not his legs. It was slow going, but twenty minutes later he made it halfway up the tree and found a stable branch to sit and catch his breath. It was only an hour since he'd taken the Oxy, but his leg was starting to ache again. His fingertips were raw from the rough bark and his chest was heaving from the exertion. He hadn't realized he was so out of shape.

Once his breathing settled, he reached for the phone, relieved he hadn't dropped it in on the way up. The screen showed a solid single bar, and a fraction of a second. It was the best he was going to do. This was his only chance. Cody punched 911. As he hit send, his left hand lost its grip on the overhead bough, and he began to fall. He tried to catch himself on the next branch, but his flailing arms met only air. He plummeted twenty feet to the ground, landing on his good ankle with a sickening crunch as it gave way.

He pulled himself into a sitting position and leaned back against the tree, gasping to catch his breath. He cried out in pain and swore, glad he was out of ear range from the trailer. He grimaced as he reached down and loosened the shoelaces, but it was too painful to remove the boot. Cody knew he fucked up his good leg and he had no idea if the call had gone through. Had he managed to hit send before he fell? He spotted the glow of the phone screen ten feet away, face down on the dirt. He needed to reach the phone. He checked his pockets. Like his phone, the gun was lost in the fall. Luckily, he still had his Oxy.

Cody pulled out the small packet and shook four pills into the palm of his hand. He'd never taken this many at one time, but he'd never been in such pain before, even in Afghanistan when he'd been in shock after the IED. He would let the medication kick in, then crawl over and get his phone. What was the point, he thought as the pain began to ease? The police were either coming or they weren't. It wasn't like he could climb the tree and try again.

He shut his eyes. He'd tried, but now he needed to sleep. He'd let Erin down. And Lindsey. And now they were going to die. And the girls would have no one. It was his last thought before he lapsed into unconsciousness.

Chapter Fifty-Four

Erin needed to get to one of her guns or find another weapon. She faked a fainting spell and fell to the floor landing on her side, her cheek digging into the disgusting carpet which reeked of mildew and cat pee. It was all she could do to keep her head planted in place.

Veronica wasn't going to kill Lindsey without a full audience. Fitzpatrick had shown her a key fob claiming it belonged to Cody's truck, but she wasn't sure whether to believe him. Her husband had left her alone, knowing she was planning to search for her sister. He ignored her phone calls and texts. It wasn't likely he'd come to her rescue. She needed to play for time.

Ten minutes later a huge gush of cold water splashed her face, and she opened her eyes, gasping for air. Veronica stood over her with a now empty bucket, cackling with pleasure.

"Playing possum, weren't you?" Veronica said. "You fooled us back then, but it's not going to work anymore. Back on the couch."

Veronica delivered a vicious kick to her lower leg. Erin slowly climbed to her feet and sat back on the couch. She'd heard the front door open while she'd been down and saw Fitzpatrick had gone outside. Had he really gone looking for Cody or was he lying about seeing his truck? She saw the black key fob he'd dropped on the kitchen table, claiming it belonged to her husband.

If that was true, her husband was on foot, but with a large head start. She prayed he made it to the road and had the sense to hide. She thought of Gracie and Charlotte and a painful lump formed in her throat.

"We'll wait till he gets back. We heard a noise by the back door again. I still think it's the damned squirrels, but it doesn't hurt to be cautious. He went to find that worthless husband of yours."

Erin knew Cody wouldn't have made it over the fence.

"You'll never get away with this," Erin said. "I called Detective Osborne and told him I was coming here. We gave him the address and Trudy Bell's name."

"Bullshit, honey. He's had plenty of time to get here. The cavalry's not coming to save you."

"How did you get mixed up with Fitzpatrick?" Erin needed to buy time and find a way to get to her gun.

"I helped him out twenty-some years ago. Who do you think tipped him off where you were being held? That was his big story, even got him some awards. He was going to work for the New York Times someday. Big talker."

"Why would you do that? I thought you loved Duggan?"

"I did, still do, although I don't see that's any of your business. But he'd decided he wanted you. Once you weren't as plump. I knew it was only a matter of time, once he started to visit the basement every night to watch you sleep. I wasn't going to let you have him, even if that's what he wanted. And I could tell you wanted it. You were such a slut. It wasn't an easy decision, either slit your throat or turn him in. Consider yourself lucky. Until tonight, of course."

Erin shuddered. She thought back to the sleepless nights two decades earlier, Stanley Duggan coming down into the basement at night and standing just past the reach of her chains while she feigned sleep.

"Why didn't Fitzpatrick tell the police where to find you?"

"He owed me, for one thing, helping him get the story of a lifetime. Plus, he couldn't risk the police finding out that he knew your whereabouts for nearly two weeks before he broke the story. There was a more senior writer on the paper who would have taken all the headlines, and he waited until the guy left town on a vacation."

The bastard, she thought, thinking of what could have happened in those two weeks.

"Did you know Osborne testified at Duggan's hearing? He supported his release. Do you know why?"

"Because he's an idiot?"

"To find you. He figured eventually you would make contact and it was his only chance."

"That makes sense, I guess," she said.

"That's why you should understand I wouldn't kill Duggan. I also knew he would eventually lead Osborne to you, and I wanted you captured more than I feared his release."

Veronica said nothing, appearing to consider what she'd heard. Her brow furrowed. She stood and paced.

"I don't know for sure who killed him, but it had to be someone who stood to benefit, right?" Erin said. "And someone with access to your property."

"What do you mean, access to my property?"

"Stanley Duggan is buried in the woods behind your trailer. You didn't know?"

"Bullshit."

"I can show you," Erin said. "It's about fifty yards back, well into the tree line."

"And you happened to be digging a hole out there and found him?" Veronica shook her head. "You were a lying bitch then, and nothing's changed."

"I can show you. Animals must have uncovered his leg. It's sticking out of the ground in plain sight. The foot is missing." Erin should have taken a photo when she'd had a chance, but she'd been too busy looking for a place to vomit.

Lindsey was awake now, watching the exchange. Veronica continued to pace, pointing the Smith and Wesson at the front door.

"Who gained anything from Stanley's death? Not Osborne and not me. The only person I can think of who benefited is Fitzpatrick. He bragged that the subscriptions to his blog have gone through the roof since Stanley was released. I imagine they took another leap after his disappearance."

"After all I've done for him…" Veronica spat on the floor. "He wouldn't have the guts to kill a man."

"He didn't seem to have a problem watching you stick a bag over my sister's head or slicing up her arm. Are you sure he couldn't have killed him?"

"He wouldn't do that to me."

"Maybe he didn't intend to kill him and just went there to get information for his blog. I know he tried to interview Stanley when he first got out of prison, and he'd refused to talk to him. He'd likely try again, wouldn't he? I can't tell you how many times he stopped by my house even after I told him not to come back."

"He's persistent, all right." She eyed the door

suspiciously and stepped closer.

"Things got out of hand and Fitzpatrick had to protect himself. That's his own gun he's carrying, isn't it? Then you know he had access to a weapon. He shot Stanley, then cut off his foot to get the monitor off. He didn't want the police to track the body."

An overweight orange tabby meandered into the room. It sized up Erin and Lindsey, then walked over to the mound of vomit in front of Lindsey's chair and started to lap it up.

"No, Pumpkin, stop. That's nasty." She reached down and scooped up the enormous cat, which was probably over twenty-five pounds. Pumpkin squirmed in her arms, finally leapt free and darted down the hallway.

"Ask him when he comes back," Erin said. "He's not going to admit he killed Stanley but see how he reacts."

Veronica put the Smith and Wesson down on the kitchen counter and picked up the boning knife. She wiped Lindsey's blood on her jeans and examined the tip. Erin calculated she could get to the Glock on the kitchen table in two seconds. It would take longer to fire than normal, with her hands taped. Veronica was two feet from Lindsey, with a knife in her hand. She may reach the gun, but her sister would end up dead.

The front door swung open. Erin prayed it would be Fitzpatrick alone and that he hadn't captured Cody. If she and Lindsey didn't make it, the girls would still have a parent.

"I opened the gate and made it all the way to the road. No sign of him. I wasn't sure which direction he might have headed, so I came back."

"You should have taken his truck to look for him."

"I couldn't. I left the keys on the counter. Besides, I figure he's more likely hiding out in the woods. Probably popping drugs and wondering where he's going to get his next dose."

Erin watched Veronica. She pushed her index finger to the top of the boning knife until a few drops of blood ran down the blade. Fitzpatrick had his gun drawn, pointing it at the floor. Neither noticed as she slid closer to the end of the couch and a few feet closer to the table and the gun. It would still be two seconds to pick it up and aim. Veronica and her boning knife were closer to Fitzpatrick than her sister at this point, but surely the reporter could shoot her before she could fire. She needed a distraction and wondered if Pumpkin would come if she called.

"She had some interesting things to say while you were out." Veronica pointed the knife tip in Erin's direction.

Erin saw a flicker of doubt cross his face, but it vanished as quickly.

Fitzpatrick said nothing.

"She seems to think it might have been you who killed Stanley."

"Why would I do that?"

"She's right, it stirred up a lot of interest in your column. It did. Tell me she's wrong."

Veronica continued to test the sharpness of the knife tip. Fitzpatrick backed away from her.

"It would have helped if he'd given me an interview, but I managed without. It wasn't a dealbreaker."

"Maybe you went to his house to try to get a story."

"I did go there, more than once. He refused. He was out in that barn of his, lifting weights. He threatened me with a barbell."

"Then you shot him in self-defense," Erin said.

"No. Shut the fuck up." He pointed the gun directly at Erin. "I turned around and left. He's turned me down for interviews in the past. If I shot everyone who refused to talk to me… Well, that would be a lot of dead bodies."

Veronica took a step closer to Fitzpatrick. He swung the gun towards her.

"Step back," he said. "Don't make me shoot you."

"Like you did Stanley," Lindsey said, her voice hoarse and low.

Erin hadn't realized her sister was alert enough to speak.

"She's right. Fitzpatrick killed him. That's the only explanation that makes sense," Erin said. "Who else would bring his body here?"

Fitzpatrick swung the gun back towards Erin.

"Big time reporter with all your rules about what I could or couldn't do. I couldn't kill Erin's little girls, and I sure had the chance, but it's all right for you to kill Stanley?"

"She's trying to manipulate you."

"She found his body buried out back," Veronica said.

Fitzpatrick's face blanched and he shook his head.

"No one else knows about this place."

"Maybe this isn't the first time Erin's been out here," he said.

Veronica let out a shriek and lunged forward, thrusting the boning knife ahead at Fitzpatrick's chest. He tried to back away and fired the gun twice, hitting her in the chest both times. In the confusion, Erin leapt to her feet, darted to the table for the Glock, aimed and fired at

Fitzpatrick, hitting him in the thigh. He dropped his gun and fell to the ground, clutching his thigh and screaming in pain.

Erin held the gun out, pointing at him. She wanted to fire every round until the gun was empty, put an end to this man's life, to his hateful blogs, to his destructive supply of Oxycontin. Her hand shook, and she steadied it with a two-hand grip, the barrel pointed right at Fitzpatrick's heart.

She didn't pull the trigger again. Instead, she breathed in for three, then out for four, counting the breaths until she heard sirens in the distance. Lindsey began to sob.

Erin approached Fitzpatrick and kicked his gun farther from his reach.

Chapter Fifty-Five

The shooting had stopped, and all was quiet. Deputies Joshua Lippmann and Marilyn Wren bound up the short flight of stairs to the trailer. He flung the door open, and they both entered, guns drawn.

The noise startled Erin, who was seated on a filthy plaid sofa trying to undo the tape around her wrists with her teeth. A small Glock sat next to her. A few feet away Lindsey was awake but looked dazed, taped sitting upright on a kitchen chair, blood soaking both of her sleeves. Joshua expected to see Erin and her sister, but to his surprise the reporter sat on the floor to the right of the door, leaning up against the wall, his right pant leg soaked in blood, conscious and alternating between whimpering and swearing. How in the hell had the reporter gotten to the crime scene before them? A handgun rested about ten feet away on the floor towards the kitchen.

A gray-haired woman lay sprawled on her back in the middle of the floor, a large blood stain soaking the front of her shirt. Her lifeless eyes were open and fixed on a slowly rotating, wobbly ceiling fan. The room reeked of ammonia and vomit, as well as the distinctive acrid smell of recently fired guns.

Joshua headed for the couch, gloved up and snatched up the small Glock, placing it on the kitchen counter next to a Smith and Wesson, both now well out of Erin's reach. He had no idea what had gone down in the trailer, wasn't sure who had done the shooting, but he needed to secure the firearms. He picked up the third gun from the floor and added it to the stockpile.

Deputy Wren gloved up and went to the elderly woman on the floor, verifying she was indeed dead.

"Let me help." Joshua pulled out a small pen knife and cut through the binding on Erin's hands and wrists.

She rubbed her hands together to get rid of the tingling, and then she slumped back on the couch, wrapping her newly freed arms around her chest as if trying to stop the shaking.

"Help me. I'm bleeding out," Fitzpatrick called from the floor, pointing at Erin. "She fucking shot me. She's crazy."

Wren grabbed a grungy dish towel from the kitchen counter, wadded it up and positioned it against the bullet wound on the front of Fitzpatrick's thigh and pushed hard. The reporter yelped and swore but didn't push away her hand.

Joshua spoke into his radio and called for two additional rescue squads, the medical examiner, and the homicide detectives.

"Hold this," Wren said, and positioned Fitzpatrick's own hands over the wound. "Now push down hard."

"You want me to hold it myself?"

"Erin, this is Deputy Marilyn Wren." Joshua nodded towards the second deputy, who by then was in the process of cutting through Lindsey's restraints.

She gave Erin a quick nod. Joshua pulled out his phone and snapped photos of the woman lying still on the floor, then stepped back and got a photo with both Fitzpatrick and the dead woman in the shot. He captured

Lindsey in the chair as she was being freed. He took a photo of Erin, now sitting on the couch looking exhausted.

"Is that necessary?" she asked.

"The crime scene unit will take a lot more photos, but I wanted to document everyone's initial position."

"I need an ambulance," Fitzpatrick said. "It's bleeding heavier, and I'm too weak to hold pressure."

"Lay down." Wren took the bloody towel from Fitzpatrick and repositioned it over the wound, applying firm pressure.

"Not so hard. It hurts like hell."

"Do you want me to stop the bleeding or not?"

He turned his head to the side, whimpered and said nothing. Erin rose from the couch, pulled a kitchen chair next to Lindsey and sat, wrapping her arm around her sister. Lindsey leaned her head on Erin's shoulder.

"Erin, does one of those handguns belong to you?"

"The baby Glock and the Smith and Wesson over on the kitchen counter are both mine. I have a concealed carry permit for both." She pointed at Fitzpatrick. "That gun you picked up off the floor is his, or at least he was carrying it. It may belong to Veronica. He pulled it on me and forced me into the trailer."

Joshua turned in surprise. He stood over the dead woman and looked down. "That's actually Veronica?"

Erin nodded. "They were in this together."

"She's lying," Fitzpatrick said. " I had nothing to do with Veronica snatching her sister. You can even ask Lindsey."

"But you forced Erin into the trailer and taped her wrists?" Joshua asked.

"She was trespassing. The land was clearly posted.

I had no idea Lindsey was inside the trailer. I just got here myself. She had already shot Veronica by the time I arrived."

"That's bullshit," Erin said. "They started to argue about whether or not he killed Duggan, and he shot her."

"I shot her in self-defense." Fitzpatrick glared at Erin. "She had a kitchen knife. She lunged at me with it. She may have fallen onto it when I shot her. But you'll find a knife."

Joshua made a mental note to warn the Medical Examiner there might be a knife on or underneath the dead woman.

"And Erin shot him in the leg," Lindsey said quietly. "With her hands taped together. She should have shot him right between the eyes. It's what I would have done."

Erin hugged her sister.

"Lindsey needs to get to a hospital. Veronica hit her hard on the back of the head with my gun and knocked her out. Plus, she'd been drugged. I don't know what they gave her. Maybe there's a bottle sitting around, or in the medicine cabinet. And her arms." Erin traced a finger down the thin line of dried blood on Lindsey's forearm.

Erin pushed up her sister's sleeves to reveal the full length of the cuts. Joshua retrieved a handful of paper towels from the kitchen and held pressure on Lindsey's left forearm, the only area still actively oozing. Lindsey winced but said nothing.

"The EMTs should be here in a few minutes. What about you, Erin? Are you hurt?"

She shook her head.

"Was Cody out there?" Erin asked.

\# \# \#

Erin saw Joshua and Deputy Wren exchange glances.

"Is he…?"

"I was only ten minutes away when his 911 call came through."

He hadn't answered her question.

"How did he call 911? I couldn't get a signal on my phone."

"I caught the address when you called Osborne earlier, and I wanted to make sure you were all right. I had a bad feeling about this whole mess, but I couldn't leave until the car crash had been handled. When I got here, I found Cody out near the road."

"Please tell me he's alive," Erin said.

"He's alive, Erin. Luckily, my headlights lit him up when I made the turn into the driveway. It would have been easy to miss him in the dark. He was a good twenty feet off the road. I gave him Narcan as soon as I found him. He was breathing, but barely. He improved almost immediately."

"He overdosed again."

It wasn't a question, but he nodded.

"The EMTs are with him now, plus Wren's partner. They've got additional doses of Narcan if they need it. It looks like he messed up his good leg. I wonder if he fell from a tree. Wren and her partner got there at the same time as the EMTs. That's when we heard the gunshots."

"Your car and your husband's truck are blocking the driveway. We ran the rest of the way."

"Fitzpatrick said he had Cody's car keys, but I thought he was lying. They may be in his pocket."

"There is a set of keys on the kitchen counter," Wren

said. "Joshua, if you can hold pressure here, I'm going to move the Volvo and the truck to allow the rescue squads to get past."

Joshua took over the bloody dish towel, and Wren pocketed the keys from the kitchen counter.

"I'm assuming these are for the truck. Do you have the keys for the SUV?" she asked Erin.

"I left them in the car. They're tucked under the floor mat on the back seat driver's side."

Wren stopped at the door and sniffed the air, her eyes beginning to water. "What's that awful stench? It smells worse than a meth lab."

"Pumpkin," Erin and Lindsey answered in unison.

A half hour later additional rescue squads pulled up, loaded Lindsey and Fitzpatrick, and left, lights flashing. Fitzpatrick was handcuffed and Wren's partner rode along.

"Would you mind sitting in the back of the police cruiser?" Wren asked Erin. "We'd like to get you out of the trailer."

"Can't I have my car keys back? I need to get to the hospital to check on Cody and Lindsey."

"They took them both to hospital in Mauston. It's the closest," Joshua said. "You'll have to wait until the homicide detective arrives. He'll have questions.

"Is that where they'll take Fitzpatrick?" she asked.

"Initially, but I wouldn't be surprised if they transfer him to Madison for surgery."

She agreed to wait out in the police cruiser and Wren led her out of the trailer. Detective Simon Barrett from the Juneau County Sheriff's Department joined them fifteen minutes later. Erin was relieved it wasn't Osborne.

Erin told Barrett about the partially buried body in the woods behind the trailer, almost certainly Stanley Duggan, and offered to lead him to the spot. He declined but asked her to describe in detail what she'd seen. He said they'd secure the property for the night and be back with cadaver dogs in the morning. When he finished, Joshua offered to drive her to the hospital in her own car. He could get a ride back to the department.

She was buckled into the passenger's seat when Detective Barrett stopped and motioned for her to roll down the window.

"You should plan on coming into the sheriff's department tomorrow, in Juneau County, not Sauk County. Let's say ten in the morning. We will likely have more questions, and you'll need to review and sign your statement. Hope your husband and sister do well. We'll be getting statements from them once they're stable." He started back towards the trailer.

"Wait," Erin called.

He turned.

"What about Pumpkin?"

He looked puzzled.

"The woman owns a cat, a massive ugly cat. You must have smelled the litter box. You can't just leave it here."

"Jesus Christ, we wondered where the smell was coming from?" The detective laughed. "Don't worry, we'll save the cat."

Chapter Fifty-Six

The drive down to UW-Madison Hospital took over an hour due to road construction. Erin made her way through the maze of parking structures and buildings to the Orthopedic wing, where Cody was recovering from his ankle reconstruction two days before. He spent the first few days in the ICU going through withdrawal before he was considered stable enough for the surgery. Now that he was on a general surgical floor, there was less restriction on visitation.

He was seated in a wheelchair by the window which overlooked a line of dumpsters. The TV was muted on a home improvement channel.

"Lindsey sent these," Erin said, holding out an offering.

She placed the vase of autumn-colored flowers on the windowsill, next to the irises she'd brought two days before. He was still pale, with an IV line secured to his left arm as well as a second line taped to his neck. A light on the wall-mounted monitor pulsed with each heartbeat. His lunch tray looked untouched, and she saw his hand tremble as he set down his Styrofoam cup of water. At least he was out of the surgical ICU, which was a major step.

Cody smiled weakly. "Tell her I said thanks. How is she doing? Is she still in the hospital?"

"No, they only kept her one night. She's still

following concussion protocol for a few more days, but the drugs are out of her system. We went for a walk yesterday and she did fine."

"How did she get a concussion?"

"I wasn't sure how much you'd remember. You were groggy before your surgery and even worse after. Veronica had given her a strong sedative to keep her from struggling. Then she pistol-whipped her to the back of her head and knocked her out, which is the reason for the concussion protocol. They performed a CT scan, and she should be fine."

"I remember some of this." His hand reached up and lightly rubbed the gauze dressing over his neck. "I remember Veronica is dead."

Erin nodded.

"Fitzpatrick shot her."

"Twice. And I shot him in the leg. He's here in this hospital somewhere, or at least he had his surgery here. They may have transferred him to a jail ward."

"You know about the Oxycontin?"

She nodded.

"I'd been buying it on the street after the pain doc at the VA refused to write any more prescriptions, and it was getting incredibly expensive. I took money from Charlotte's college account. Then Fitzpatrick came along and started giving it to me like it was candy." He stopped and stared out at the dumpsters.

"We'll deal with this once you're discharged," she said, hoping the financial damage wasn't too severe. She had more than twelve years to make up the difference before either girl was ready for college. She froze his access to their joint accounts but neglected to check on the college savings plans.

"I deserve to have died under that tree."

"Don't say that. The girls need you in their lives. When Lindsey and I needed you most, you were there for us."

"I can't believe I broke my good ankle. They said I'd be in a wheelchair for a while."

"That's what the surgeon said. Maybe when you were falling from the tree, you instinctively tried to protect your prosthesis."

"You're giving me too much credit. I was stoned. After I fell and was sitting on the ground with this ankle…well, I knew one way to make the pain go away," he said. "They said I almost died. If I hadn't received the Narcan in time…"

She nodded. If Joshua hadn't headed in the direction of the trailer, on a hunch more than anything, it might have been too late for Cody. By the time Deputy Wren and her partner arrived in response to the 911 call, he may have stopped breathing altogether.

"Joshua saved my life, didn't he?" he asked.

"He overheard Osborne on the phone and knew we were in trouble."

"My mom called earlier this morning and let me talk to the girls," Cody said. "I didn't know how much to tell them. I said I hurt my ankle and would see them soon."

"I know. I spoke to her on my drive down."

"Did you tell her everything, about the drugs?"

Erin shook her head. That was his story to tell when he was ready.

"I'm heading to Milwaukee from here. It helped that your parents could take them for a few days. I'm sure it wasn't easy with your dad recently discharged from the hospital. They are supposed to start school later this week. They may still miss a day or two, but I need them back home. And I'm sure they're driving your father crazy by now."

Cody nodded.

"If you're feeling up to it, we can stop by on our way home for a short visit."

"No, I don't want them to see me like this. Not because of the ankle. I know I look like shit. I'll get clean, Erin."

She nodded.

"Did your surgeon say how much longer he'll keep you here?"

"Three more days, if everything goes well. They're loading me with IV antibiotics since it was an open fracture."

"I can try to get a temporary wheelchair ramp installed, although I doubt if I can get it done in three days." She wondered about handicap access at his friend Gunther's apartment, since he'd be in a wheelchair for potentially months. It was also possible Cody could temporarily use Lindsey's apartment, which had an elevator, since her sister was still staying with her and the girls.

"You can relax. I'm not coming home in three days. I talked with a woman from social services yesterday and again this morning. She's helping me arrange a month of inpatient drug rehab. It'll likely be in Minnesota. If she can get me into the program, you need to know the insurance isn't going to cover it. Some of the programs offer a discount for veterans, and she's checking in to that, but even then, it isn't going to be cheap."

"We'll find the money. It might mean a home equity loan, but I'm starting back at work next week, part time at first."

"Thank you."

Erin wasn't sure she'd make it back to Madison before Cody left for his inpatient rehab, in Minnesota or wherever he ended up. She didn't know whether she'd be able to visit him during his rehab month. He needed to understand their marriage was irretrievably broken, and there was plenty of blame to go around. Should she wait until he completed his treatment to discuss it, or was it likely going to send him into a tailspin that would be a huge setback? She had no idea which would be worse. She'd already scheduled an appointment with a family law attorney. She would wait until Cody was stronger for these discussions.

Cody's nurse came to check his vitals and help him to the bathroom, and Erin snuck out the door.

Erin wouldn't be going back to Alex or any man like Alex. She also couldn't stay in a marriage with Cody, whom she would never fully trust again, neither as a partner nor as a full-time father to Gracie and Charlotte. She would forgive, but she could never forget.

Erin needed to be alone to be whole for now and perhaps that had been her fate from the beginning.

Chapter Fifty-Seven

"I heard Cody had his surgery this week. When will he be coming home?" Joshua joined Lindsey and Erin at a café table outside the coffee shop. He set down the cardboard tray and distributed the three beverages around the table.

"He'll be discharged in two days, if nothing changes." Erin leaned back in the chair. "But he's not coming home for a while. He's going into an inpatient drug treatment center in St. Paul. I need to pick him up in Madison and drive him up."

"How long does he expect to be there?" he asked.

"Four to five weeks," Erin said.

"Good for him. Has he ever done inpatient treatment before?"

"A long time ago. But he's optimistic this will be what he needs. Anyway, it's worth a try."

"Are visitors allowed?" he asked.

"Yes, but the visits must be scheduled around the therapy sessions, which makes sense. I'll give him a week or two to get settled in, then drive the girls up for a visit."

"I'd like to go along," Lindsey said.

"I'm sure he'd love to see you."

"Are the girls back in school?" he asked.

"Yes, their classes started yesterday, so they only missed one day. They were excited to see all their friends this morning. I'm starting back at the clinic next week."

"Did the school principal talk to you?" he asked. "Mr. Evans."

"They call him a headmaster. I know it sounds pretentious. I've met him at fundraisers in the past but haven't talked to him recently."

Joshua scratched his chin and studied his coffee cup for a long time.

"Why are you asking?"

"When we searched the trailer, we found a driver's license with a picture of Veronica using her sister's name, Trudy Bell. We also found a work ID under that name from Heritage Learning Academy. Detective Barrett talked to the administration there. Mr. Evans has been fully cooperative. It turns out Veronica has been working in the school cafeteria for the past eighteen months, including the summer session, under her sister's name."

Erin nearly dropped her cup of coffee on the table. That woman had been in her daughters' school, seeing them every day and having access to the food they ate. She could have hurt them, even poisoned them. She remembered Veronica's comment in the trailer, admonishing Fitzpatrick for not allowing her to kill the girls. Perhaps that was the only good thing he'd done.

"How could this happen?"

"They ran a background check, but under the name of Trudy Bell. Honestly, I don't think there's any way they could have known."

Erin thought they sure as hell should have known, for that kind of tuition.

"What ever happened to Trudy Bell?" Lindsey asked.

"At this point we aren't sure, but we're assuming she's dead. The crime scene unit is still processing the property. One of those outbuildings was filled to the ceiling with junk. That trailer was beyond filthy, but the shed suggests someone was also a hoarder. Maybe Trudy. Maybe Veronica."

"Maybe they'll find her at the bottom of the pile. I saw that one time on one of the Hoarder shows," Lindsey said.

"I still don't understand why she would blame me for her sister's death?" Erin asked. "If she's actually dead."

"I don't even have a theory to offer you," Joshua said. "We'll share aspects of the findings with you as we get more information, but at this point it's still an active crime investigation."

"Would Fitzpatrick know about her sister?" Lindsey asked. "Know if she's dead?"

"I wouldn't doubt it, but he's not saying much about anything."

He looked uneasy and again way too interested in his cardboard cup.

"There's more, isn't there?"

"Trudy…Veronica had a locker in the school basement, and Evans allowed us to cut off the padlock. Like I said, he's being fully cooperative."

"More pictures." Erin said. She couldn't be shocked any more.

He nodded. "Some new ones, compared to the pile at Duggan's house and the one's dropped off in your mailbox, but similar pictures. Nothing to suggest she ever took your children out of the classroom or been alone with them."

"Thanks for letting me know. I have been debating about letting the girls ride the bus this year. They'd pick them up right outside our gate. Maybe I should wait another year."

"They're safe at school now, Erin," Lindsey said. "Safer than they've been in a long time. You didn't know how close she was to the girls before."

"That doesn't make me feel any better," Erin said. "I'll think about the bus."

"I can give you a brief update on Fitzpatrick. He's being held in a jail medical ward in Madison awaiting trial and it's possible you will both have to testify, since he's pleading not guilty. That may change. Too early to tell. He should make a full recovery from the gunshot wound. He still denies killing Duggan, but we're waiting on ballistics comparing the gun he shot Veronica with to the shells removed from Duggan's kitchen. My guess is they'll match."

"It explains how he knew about the child porn on the computer and pictures of my family. He searched the house after he killed Duggan."

"He's not denying he was working with Veronica, is he?" Lindsey asked.

"He's denying absolutely everything. He claims he showed up to try to rescue the two of you, and things went south. We found a burner phone in his home, and it didn't take too long to find he made lots of phone calls to Veronica. The GPS on his car was also a giveaway. He'd been out at the property several times in the past year."

"I don't understand their connection, Fitzpatrick and Veronica, I mean. He was an awful human being, but why was he working with her? It doesn't make sense,"

Lindsey said.

"Veronica told me she gave Fitzpatrick the information where to find me in the first place, but she used it for leverage all these years because he waited a few weeks to take it to the police," Erin said. "You don't remember everything that happened in the trailer, do you?"

Lindsey shook her head.

"I talked to one of the detectives who was working on the case with Osborne, back when you were kidnapped. He said they were suspicious of Fitzpatrick even back then, especially when he came up with the tip you were being held on Duggan's farm," Joshua said.

"Did they suspect she was his source?" Erin asked.

"It was their working theory twenty-one years ago, but they couldn't prove it. It rankled them to no end when he got the journalism award for the coverage."

"Why would she report Duggan, especially since she was involved?" Lindsey asked. "Weren't they lovers?"

Erin thought back to the remarks Veronica made in the trailer about Stanley watching her while she slept. Veronica turned him in as an act of revenge when he turned his attention to Erin. She had escaped just in time. She told Joshua about their conversation.

"Why would Fitzpatrick kill Duggan?" Lindsey asked.

"We know he'd been out to Duggan's farm a few times since he was released, presumably to get an interview. He took one of the photographers along with him once, who told us Duggan refused to talk to him and it had almost come to blows between the two. Our theory is he confronted Duggan when he refused to talk to him again, and things got out of hand."

"But why move the body?"

"It was risky, no doubt about that. It's likely he did it to create uncertainty as to whether Duggan was dead or just managed to run off. Maybe he was afraid to have Veronica find out he had killed him."

"I saw in the paper you recovered Duggan's body," Lindsey said.

"Yes, and just like your sister saw that night, the foot had been severed. It's an extreme step to remove the ankle monitor, and it was a clean cut, like he used a power saw. We didn't find a saw at the trailer or anywhere on Duggan's property. Nothing in Fitzpatrick's apartment. We figure there may be an additional crime scene out there."

Erin shuddered, remembering the bright white bones of Duggan's lower leg, glimmering in the beam from her phone.

"We're still looking for the foot. We've taken the cadaver dog out to the property twice. But like I said, there's a lot of garbage piled up in that shed and the crime scene people aren't finished." Joshua drained his cup of coffee. "The GPS on Fitzpatrick's car showed he was out at that trailer late morning the day after Duggan disappeared, when Veronica would have been at work. We figured that's when he buried the body. He denies it, of course."

"Why would he take it there of all places?" Erin asked.

"Good question, and like I said, he claims to be completely innocent. But her trailer site is secluded, and he may have assumed she never went far into the woods."

"I know another thing he'll probably deny. Fitzpatrick was supplying Cody with Oxycontin in exchange for details on our family for the book he was writing."

"It nearly killed him," he said.

Erin nodded. She could never repay this man for saving Cody's life.

"One more thing that may interest you. Osborne has resigned from the force. It becomes official at the end of the month, but he's already turned in his weapon and badge. We're not exactly on speaking terms, but I am sure he regrets his decisions that led up to what happened in the trailer."

"You said you'd been suspended for a week. Is that because you opposed some of those decisions?" Erin asked.

He nodded. "But it's also because I didn't follow protocol the way I should have. I should have taken it directly to Sheriff Carter instead of trying to work around Osborne, and that's on me."

"We're grateful," Lindsey said. "And it should have been one of us buying the coffee today."

Joshua smiled and excused himself to go back to work. Lindsey watched him walk the half block to his car and climb in.

"I wonder if he's single," she said.

Her sister could certainly do worse.

Chapter Fifty-Eight

"I'm sure you've heard I've left the force," Osborne said.

Erin nodded, again wondering why she agreed to meet him in the first place. He'd said he needed closure. Fine, she'd give him that, but not absolution. Not forgiveness. It wasn't in her DNA. His actions had put her entire family in danger. If he'd done his job properly, Cody wouldn't be in a wheelchair and her sister wouldn't be waking up screaming during the night.

They'd arranged a meeting place in Baraboo, the same park where Osborne had followed Duggan and his dates. She'd run some errands first and thought about standing him up. She showed. She'd let him speak and then she'd never have to talk to him again. He commandeered a picnic table in the sun. The park was quiet, with the children back in school, a few dog walkers and parents pushing strollers. The leaves overhead were a mixture of crimson, gold and rust and fluttered to the ground around them. Autumn was in full swing.

"I appreciate your meeting me. I'm sure you're still understandably upset about the way I handled everything."

No shit. She said nothing. She'd agreed to listen, that was it.

"I'm not going to make excuses. I made mistakes. I never should have enabled Duggan to get out of prison.

I trusted Fitzpatrick when I should have trusted you. I want to let you know I'm sorry."

Not only hadn't he believed her, but he'd also implied she was a liar or mentally ill. Made mistakes? It was an appalling understatement.

"How is Cody doing? I talked to Lippmann a few days ago, and he told me your husband went to a rehab center out of state."

"There are a few weeks left, but he seems to be making headway. He's clean. He's optimistic. Time will tell."

"I understand Fitzpatrick was supplying him with drugs in exchange for dirt on your family. What a sleaze he turned out to be. I knew he had to have a source for his information, but I thought it was a leak in our department."

"You may have had a leak, but some of it came from my husband."

"Not to mention Veronica herself. No wonder Fitzpatrick knew about the photos. He might have been by her side when she marked them up."

She studied him closely. He looked a decade older than he did a few months earlier, with dark bags under his eyes. His skin was pasty as if he hadn't been out in the sun in ages, and he had shaved off his mustache. His long sleeve dress shirt was neatly pressed as always, and he wore dress slacks, but still there was an air of disarray she couldn't pinpoint, even with her psychology background. He noticed her watching him and blushed and looked away.

"If it's any consolation, they found a sizable stash of Oxycontin in Fitzpatrick's apartment, all illegally obtained, which means additional charges for felony possession."

"I hope he goes away for a long time," she said.

He nodded and stared down at his hands.

"Lippmann also told me the law firm out of Madison came clean about who hired them to represent Duggan. It had nothing to do with Veronica or Fitzpatrick. It was a female pen pal who had been writing to Duggan for nearly ten years and imagined a future with him after he was released."

"Was it one of the women you photographed?"

"No, ironically. Lippmann contacted her and she said Duggan unceremoniously blew her off a few days after his release. She sees now she dodged a bullet."

"She could have been hurt when Fitzpatrick murdered Duggan if their relationship had progressed. She was lucky."

"If you call shelling out seventy thousand dollars for legal bills, only to be dumped as lucky, then I agree."

They sat in something approaching companionable silence. This was easier than Erin had anticipated.

"Detective Morgan also told me the ballistics from the bullet removed from Duggan's body as well as the wall in his kitchen came back and they showed a match to the gun Fitzpatrick pulled on you. The one he used to shoot Veronica."

"I had heard Duggan had been shot."

He nodded. "He killed Duggan before he tried to remove the ankle monitor."

"I was fairly sure it was Fitzpatrick who killed Duggan, once I saw him with Veronica. Fortunately, I was able to convince her that night, and she turned on him rather than killing Lindsey and me."

"There's not a good explanation as to why he would

have killed Duggan in the first place."

"It's even harder to explain why he would have risked moving the body onto Veronica's property. That was unnecessary and she could have caught him."

He nodded in agreement.

"Maybe he'll write about it in his next blog," she said, and they exchanged smiles for the first time.

"There's one thing that bothered me. I don't understand why you refused to allow us to run ballistics on your handguns. It just made us more suspicious."

In the spirit of fair play, Erin answered. "I knew I hadn't shot Duggan, but there was a small part of me that was less sure about Cody. If he'd killed him, I wanted him to be able to hide behind my refusal."

He nodded. "I wondered about that. I didn't think it was you, because you were always more afraid of Veronica than Duggan."

That was true, she admitted to herself, with good reason. She had always been the more sadistic of the pair. She often wished it was Veronica who had gone to prison instead of Duggan.

"Lippmann suspected I might have killed Duggan. I was admittedly alarmed at how strong and fit he appeared to be, and he was parking his van by city parks and playgrounds. We visited him in prison a month before his parole hearing and he truly looked sickly. I believed he was in bad shape. I never would have tried to get him released otherwise. Once I saw how capable he was, I was afraid he'd hurt another kid. I'm not sad he's gone, but I wouldn't have killed him."

"Is that why Joshua got a week of suspension?"

"He told you about that, huh?" He had the good grace to look ashamed. "Yes, he asked the crime lab to compare the bullets taken out of the kitchen wall to my gun. I shouldn't have got him in trouble for that, but at the time it pissed me off. He's a good cop, better than I ever was."

"Did they ever find Veronica's sister? I heard one of the outbuildings looked like a hoarder's paradise."

"Funny you should ask. They found an old well at the back of the property, long dry. A new well had been dug years ago up closer to the trailer. There was a woman's skeleton at the bottom of the original well. She'd had a lot of dental work done. It took some digging, but they were able to track down the sister's dentist, who was retired, but never threw away his patient records."

"It was a match?" she asked.

He nodded and sighed.

"There's more?" Why did men always sigh when there was more?

"There was a second skeleton underneath Trudy's. It was a small animal. The forensic pathologist said it was a young dog, not much past puppyhood."

"The King Charles Cavalier. Scooter," she said.

"I'll be honest, I didn't believe you twenty years ago. I didn't believe there had ever been a dog. But I always believed there had been a Veronica."

It was her turn to nod and sigh.

"What's next for you?" she asked. "Do you plan to look for another job in law enforcement?"

"Hardly," he said. "I've put in enough service time to get my full pension. I should have retired five years ago. I'm not going to be rolling in the dough, but I'll be comfortable."

"Good for you," she said, surprised she meant it.

"I even thought about getting a dog, now that I'm not putting in the long hours. I went down to the county humane society last week to adopt a rescue."

"My girls have been begging for a puppy. I'm tempted."

"Well, as fate would have it, I ended up falling in love with a cat. She's a big girl, pretty orange tabby, cuddly as can be."

"I wouldn't have pegged you as a cat person," she said.

"I grew up with cats. We had them when I was married but I haven't owned one since my divorce. Anyway, this girl has an intelligent, intense look in her eyes, like she knows things I'll never understand. I can tell she's led an interesting life. If only she could tell me about it."

"You sound smitten," she said.

"I guess I am. I know some people change their pet's name after adoption, but it fits her. Pumpkin."

Erin gasped, then smiled.

"Let me know how it works out for you and Pumpkin."

"I'll do that. Again, thanks for meeting."

"You're welcome."

Erin thought about forgiveness as she walked back to her car. Her mother hadn't raised a forgiving daughter, but maybe it was something she could change.

A word about the author...

Cynthia Rice presents her debut novel THE LAST BROKEN GIRL set in rural Wisconsin, where she has strong family ties. She is a recently retired physician living in the Milwaukee area and a proud member of Mystery Writers of America and Sisters in Crime.

Thank you for purchasing
this publication of The Wild Rose Press, Inc.

For questions or more information
contact us at
info@thewildrosepress.com.

The Wild Rose Press, Inc.
www.thewildrosepress.com

Printed in the USA
CPSIA information can be obtained
at www.ICGtesting.com
LVHW052225240624
783922LV00037B/1030

9 781509 255399